O GENTEEL LADY!

O GENTEEL LADY!

Esther Forbes

**Cassandra
Editions**

Published in 1986 by

Academy Chicago Publishers
425 North Michigan Avenue
Chicago, Illinois 60611

Copyright © 1926 by
Esther Forbes Hoskins

Published by arrangement
with Houghton Mifflin Co.

Printed and bound in the USA

Library of Congress Cataloging-in-Publication Data

Forbes, Esther.
    O genteel lady!

    I. Title.
PS3511.0349502   1986   813′.52   86-22149
ISBN 0-89733-234-2 (pbk.)

To
My Father and Mother

CONTENTS

O GENTEEL LADY!

CHAPTER I

A LADY LEAVES HOME

1

'I HAVE nothing,' she thought, 'but myself. No parents that count; no longer a fiancé; no home. I'm not even young any more, actually twenty-four. Ladies in novels are never out of their teens. Well, at least I've myself.'

She straightened her long, slim body, straightened her bonnet, and looked about the railroad coach and the miserable cold companions of her journey.

'Myself . . . and a mink pelisse,' she added, and was sorry for the women in frayed shawls and shabby bonnets gathered close about the pot-bellied stove standing midway in the coach. A man, almost a gentleman but not quite, continually stooped to feed more wood to the fire.

'Disgraceful,' said the man. 'That brakeman ought to come around oftener, and we'll run short of wood before we reach Worcester.'

'Gimme,' said an old fellow with a muffler tied about his ears — 'gimme the good old days and hosses. Nobody then tried to carry a stove around on wheels, but at least we had straw in the wagon bed right up to your calves, if the ladies will excuse my language.' He spat fluently and accurately against the belly of the red-hot stove.

'Ugh,' thought Lanice, and wrapped her costly furs about her. She was quite alone now in the cold, far end of the coach close to the ill-fitting door and empty ice-water tank. The seat upon which she sat had been designed for two, but her skirts of fine, pale wool and brown velvet filled this space and flowed out into the aisle. She looked down and saw the points of her bronze slippers resting side by side upon the dirty floor, exactly as a lady's shoes should rest, and smiled a lingering and secret smile. Exactly as a lady's shoes should rest . . . no one would guess that they were empty and that her feet were drawn up under her warm body. She herself was nestled inside her formidable shell of clothing as snug and compact as a worm at the heart of a chestnut. The hoops and crinoline hid how she really sat and what she really was.

No one would have guessed that this elegant and exotic creature had any legs, or, if she were so carnal as to possess such things, that they could bend so subtly beneath her. Long ago, when first out of pantalettes, she had learned this trick of taking her ease and preserving her dignity during the protracted dull sermons in the Congregational Church in Amherst. To the man who hoped that the cold would eventually drive her to share the fire he so laboriously tended, she seemed only a pale, oval face with tightly tied red mouth and black lacquer eyes. Occasionally two alabaster hands emerged delicately from the

[2]

great sleeves of her pelisse and wandered upon the surface of the dark fur. Her eyes moved, glittered and drooped down. Her expression seemed to reflect the ideal of a fashion-plate artist rather than the heart which supposedly beat beneath the tight basque and tighter stays.

No one would have guessed that for two nights and a day she had cried almost without stopping, or that she had had the audacity to run away from home, or the intellectual conceit to believe herself a genius. In Amherst her talents had been recognized. In Boston she would at last receive the proper training and be launched upon a career.

She shut her eyes and savored a sensuous pleasure from the greatness that was to be hers. Yet at her heart she knew that if Augustus had been a different man, she would not now be planning her career but the furnishing of her house, and she was honest enough to realize that one occupation would have been as absorbing as the other. Augustus! what a white rabbit of a man, and so good, so uncarnal, so considerate of her purity. Not many men like that; one should appreciate them. She touched her sleek mouth with a finger tip. 'Dear God,' she returned thanks, 'we thank Thee that he has never kissed me on the mouth, only here,' and she smoothed her cold cheek. Her mind, with its extravagant bursts of day-dreaming, abandoned the career before she had even decided whether her genius lay in art or litera-ture, and spread before her the thought of other men, not Augustuses, not 'young gentlemen from the college,' but strangers coming from far lands and fine adventure. She shuddered and shut her narrow jaw. 'Dear God, please help me to think only of Higher Things.' She hated the thought of marriage. She hated the thought of men. Most of all she hated Mamma.

It could not be that she herself inherited something of Mamma's wicked wantonness, Mamma who had disgraced them all and had made Amherst an impossible place for her daughter to live. 'You must not think of Mamma. You must never think of her again. She is a bad woman, and you must be twice as good because she is so bad.'

But memory of that sweet, beguiling face was upon her, lips, currant smooth and ripely red, and dimples eddying high upon her left cheek. She could see her in a dozen characteristic postures. Mamma! How, on a sunny day, she would come sparkling out of the fashionable villa in Amherst ruffled in grey, a bit of a grey bonnet perched like a bird on her chestnut curls, and look up at the sky and smile at the sunshine as though the June day were her lover nervously waiting her approval. Mamma . . . never again Mamma. How could she have run off to Italy with one of Papa's own students in natural philosophy, young Roger Cuncliffe! Cuncliffe — the pretty boy with the light walk and feverish color and black curls. The rich boy who had been brought up in Europe. The sick boy for whom people felt so sorry.

Her white hands clenched in the depths of the fur. Her heart thumped and she was swept with a sense

[4]

of physical nausea. Strange how things went to-gether. Because Mamma had run off with Mr. Cuncliffe, she had been violently sick all the time she wasn't actually crying during the next two nights and intervening day. If she thought enough of Mamma she would begin again, and she would much rather have died than begin again. It was sleep she needed. 'Oh, dear, I shall never sleep again; I shall never be happy again. Everything is gone, except myself.'

The train swayed upon its little rails. Outside was a white-wrapped world slipping back towards Amherst as the train forged forward to Boston; inside the group about the stove, the inelegant women, the men who were not quite gentlemen, and three bundles of cloth with children within.

'Toot toot to-to-o-o.' Another station. The train drew to a ponderous stop. She looked out and saw that it was Worcester. The lady with the green dolman was getting out, and the brakeman was coming in carrying a big basket of wood. Behind him two little girls, obviously orphans with black frocks and almost professionally pinched faces, held out in their little thin hands trays of gingerbread and cold cup custards. They did not say a word, but clung to each other like unfortunate orphans in moral tracts and gazed piteously at the passengers. Lanice motioned them to her. 'I'd like some gingerbread,' she said, and liberally opened her bead purse to pay them. The little creatures whispered their thanks, then sank into abysmal woe.

'Are you alone in the world?' asked Lanice gently.

'Not alone,' piped the littlest of the two. 'God cares for us. He loves us.'

'How selfish I am,' thought Lanice, and gave them all her silver.

When they were gone she heard one passenger tell the others that children often rigged up in black and boarded trains and made soft-hearted females give them money. The almost-gentleman laughed loudly and glanced at Lanice. She flushed with chagrin, but remembering their thin hands was glad she had been generous. She moved slightly lest her folded legs should go to sleep. Her head fell back, the pelisse slipped from her shoulders showing the seed pearl brooch at her throat. 'Asleep,' said the man in the muffler, pointing with his thumb.

She was back again in Amherst with Mamma, in the garden of the sumptuous 'villa.' Mamma was pulling up plants by the roots. The roots were hair. She jerked up out of the clotting earth a succession of writhing human bodies.

'Oh, Mamma, stop, please stop! I can't bear it, expecially those purplish ones without any legs!'

Mamma leered at her. Usually the heads were half out of the ground like turnips. Sometimes there was only a head. The most ghastly of all had but a leg and a splay foot.

'Mamma!' The pretty woman chirped and clapped her hands. She wore her fashionable cherry-red *pelisse de voyage* and whirled her tiny ermine muff. So it was Lanice had last seen her. In the nightmare Mamma pointed at her and the imps fixed her with hideous vegetable eyes and patted their chests and thighs. She struggled to run. Little fiends were upon her, pinching and pulling. Her feet stuck. She had taken root. The earth, which had so recently borne this strange crop, was sinking beneath her.

Lanice knew she slept and wanted to wake. She moaned piteously. Papa watched her fall and did not help, but his red mouth moved sarcastically in the midst of his black silk beard. 'Augustus!' she cried, and desperately resented the look of superior virtue he cast towards his erstwhile fiancée. 'I am purer than thou art,' he said, 'as high as the Heavens are above the earth . . .'

She woke, half falling to the floor, her bronze slippers several feet away from the edge of her skirt. She was corpse-cold, but drenched with sweat. Her icicle fingers were pressed to her pounding heart.

'Where am I, where am I? Oh, dear Lord, save me!'

Struggling inside her hoopskirt she got to her feet, and stared about her. Only the dirty train and the cold people by the fire. She wanted to laugh, almost cried, and suddenly felt a return of the sickly sense of nausea. Then she sat down, ashamed of her display. A passenger, who an hour before could not have imagined that this doll even had legs, noticed with amazement and intense interest that she seemed to be a quadruped. The points of four feet protruded from under the pale skirt flounced with velvet.

2

It was only five o'clock, but the February day was

already darkening. The train on its little single track bored on towards Boston. 'Boston — Boston' sang the wheels upon the tracks, and Lanice, released from her bad dreams, had, as the train curved, a glimpse of foul shallow water criss-crossed with tracks and carelessly filled with ashes and the sordid débris of a city. The sight was not ugly, for the sunset reflected in the dirty Back Bay and beyond it, rising grandly in stages of staggered red-brick buildings vivified by the spires of churches, crowned by the bald dome of the State House, delicately veiled by smoke — loveliest of cities — beyond the pink waste of water was Boston!

The girl was frightened. She wished that she had stayed in Amherst with Papa, until she thought of Augustus and the pastor's lean she-wolf of a wife, and the social structure of Amherst tumbling about her ears. She knew she could not endure that. Better the unknown terrors of a strange city and strange relatives than the familiar, impossible situation at home. She had telegraphed her cousin Pauline that she was coming, and then, before she had had time to receive an answer, had set out. This Pauline she had never seen, but from a correspondence which had started two years before, when Pauline had tried to interest Lanice in writing a series of articles about women's rights for the 'Godey's Lady's Book,' she guessed that she was very purposeful, very high-minded, and probably the possessor of a beautiful soul. A beautiful face was undoubtedly too much to expect. She was wealthy, the only child of a retired merchant who had been widowed for years. Of course she would be elegantly costumed and prepared to sneer at her country cousin. She would not know that Mamma and Lanice always had *their* accoutrements from New York. 'Dear God, I am so alone in the world, I hope to like Pauline. I hope she really meant it last year when she wanted me to live with them on Beacon Street and study art.'

'*Every*body out,' yelled the captain of the train. The interested passenger presented himself blushing and looking foolish.

'Madam,' he said, 'may I not help you with your boxes?'

She had four, and a folio of her paintings, a reticule, a small carpetbag, a muff, and an armful of skirts. Shyly, but with a certain sophistication in her shyness, she accepted his offer.

'That's unnecessary,' said a positive, well-bred voice. 'The man is here. He'll attend to your baggage.'

Lanice jumped about, flushing as though her intellectual cousin had caught her amorously smirking at the stranger.

'Cousin Pauline? How good of you to come to meet me. I was beginning to feel really quite alone and in need of being met.'

'I understand,' said Pauline very clearly, and withered the trembling semi-gentleman with a well-bred Boston look. He disappeared as if by magic.

'You poor girl! Has he been annoying you all the way from Springfield? You might have spoken to the captain of the train. He would have put him out.'

'Oh, no, Cousin Pauline. Every one was most respectful. He saw I needed help and . . .'

It was useless. Pauline evidently knew the Truth, whether or not it existed. She tactfully changed the conversation.

'Patrick will fetch your things; we will go to the carriage. You are very fatigued.'

Lanice found, on stepping out into the grey station, that the cold weather of the central part of the State had been left behind. She knew by the smell of the air as it blew in under the train sheds that it had thawed all day and only now at sunset had stopped dripping and begun to freeze again. The station was confusing, but not as large as she had expected in so vast a metropolis.

'But,' Pauline defended her city, 'we have eight stations, you know, and some are much more sumptuous than the Western Railway Depot. Come this way; take my arm. There, those white horses are ours.'

The two young women climbed into the swaying open barouche and drew the bear rug about them. It was lighter on the street than in the train or station. Patrick packed in the baggage, mounted the box, and the ugly fat white horses jogged off up Kneeland Street. Lanice, who had her mother's fondness for clothes, looked at the animals critically. 'If I had them,' she thought, 'I'd have them painted a dark color; or perhaps longitudinally striped, like a

Parisian lady's mantua. It is a shame they must always wear such stuffy white and look like harnessed polar bears.' And her mind went back poignantly to the flashing and dainty horses her mother had owned. Black, they were usually, or bays, and when you rode them you were like a bird flying down the sky upon the wind. Papa would sell them, now Mamma was gone forever.

'I knew you,' Pauline said, 'the moment I put my eyes on you. I saw your profile as you ... shrank away from that man, and I knew that you were my cousin. Not, of course, that we look alike, as I am light and at least ten years older.'

Lanice glanced sidewise at her companion and saw with dismay and distaste that there was between the two of them a fundamental resemblance, hidden deep down in the bony structure of the face. Her cousin had an eager, intelligent face and a waspish manner. Her skin was blotched, and the parentheses marks were beginning to close grimly about her mouth. It was humiliating to think that any one could see a likeness between them. She was glad her hair was not ash blond nor her skin broken. There was a mysterious contagion about Pauline's ugliness. Some plain girls made Lanice believe herself a beauty, but Pauline made her feel irritated with herself.

Pauline was speaking. 'You must get your black eyes from your father's side of the house; the Poggys are quite fair.'

'Yes, Papa is black as the ace of spades, but his skin is very light. Mamma was a chestnut blonde. I

[11]

think that is the prettiest thing in the world. Mamma
had, *has*, grey eyes and . . .' Her description trailed
off. She was conscious of Pauline stiffening beside
her and a piercing intensity in her blue eyes.

'Cousin Lanice, I wish to begin at the beginning —
perfectly honestly with you. I want you to know that
I have heard — all.'

'About — Mamma?'

'Yes.'

There was a long pause, and Lanice knew that
Pauline was tactfully avoiding a direct question,
waiting for Lanice to speak of her own volition. She
could not. She drew her breath in with a trembling
sigh and pressed her lace handkerchief against her
mouth. The pause grew, and when at last Lanice
flung her words into the hiatus they echoed and gained
momentous weight.

'It is the most terrible thing in the world —,
hideous.'

'What?'

'Our lower natures. Mamma's got the upper hand
and — destroyed her. I almost wish it really had
killed her. And I am determined to live always on the
higher, the highest plane.'

'Yes, yes, Lanice. I can see, in spite of all these
absurd fashionable clothes that you affect, that you
are really a Mind. I can see . . .'

Already Lanice regretted her burst of confidence,
and drew back somewhat sulkily into her corner of
the barouche. She interrupted with a catch of heart-
break in her voice. 'How can I love her any more?

To think of running off with one of Papa's own students. Every one in Amherst is astounded. Papa's the only one who doesn't seem to be surprised.'

'You mean, previously, other men, some other time . . .'

'No!' cried Lanice hotly, and her cheeks were suffused with color, as she lied desperately, remembering Mr. Alpheus Matthews of New York. She knew that for years this man, greatest of cotton brokers and managing director of Mamma's mills, had worshipped the pretty woman in his own arrogant way. It had been terrible, when she first had found out. Mamma had given her a red riding-habit she no longer fancied, and then had gone humming and smiling out of the house. The young girl, arrayed in her first adult finery, had slipped to the darkened best parlor where the Venetian blinds were always drawn, and the smell of moth preventatives was never relieved by an open window. She had been forbidden since childhood to enter this Blue Beard's chamber, yet confidently she pulled up a blind and became absorbed in her own newly found beauty reflected in the glass, mimicked Mamma's coquettish graces. That was the way Mamma felt all the time, light on her feet, giddy in the head, secret happiness springing up and up through her veins. Lanice shook the long scarlet plume on the beaver hat, threw back her head with shut eyes. Mr. Matthews, tiptoeing into the room, saw only the familiar red habit and the loved pretty gestures. A moment too late he discovered it was not the mill owner playfully protesting his caresses, but

[13]

her 'brat,' in deadly earnest. They stood at last
facing each other in the most ghastly of comedies.
No explanation could explain. Later, at supper,
Lanice watched her father, reading, as was his
custom, from the classics as he ate, knew in some
subtle and shamefully intimate way that he, too,
knew about Mr. Matthews. Even the meek, pale
servant seemed omniscient. Mamma alone was un-
touched by her own sin. She was in rust-colored silk,
which matched her hair. She wore topaz in her ears,
and little gold French slippers with delicately immoral heels upon her feet.

Pauline was speaking.

'Italy — or France — perhaps France even more
than Italy is the place to go for sin. It never would
be tolerated in *this* State.'

'How did you hear?'

'Our Springfield cousins have written. And I know
that you have broken with the man whom you
love.'

'Cousin Pauline, I don't love him any more.
Perhaps I never did. I think I wanted to be married.
There seemed to be nothing else to do there and I was
getting too old for students, and . . .'

'There is plenty else to do here in Boston,' said
Pauline energetically. 'Why, only three weeks ago a
committee of dear, good women opened a philan-
thropic Boarding House for Industrious Females. It
is work one could absolutely lose one's self in if one
had the time. I personally am consecrated to other
things. Abolition moves me intensely, when I think

[14]

of God's Black Children sold as chattels. Children torn from their mothers and . . .' she glanced cautiously at Patrick's purple cloth back hunched upon the box — 'and no chance for colored females to retain their virtue — none.' She whispered, out of respect for Patrick's delicate masculine ears. 'I am much engaged in Women's Rights and in Higher Education for Females. Oh, so many, many things! My days are full, I assure you. That is the secret of a happy life. But you, Cousin Lanice, you have your genius. You have only to choose between literature and painting. But you must be very serious in your chosen field.'

'Oh, I am. What pleasure I henceforth get out of life must be quite independent of my gender. From now on I am not a woman, merely a human being. I want to be an artist or an authoress, and,' she added naïvely, 'I've stopped curling my hair.'

'Oh,' cried Pauline, 'I wish all women would, but even Mrs. Stowe, that high-minded, noble woman, wears a perfect galaxy of these female adornments.'

So it was for principle that Pauline screwed back her dull hair and buttoned her eager, stooping figure into such plain black basques. Her searching nose seemed made for the smelling-out of new fancies or old truths. Lanice remembered hearing that in Boston ladies did not greet each other with a 'How do you do, my dear?' but, 'Have you heard the latest thought out, my love?' Cousin Poggy's blotched skin and nervous manner made her slightly repellent, but she had the undaunted interest of a born confidante and

[15]

her willingness to set the world right showed her
generous spirit.

'Women must conduct themselves in such a way as
to win not the patronizing affection of men, but their
respect. I protest . . .' (there seemed some danger
that the jet buttons might leap off the tight basque)
'I protest . . .' Suddenly her keen, almost lovely
eyes narrowed, 'Cousin Lanice, are you at heart an
artist?'

'Oh, I hope I am, Cousin Pauline. I love to paint.
That's all I have done for five years, except a few
romances. I've never had proper lessons; Amherst is
so small.'

'Lanice, you shall have everything, *everything*:
masters and studios, and trips to Europe if you can
only promise to paint one picture, I care not how
small, but one picture that will rank high with the
work of the great male brushes.'

So compelling were the strange, eager eyes, Lanice
took fire. She felt a spiritual quickening that left her
ecstatic and throbbing.

'Pauline, I think I could.'

'Not a mere picture such as other female artists
could paint, but a real artistic triumph fit to hang in
the Uffizi or the Louvre, I care not how small.' The
size-clause reassured the young artist.

'I do feel as if I could, Cousin Pauline. I . . . To-
day . . . I know I could.'

'You mean,' said Pauline with flat suspicion, 'you
want to paint a masterpiece now, to-day, without
sufficient learning?'

'Oh, no. I must be taught, but do you think I could ever learn?'

'Dear cousin, I've never doubted but you are a . . . Genius!'

Lanice, her face flushed to a precocious pinkness, her eyes flooded with light, her tight lips trembling, gazed with rapture at this *dea ex machina* who could, by some alchemy, make her a great artist.

Pauline hastily outlined a plan. Lanice was to live with the Poggys and study with any half-dozen artists of established reputations who conducted informal classes. Little by little she was to realize that in her artistic career she worked, not merely for Art, but for the Freedom of Women. She should serve Minerva, not Apollo. She would, during her training, attend many lectures, conversations, meetings, unions, and institutes with Pauline. Social life, except an occasional soirée at the home of a Harvard professor, was forbidden. For all these good things Lanice was not to pay a cent. The girl demurred. She had a generous monthly allowance. How strange Papa had looked when she had asked if it would be continued, his face white, his eyes like onyx. Not a word suggested pain at his wife's or daughter's desertion, but if you watched him very closely you saw that every so often his head moved slightly up and to the left. His lips were so dry they rustled as he pressed his handkerchief against them.

It was decided that Lanice, in her spare hours, should serve as amanuensis to Captain Poggy. The old merchant, senior member of Poggy, Banks &

Poggy, had been, since he 'fell off Cape Horn,' very
lame. First he gave up his sea life and, some five
years before, all but a nominal interest in his great
shipping firm. For years he had been engaged in
writing an historical study of Salem witchcraft, 'not
that the past really matters, only the future.' Lanice
had never heard of this dark chapter in New England
history. She urged her cousin to tell her of it in
detail, but soon Pauline glanced at her with sly,
questioning eyes as if trying to fathom this pretended interest in so unimportant a subject. Yet, for
a moment, such was the power of Pauline's tongue,
she had actually seen them — stubborn Giles Corey
pressed to death for 'standing mute'; the flaunting
witch who ran an inn and made her death-dealing
poppets of hogs' bristles and human hair; and a poor,
ancient gentleman who walked about on two 'staves.'

Lanice saw the gruesome bodies swing upon
Gallows Hill against a fleecy spring sky.

'Father is so serious about this history, and only
last week the young man who has been helping him
left to teach school in Needham.'

Lanice would go with him to the Athenæum —
whatever that was — and to Salem. She would copy
records, write letters, take down his dictation, for the
disaster off Cape Horn that had lamed him had also
injured his hand. She could not believe her fabulous
good fortune.

'I'll work to the bone, both at my Art and for your
father,' she cried. 'It's wonderful. Oh, Cousin
Polly,' she exclaimed, using this diminutive for the

first and last time, 'I've never been so happy, not for years. Now I won't dream about Mamma ever again. You are an angel.'

She turned away her head again and sat with her profile turned towards Pauline, who was encouraged in her proselyting by a certain intellectuality she found in it. The nose especially, in spite of its neatness, might easily belong to a Great Mind.

'Now you are in Boston you shall have everything — why, to a girl of your genius the world lies open like a flower.'

Lanice turned towards her. Her face, seen from the front, was of a different calibre. It held a veiled suggestion of earthiness, perhaps more threatening to the owner's happiness than Mamma's frank paganism. Almost as if by an act of will, however, the expression changed, or, rather, wiped itself out. She looked, with her small pointed chin, open brow, and eyes like a maiden's prayer, rather like a fashion-plate drawing from a 'Godey's Book.'

3

Boston Common at last, and the still, small light of dusk lacing the naked trees. Cousin Poggy commanded her coachman to make a turn about the Common. Ranks of ordered brick houses, pleasing in proportion and fastidious in detail, were drawn up on three sides of the Common and slightly superciliously gazed at this tattered Eden from which the cows had been but recently banished. Lanice had not dreamed that in the whole country there were so many gleaming brass knockers and glass doorknobs, so many shallow bow windows, lacy iron balconies, and classic white porticoes. New York was not so chastely elegant.

A little, active creature in high stock, high hat, gaiters, and tightly buttoned overcoat see-sawed past her. His face was alive with benign intelligence. He must be famous — perhaps Dr. Holmes, who was *so droll*. The powerful Olympian with flowing cape and beard and majestic stride, why, he might be Professor Longfellow! Perhaps it is Harriet Beecher Stowe herself, this lady with the pointed face, draggled petticoats, and ancient straw hat. Even the children looked distinguished and well-grounded in Greek. Lanice remembered that Margaret Fuller had read the classics at seven, and gazed reverently at a little girl with bulging forehead and dangling legs and arms. She gaped at Boston coming and going over its criss-cross little board walks raised above the mundane slush. Boston, *Boston*, BOSTON! In her excitement she forgot the ideal expression for one of her sex, which should be chaste and sober and elegant, and something delightful flamed up and fled over her slim red mouth and glittered in her long black eyes. So with beauty she looked upon Boston. 'This,' she thought, 'is my oyster, as somebody — perhaps George Washington — once said of something else.' Boston, Boston! She saw its doorways, its Common, its chimney pots. She saw the sky. She saw herself suddenly as a part of all this and wondered why she had been frightened at the station.

They jogged up Park Street, turned left upon Beacon, and before a graceful Doric portico the fat white horses came to a willing stop. The ladies clambered out, and with secret admiration Lanice saw her emancipated cousin draw from her petticoat pocket a doorkey and quite like a man open the white door. With a certain pride in the fine house, Pauline pushed her in and through the hall into one of the two self-possessed living-rooms which ran the width of the mansion. The walls were papered with an exotic tropical landscape. Dark, flaunting trees shaded joyous revels of nymph and faun. Ruins twisted with faded roses. Goddesses in the unladylike costume of the First Empire disported themselves. When Lanice herself drew Venus, Calypso, or Ariadne, it was with difficulty that she kept the telltale hoop from under their skirts. She arranged their hair exactly as she did her own, nor might their freer spirits escape her tight stays. For this was beautiful and elegant. Skimpy draperies and snood-bound Psyches were wanton and ugly, and in the case of one nymph sporting by the fountain, actually indelicate.

Mahogany, sleek as the haunch of a polished horse, twinkling chandeliers, dripping their bright prisms, crimson curtains, fastidious woodwork. The more intimate of the two rooms was partly cut off by folding doors, and a massive screen of teak and fat jade.

Pauline's flea-like mind was leaping ahead in all sorts of wrong directions. She thought her young cousin still suffering from terror at the stranger's approach in the train. 'There, there,' she said, and saw the tears in Lanice's eyes before the girl knew that they had gathered. 'Men are such brutes. Do not think of that . . . unpleasant experience, think only of the great things that your brush shall do.'

She took her by her slender arms and shook her enthusiastically. Lanice felt the terrible nausea return with the tears that constricted her throat. The prodigious tropical trees upon the walls and her cousin's narrow ash blond face suddenly fogged with tears. Her own mouth squared childishly.

'Would you like some hot milk?'

She shook her head.

'Your room?'

'Yes,' she assented mournfully.

Pauline patted her hand, and chatted as she led her up two flights of stairs to a lovely yellow room whose walls were quaintly printed with emerald pagodas, red Chinese mandarins, and blue birds. Pauline whispered to her the tea hour in the tone of a conspirator, left her alone, and with elaborate tact tiptoed downstairs.

CHAPTER II

AND GOES TO WORK

1

My dear Papa,

I wish to assure you that I am settled most auspiciously in Boston and intend to stay here and study for a year at least. When I think I can endure Amherst I will come back and visit for a few days, but now I could not; Papa, if you were very angry with me you would not still be paying me my allowance, would you? I hope this means you forgive me. Amherst is no place for one who wishes to be an artist, as there is no one there any better than myself to teach me, and you must understand why I prefer not to be in Amherst where all the Old Hens, and what is worse, the Male Gossips like Mr. Goochey (I do not care if he is the minister), will talk of nothing else but the Bardeens for six months. I know you will not miss me, for you have always preferred the society of books to any human companionship. You may not believe me, but I am glad to leave Mr. Augustus Trainer forever. I do not think Heaven would have *smiled* upon our Union, and just as soon as he heard about Mamma he promised to protect me from any inherent *sinfulness* I might have inherited, and proposed postponing our nuptials for a year, so if I had any flightiness it might be manifest. Please tell Mr. Trainer that yes, I am flighty, and that I never in the world will marry him. I hope he is not languishing away, but if he is I think it would do him good. I have decided that Marriage is not an enviable state. I intend to offer myself heart and soul to Art. I have stopped curling my hair and now am working at Mrs. Dummer's studio. It is very inspiring and the instruction so good. Mrs. Dummer is considered the first lady artist in the city — perhaps in this country. She is painting a series of twenty-four scenes from the Old Testament. The canvases are six by four, and sublimely conceived as well as perfectly executed. She is now working on her 'Drunkenness of Noah.' It is immense. She has done some of the New Testament, but when she tried to paint the 'Miracle of the Loaves and Fishes' I had to show her how fish scales really fit on, as I do not think she has ever looked with great accuracy at fish. I went to the Market and had a basket filled with one of every kind. But Mrs. D. did not like the smell. I did not mind, and painted fishes all that day, and at night divided them between a model and Willy, the Poggys' cat, who in spite of her name has just had a mess of kittens. Her (I mean Mrs. Dummer's) ideals are of the Highest. We both agree that there is enough wickedness and ugliness in the world without putting it in pictures or stories. It is the duty of Art to see only the Beautiful. And this noble theme she is able to carry out, even when treating nasty old Noah, who, on re-reading this particular part of the Good Book, strikes me as being a very worldly gentleman, unworthy of his place in Sacred Literature.

It is almost more interesting to work as Captain Poggy's amanuensis. This task commands half of my time, usually the afternoons. All are agreed that ART can be best served by judicious application and that both morning and afternoon at my easel would soon render me *stale*. So it is without detriment to my Chosen Muse that I help Captain Poggy on his witch-craft history. It is like spring already, although but the middle of March. Early in April Captain Poggy and I will spend several days in Salem, which city I would now rather see than any the New World has to offer.

Papa, if you are too lonely, write me and I will return to Amherst, much as I now hate it. I hope the horses are well, or have you sold them?

I am, dutifully, your daughter

LANICE BARDEEN

2

When Captain Poggy tried to explain to Lanice the purport of the book and the duties expected of his amanuensis, Pauline would flit restlessly before his bookshelves, pulling down one volume after another and often replacing it wrong side up. All the time Lanice was conscious of her eager, sidelong glances. Finally Captain Poggy politely asked his daughter, as long as she had so kindly furnished him with this clever secretary, to leave them undisturbed. Pauline inexplicably burst into tears and left the room. Captain Poggy, a seraphic man with white hair as silvery as a gone-by dandelion, paid no heed to this outburst and calmly went on with the subject of his

discourse. Land rights, church conflicts, jealousies —
all these petty things one must understand thoroughly
if one would understand Salem witchcraft. In his
book he would show not only the courage but also
the terrors of the early settlers confronted, as they
believed, on all sides by the power of Beelzebub.
They really thought the Red Men to be devils and
the wolves were were-wolves. They themselves were
from a little land of hedges, lanes, and small fields,
but here was the unutterable weight of endless forest
at their backs, and the dark sea beating at their feet.
As Lanice wrote, the subject enchanted her. When
Captain Poggy was done she could hardly bear to
lay her pen down, although her fingers ached.

While engaged in her art lessons with Mrs. Dummer, she thought more often of the witches than of
the Biblical scenes growing up about her. Once she
painted a convent on Mount Tom, but this she replaced with a gallows. For the shepherds she sub-
stituted witch-fire. It would not have occurred to
her to paint old Jabez, the actual shepherd of Amherst
sheep, who smoked and did not play his pipe.

3

A month later Lanice received a roundabout
response to her letter. Mrs. Andrews, the housekeeper, found her at work by the Chippendale table
in the library. She glared at the pale young lady
through her rectangular spectacles.

'If I may interrupt, there is a gentleman at the
door asking for Miss Bardeen.'

The girl, absorbed in her work, sleeked her jet-black hair, frowned and shook her head. She knew no one in Boston.

'But, Miss . . .'

'I must finish this before Captain Poggy comes back. If any one really does want to see me, ask him to come back later.'

The gentleman left a large box. Evidently this box had come from afar. It was wrapped in Italian paper, and stuck with labels and customs seals. When Lanice saw the handwriting, she drew back. 'I'll open it later; I'll rest now.' Her silk skirts swished up the stairs. Mamma had addressed the label. Wicked, wicked Mamma had sent the box.

She lay in her small yellow room and composed herself. Perhaps it was a little statue that Mamma had sent her to Amherst and which some one had carried to her here. Perhaps it was a Swiss music box, or an alabaster Leaning Tower of Pisa, or a Roman vase. She wished it had never reached her. An uncomfortable tenderness towards Mamma stirred in her heart and hurt her. Mamma with her apple-blossom face. . . . Surely Mamma was the happiest person in Lanice's world. Even now she was seeing the Wonders of the Old World, Switzerland and Italy . . . Italy! Italy! Roger Cuncliffe — the pretty boy with the light walk and feverish cheeks. The awfully sick boy who had been brought up in Europe. Lanice could instantly recall his narrow face, black curls, burning color, and cattish grace contrasting with the heavier virtues of the other students. Some-

thing symbolical . . . symbolical of what? Mamma
was in Italy with this symbolical young man. Venice
and the Grand Canal; Naples and Pompeii; Florence
and the Arno; Rome and the Colosseum — and Roger
Cuncliffe.

Mrs. Andrews rat-tatted on her door. The gentleman who had left the box had returned. Perhaps it
was Papa!

Had the gentleman fine brown whiskers? Did he
wear a green cape?

The gentleman had a very small flaxen Dundreary.
The gentleman wore a plaid ulster and a small High-
land shawl beneath.

Not Papa, who was prouder of the almost feminine
beauty of his beard than of his great classical learning. Not Papa, but Augustus. 'Oh, God,' she
prayed, 'guide me. Give me strength to send him
away and forgive my disliking him.'

Strangely enough she stopped, before descending
to see this hated young man, to lay off the ugly
brown merino that she had much affected since life
had grown so serious, and hooked herself into her
black glacé silk. She adjusted her point d'esprit
collars and cuffs. This slightly tragic dress she knew
always had had a disturbing effect upon Mr. Augustus Trainer. Although she intended to 'part with
him forever,' she was almost as anxious to appear
handsome in his eyes as she had been two years
earlier when she thought him a great mind. Then the
girl ('vixen' Mr. Trainer would have called her if he
had known all) hung black onyx and pearl ear-rings

[28]

in her ears, moistened her palms from the bottle of Boudoir Liquid Hair Pomade and slicked her already glittering hair. Satisfied that Augustus should at least appreciate what he had lost, she stole darkly down two flights of stairs and saw Augustus standing beneath the hall chandelier, leaning on his cane.

'Ah . . . Lanice.'

'How courteous of you to seek me out, Mr. Trainer.'

'You left me most unceremoniously, Lanice. Could you not have trusted me with your plans?'

'No. I couldn't even trust myself . . .'

She had intended to send Augustus away without letting him sit down, but wishing privacy she motioned him into the more formal of the two drawing-rooms. She sank delicately into a red Chinese chair in front of the screen, massive as the gates of Paradise, curiously made of carved teak and fat jade. She wished to rid herself of him forever, but could not help looking up at him sadly with more meaning in her long black eyes than in her heart.

'Augustus,' she said, with the gentility of one of her own mawkish heroines, 'it is best for you, as well as for me, that we part. I am more definitely pledged to my Art than I ever could be to you.'

'No, no, Miss. It is not your art that has come between us, although I admit that you have talent. It is the chagrin you feel at your mother's ridiculous conduct.'

'Ridiculous?' The girl's heart was pounding and her neat ivory hands twisted the bracelets on her

[29]

wrists. It was one thing to hate Mamma herself, and another for Augustus to sneer. 'Is it ridiculous to prefer the wonders of the Old World to — Amherst?'

'It is ridiculous to prefer the company of a scatter-brained boy to one's lawful spouse.'

'Ugh.'

'Why do you say "ugh" Lanice?'

'I do not like the word "spouse."'

'"Spouse?" It is one of the most hallowed words in the English language. Its associations . . . but to leave philology and return to ourselves. I have come to tell you that, in spite of what I once said, in *my* eyes you are as untainted as before your mother's fall. I spoke hastily, I fear. I suggested that the mischievous wantonness of your parent . . . Lanice . . .' The young man, for he was young in spite of his impeccable dignity, faltered slightly. 'There are certain barriers with which womanly modesties and delicacies guard themselves. I never have known you, even in moments of enthusiasm over our approaching nuptials, to transgress one of these barriers. I have never seen in you a suggestion of gross passion. Because I believe entirely in your own purity, I am willing to overlook your mother, and once again offer you my hand.' His forehead was dank with sweat. His earnest, grasping eyes stuck out from under the piggish-white lashes.

'Mr. Trainer, you do me honor, but I can see now that I have never really loved you.'

'How many a pure woman has said that! It is only

with marriage the truly womanly woman comes to understand love.'

'That may be true, but, perhaps I am not womanly, for my *poor* Augustus, I think I could understand so much more, even before marriage, from some one else.'

The young man empurpled.

'Lanice! That does not sound like you. I am afraid I do not approve of studio life for a young female; such thoughts are unbecoming.'

'But please realize that I think them.' Then, as if to counteract any impression of wantonness, the girl cast down her black-fringed lids, crossed her slim feet and gentle hands.

'Lanice.' The young man was oppressed with the desire to crush the primly corseted female form. Some one else would teach the minx to love! She sat in her red lacquer chair and black glacé dress, her eyes veiled, but a provocative, mocking smile shadowing her mouth.

'Lanice.'

'You said that before.'

'I beg of you to consider my suit.' She innocently regarded his two thick layers of plaid.

'A new one, Mr. Trainer?'

'It pleases you to be frivolous.'

She raised her pointed chin and put out her hands with a direct, boyish grace. 'No, only silly. But it's no use. I'll never go back to Amherst and I'll never unite my fortunes with yours. Nor even have an understanding with you nor permit you to call upon me again. You'll fall just as much in love with some one else.'

She stood up, her hoops swaying delicately beneath her glossy skirts. It was a trick of hers, learned from Mamma. She could start this flower-like swaying by giving the skirt a secret little push in back.

'Augustus, let's unpack Mamma's present.' She swished past him into the hall and he suffered vaguely from the fascination of a half-realized scent of lavender and sweet rose-leaves, then lurched after her and humbly set about unpacking the box.

Inside the wrappings was a strange rosewood box. It was handsomely mounted with ebony, fitted with lenses. Obviously one was intended to squat before the mystery and peer in.

'Lanice, my dear, your mother has sent you one of these wonderful modern inventions — a stereoscope! See, here are the photographs to go in the machine and the directions in French.'

While Lanice rapturously gazed at the pinkish double photographs, mounted on yellow cards bearing names of foreign dealers, Augustus studied the directions and established the machine in the shallow bow window of the drawing-room. His mechanical enthusiasm was as touched as Lanice's artistic. The girl had never in her life seen so many fine photographs of foreign wonders. Her mind thrilled under the impact. Augustus demanded the photographs and skilfully inserted them within the box. Then, adjusting the light, he called upon Lanice to see. She had not even heard of the invention. Why were

there two of every view, mounted side by side?
Why must she look at them in the box? At the last
moment Augustus decided that it was undignified
for the young female to sit on the floor and begged
her to let him rearrange the show upon a table. The
girl uttered an emphatic 'no,' and, squatting before
the box, applied her eyes to the lenses.

'Oh, Augustus!' she cried, and felt a spinal chill of
delight, a rapturous shuddering such as love had
never raced through her body. By magic the flat
photographs had become rounded realities. A jutting
rock overhung one corner of the scene. It was so real
that she wanted to put out her hands lest it fall upon
her, lest she slip into the Alpine chasm below. Whirling waterfalls and mist floating up. In the distance
snow-capped mountains. Two travellers in capes,
rucksacks, and beards leaned against the flimsy
fence that guarded the footpath. The illusion was
painful in its reality.

'Ready for the next?'

'Oh, not yet. See, even the buttons on their coats
are round.'

Many views of 'La Suisse' — and then . . . Italy.
The Alps stunned her; Italy pierced her through.
Milan's lovely lacework, layer upon layer, like a
valentine. Lake Como, with iron chairs in the garden
for Lanice to sit upon. The Rialto, so firm she might
set her eager feet upon it. Miles away Augustus was
saying that President and Mrs. Duke in Amherst —
despised Amherst — had a small machine of this
type. 'You hold it in your left hand and adjust the

pictures with the right. Amherst has some things, Miss, as soon as Boston!'

The Arno shooting through its five great bridges. Which was the one where the jewellers worked? Which sweet hill Fiesole? Saint Peter's, and the stone arms stretched out to enfold a world. The Tiber. The Campagna, stone pines and marching ruins of aqueducts. Augustus turned mechanically. He could not see the pictures himself but his voice wove mesmerizing passes about her. Out of oblivion Lanice occasionally recognized the word 'Amherst.'

'The advantages of such a town for a home ... I am afraid that for some years a humble home ...'

Pompeii and Capri and the Blue Grotto which was painted an intense blue and yawned at one like a dragon's gullet.

'The new board walks do much for our comfort in Amherst. They have been extended as far as the Dickinson house. On Pleasant Street ...'

Out of the dark of the box flashed the gleaming body of a girl. The headless, almost armless, fragment twisted in a dance. Lanice's heart gathered itself together and stopped. For the first time in her life she was touched by the beauty of nudity. With unabashed interest she followed the flowing curves of the nymph's body, and regretted that she, herself, was so thin. Apollo Belvedere next, his vapid face turned away, his hair coquettishly knotted. She admired the lines of chest and abdomen, and the sleekness of his limbs. Next, out of the darkness to meet her came a brutal bronze boxer with gaping sockets where once enamel made him eyes. His coarse muscles and rather bestial masculinity embarrassed her, but she stared with fascination. Strange, he was not as beautiful as Apollo, but she felt the spinal chill which she associated with beauty. She wished Augustus would remember to turn the crank. One should not stare too long at this animal, yet she could neither drag her eyes away, nor tell Augustus to turn on.

'... Still an instructor, next year, and live with your father ... a professor ... eight hundred a year ... little home ... settle down ... restless ... tormenting yourself with art ... Amherst. By and by in God's good time ...'

Did men look like that? Threatening, bulging muscles, fleshless thighs, corded neck and arms? She was almost afraid the creature would follow her out of the box. How terrible would be a man of bronze! Stronger than twenty men of flesh.

'Are you ready, Lanice?'

'Oh, *quite*. Turn the crank.'

'My dear, you could not have been listening. Well ...'

They moved on to the Throne Room of Versailles. Gold, crimson, polished floors, seemingly hundreds of candles actually burning in crystal chandeliers. Kings and Queens!!!

'I am a patient man by nature and I can, I will wait ... I ...'

They had come around once again to Switzerland.

'A home is not a thing to despise . . . and frankly, my dear, why should you think yourself a genius . . . few women have been that . . . a husband . . . and I will always love you Lanice, my dear.'

He straightened himself and looked hopelessly at the great hoopskirts collapsed in circles upon the floor, and at their owner gaping into the black box. He twisted at his stock and placed his palm upon the girl's waist. The girl unfolded at the touch. Her eyes, long focused on foreign wonders, blinked, and her mind, from far away, came back with difficulty.

'Thank you for bringing me this thing all the way from Amherst . . . and such a heavy box! But when you touch me suddenly you give me creeps. And, really, you must now excuse me, for I have my copying to do for Captain Poggy.'

'Lanice, when?'

'I must beg of you to believe me when I say that I can never be more than a sister to you, only a friend. And may I suggest that the way to be spared the burning is to avoid the flame? In other words, Mr. Trainer, it is best that we meet no more!'

4

She journeyed to Salem, the dirty steam packet approaching from the sea as had the first planters. At the decaying Derby Wharf where the packet docked they found a purple chaise with a wan yellow horse, and so drove in shabby state to Chestnut Street and the long dead Mrs. Poggy's sister's house, one of the most pretentious of all the houses that

McIntire had designed for the greatness of a past generation. Here they stayed their week.

Lanice, knowing the wealth of the Poggy family and realizing that the great success of the present firm of Poggy, Banks & Poggy was based upon the fortunes of this old Salem family, was shocked to find 'Miss Myra's' mansion pitifully gone in decay. Captain Poggy, conscious of her amazement, availed himself of the first moment his sister-in-law left the room to explain that, although he yearly paid over a 'proper sum' to this eccentric lady, she always refused to more than tolerate it in her bank. She would not spend it because she believed it to be the 'blood money of Salem.'

Miss Myra, even in her own house, always wore a large green silk bonnet of a long past style, and black or yellow silk mitts upon her birdlike hands. She smelled faintly but unmistakably of the past. Lanice could not analyze it, but it was not unsimilar to ancient cookies.

To Lanice, who was but a distant and inland connection, she relaxed into courtesy if not kindness, but to the Captain she remained stolidly aloof, treating him with studied old-fashioned courtesy that was ruder than the insults of common man. Even his name she would not always deign to remember and called him 'Captain ... er ...' with a belittling gesture of her hand. Lanice, angry for his dignity, asked him why they must stay here in this mouldering house, the guests of this hateful old lady, but the Captain would reply that if they had stopped any-

where else it would have hurt Miss Myra's feelings.
On the sixth day Miss Myra so far unbent as to take
Lanice to her own room where the shutters made per-
petual night, although outside the sun was bright.
Miss Myra lighted a candle and with some rheumatic
difficulties got to her knees beside a red Chinese
trunk, bound with brass.

'I took to you because I have known your face for
so many years...longer than you have lived, I
imagine.'

'Do I resemble my mother's people?'

'No, no, no, no,' the old lady frowned irritably and
laid aside the Eastern gauzes and embroideries heavy
with musk and sandalwood. She took out a gold
filigree case, and with some staggering, muttering,
and ineffectual aid from Lanice, got to her feet.
She looked baleful and evil, like a witch cat, and
Lanice, thinking of the women hanged upon the hill,
could imagine this bitter lady in a halter.

'Open it,' she commanded. 'No one has seen it for
forty years, not since Sister Poggy deserted Salem to
go with that worthless husband to Boston.'

Lanice found herself face to face with a beautiful
Indian or Persian miniature painted upon ivory.
The girl she faced had long jet eyes, black silk hair,
pale shapely face, and locked red mouth. She was
heavy with jewels, ear-rings, nose stud, bracelets,
and necklaces. Her skin was so white as to seem opalescent, and her fingers were henna-dipped. Lanice
could see the vague resemblance, but was amazed by
the almost hypnotic, unearthly expression, a promise

of intoxicating joys and subtle evils which no one had found in her, nor she in life.

'As soon as you came in, I recognized the resemblance. My uncle never married because of that face. He had the miniature in his hand when he died fifty years ago in Canton, and his partner sent it back to us.'

'Is it a picture of a real woman, some one whom he loved?'

'No. Never. No woman. Some idea . . . a dream vampire . . .' the old lady's voice sank . . . 'ghoul.'

'But perhaps it was nothing so terrible. Just a girl of flesh and blood, like me. Your uncle . . .'

'My uncle was no fool. And the men of *my* family do not commit suicide for an actual woman. This thing drove him crazy.' She turned away from the strewn contents of the chest. 'Keep it, if you want it. I'm through.'

Speechless, Lanice tucked the miniature in her voluminous petticoat pocket, and at a peremptory gesture from the old lady, left the shuttered chamber and its antique, delicately cooky-scented occupant.

Captain Poggy laughed at the idea of suicide. Every one knew, he said, that this uncle had died of dysentery, but the ladies of his family had preferred a more romantic ending, and now Sister Myra actually believed these lies. Lanice surreptitiously showed him the miniature, which he pronounced the finest thing of its kind he had ever seen. If, in some subtle way, it did resemble Lanice, evidently the fact escaped his shrewd eyes.

[39]

5

On other days she climbed the rock hill on which
the gallows of the witches had been set, and saw the
crevices where tradition believed their bodies had
been buried, some with their hands exposed above
ground for vile and simple headstones. She saw their
gnarled old houses, far away in Danvers or Beverly.
She saw the pins with which the afflicted girls had
been tormented. But much of her time was spent in
the new court-house where she deciphered and copied
old records of court procedure.

At night, on returning to Miss Myra's, supposedly
to sleep on the great sleigh bed, she would find that
the words of the witches, the questioning of the
judges, the outcries of the 'afflicted,' followed her
from the lifeless leaves.

'Have you made no contracts with the Devil?'

'No.'

(Then the afflicted did cry out.)

'Why do you torment these children?'

'I do not. I scorn it.'

(She muttered and the children were struck
speechless.)

'What do you mutter to yourself?'

'If I must tell, I will tell.'

'Tell us then.'

'It is the Commandments. I may say my Commandments, I hope.'

Lanice would turn and try to forget these long-
dead tragic folk. But again their words, forcing themselves through the quiet of the night, came to disturb

[40]

her sleep. The voice of the witch, 'I am a gospel woman and God will save me. I am a gospel woman and I hurt no man.'

'Why do you torture these children?'

'I do not. I scorn it, and God shall prove me innocent as an unborn babe.'

The accused told of red and yellow birds, hairy imps, pretty black men dressed in green leaves, and these too Lanice could see by shutting her eyes.

In odd moments she saw Salem. Where the East Indiamen and China clippers had been were now a few lumber schooners from Nova Scotia, or a shipment of hides from the South. The proud city that Captain Poggy had, in his radiant boyhood, adored as a lover, had fallen into senility. He told Lanice, as they walked the dull, echoing streets, how he had first come to Salem as a youngster without worldly goods beyond his 'Bowditch, his Testament, his quadrant, and his mother's blessing,' and how he had risen to be master at twenty, at twenty-three had married his employer's daughter, and by thirty was a shipowner. The rest of his career Lanice gathered, from the speed with which he dismissed it, was nothing. The rise of the great firm of Poggy, Banks & Poggy and all that he had accomplished since he was thirty — that any one might have done. But to be master at twenty!

He told her how, when he had come into control of the great shipping interests of Salem's most distinguished family, he decided Boston was the coming port and that Salem had had her glorious day, so

[41]

abandoned the old love for a new. For this disloyalty he had been followed by the implacable hatred of the proud families that had accepted ruin with the failing port.

Sometimes they stopped to call upon dry and haughty old dames sitting in close parlors that smelt of sandalwood and camphor, drinking rare tea out of the cups their fathers had brought back from the East fifty years before. The paint peeled from the beautiful classical doorways and weeds grew between the bricks of the sidewalk.

Walking the streets of Salem the Captain liked to take Lanice's arm. This he called 'helping her,' and she graciously accepted it as such, although, because of his lameness, his 'help' sometimes dragged. She knew he was proud of his 'Cousin Laney,' as he called her, and liked the pretty white frilled muslin she wore and her scarlet straw bonnet. His cane tapped the sidewalk. Her skirts swished against the mouldering iron fences.

One day, enough work being done, the weather fine, they idled down Chestnut Street for the beginning of their stroll.

'I believe,' said the Captain, 'that there yonder down the street is a familiar back.'

'Not to me, Cousin Poggy.'

She looked with attention at the retreating back. It was of a tall, strongly built man making considerable speed away from them.

'It's a Ripley back' said Captain Poggy positively; 'if it's not Sears Ripley it's his half-brother

[42]

Frank, or his cousin Asa. The Ripleys all have been built like that.'

'I don't see anything so particular about it.'

'Oh, that's a *fine* back.'

'Is that the Mr. Sears Ripley who lives in Concord and is so literary? And teaches at Harvard? I've heard of him; why should he be in Salem?'

'That Concord house of his was his mother's, a second wife, but all the rest of him is Salem and he ought to be thankful for it.' The Captain began to hurry.

'We can't possibly catch up with him.'

'He may turn round and see us.'

'What do you want of him? You see Mr. Sears Ripley every week in Boston, at your Literary Club.'

'I know, but it may be Asa.' The Captain was getting a little breathless, 'And Asa is still shipping out of Salem. I'd like a word or two with him. Do you know, Cousin Laney, I could still shout so as to make him hear? No, no, I'm not planning to do it.'

'What would you shout?'

'"Hoy, hoy, Ripley!" — only very loud.'

The man, unconscious of his pursuers, slackened his speed and seemed on the point of turning about.

'Ha! That vermin! And off again is he, faster than ever — with those long legs of his.'

'And that *fine* back.'

They both laughed. Lanice grew restless.

'Wait. I'll run ahead and stop him,' she offered, and lifting up her many muslin ruffles, she flew down the street after him, the scarlet clocks in her white

[43]

silk stockings visible to all the watchers behind closed blinds. She overtook him, and called in a voice made loud and uncompromising by breathlessness, 'Mr. Ripley.'

He swung about in amazement.

'If you are Mr. Ripley,' she added.

'I am,' he began, 'and. . .' He wanted to know who this bright pursuer was and what he might do for her. When he turned and faced her, she saw that he was not as young as she had judged from his back. He had a short, slightly pointed dark beard, and his eyes were amusingly triangular in shape and very deeply set. His suit was cut square, a little like a seaman's, and made of blue serge. His complexion, either by nature or exposure, was dark. She decided that he must be Asa who 'shipped out' rather than his Concord cousin, the scholarly Sears.

'I beg your pardon for running after you.'

His little, odd eyes twinkled. 'I am flattered.'

'But if you are Mr. Asa Ripley . . .'

'Oh, but I'm not. If I were Asa I would be merely a ghost. He died two months ago.'

Lanice was conscience-stricken. She begged his pardon again. 'Captain Poggy cannot know that he is dead.'

'Nobody did until the brig, Laura Burn, came in day before yesterday. But is Captain Poggy about?' He looked down the street, saw him coming, and hastily and rather joyously went to meet him.

'And my young cousin, Miss Lanice Bardeen.'

The little eyes sparkled. 'Oh,' he said, 'you need

[44]

not introduce us. We have already broken the ice splendidly.'

But later, evidently fearing that she was sensitive about her blunder, he said to her, in an aside, 'Asa and I always disliked each other — even as boys. You must not think you hurt my feelings.'

'But still I'm sorry,' said Lanice.

'You must not feel sorry,' said Sears Ripley.

They smiled and were friends.

CHAPTER III

SHE DISCOVERS MR. FOX

1

PAULINE still watched for wonders from her protegée's brush, but now from force of habit and without many illusions. When she saw how much of her father's book really was Lanice's work, she thought either Lanice's name should be on the title-page or that her father should be 'too proud' to present as his own so much of the work of another. Captain Poggy appreciated his secretary's judgment and accepted her advice in matters of style. He did not guess that it was her work that made the book something of a work of art. She suggested that he should add a chapter on the history of European witchcraft, showing backgrounds from which the tragedy of 1692 sprang.

'Go to it, Cousin Laney. If 'tis a good chapter we'll use it, and buy you the finest of Indy shawls to boot.'

Every day she read in the Athenæum. She forgot she was a lady, delicate of mind as well as body. She forgot the hoopskirts which stood out as a barrier, holding the world at a little more than arm's length. She plunged into the Stygian dark of that most ancient and terrible of religions, witchcraft. A religion rather than a superstition. The librarian found for her 'Discourses of the Subtill Practices of Devilles,'

'Pleasant Treatises of Witches,' Glanville's 'Sad-
ducismus Triumphatus,' and 'The Hammer for
Witches.'

Nothing in the Salem trials had prepared her for
the magic of the earlier European beliefs. So old was
this religion, older than Christianity. There were
lithesome devils who came to the worshippers dressed
in green leaves and danced in magic circles, and
beautiful naked witches, the black goat, and un-
baptized children with no cross to guard them. She
learned the body-marks the Devil put upon his worshippers, and, safe in the scholastic gloom of the
Athenæum, safe in Boston far, far away from the
morning of the world when such things originated,
she learned of the earth-old fertility rites. She blushed
and went cold. She hated the human race that had
thought so evilly. She tried to forget and hurry on.
She learned of strange night demons, incubi and
succubæ, and the use a cat can be put to in brewing a
storm, or a wax puppet in the slaying of man, and
how the fertility of field or beast or human may be
blasted.

The world had been clothed, and now was naked.
She gritted her teeth against its ugliness and from a
small part of what she had learned she wrote her
chapter. There was in it none of the mawkishness of
her 'Godey's Book' or 'House and Home' stories.
The thought that no one would guess her to be the
author gave her assurance and poise. She did not
have to think whether or not it was appropriate and becoming to one of the gentler sex to write such things.

2

'Your work on Father's book is done, Lanice. Surely Art will not take all your time. I wish you could give yourself, heart and soul, to some Cause. Perhaps the Cause of Women. The Society for the Promulgation of Belief in Women is to meet here as soon as Father goes to New York. I am sure that will point the way.'

'Perhaps it will, Cousin Pauline. But I cannot believe I will like live women as well as dead witches.'

The drawing-rooms were denuded of everything but chairs. Chairs brought up from the dining-room and down from the bedrooms, chairs hired from the undertaker. The meeting was to be addressed by a series of speakers who would represent various spheres of woman's success.

Mrs. Morgan would speak of their accomplishments in the cause of Temperance; Miss Cordelia Gatherall of their services to the Southern negro; Meminta Purse, author of two dozen novels, would represent literature; Mrs. Professor Channing was to explain woman's recent advancement in scholarship.

Miss Gatherall arrived first, and had to lie down to recover from her train journey. Then four or five Boston ladies in a group, and three or four from Cambridge, who came on the horse-car. More arrived in hackney coaches, in gigs, and on foot. It was really a stupendous gathering of shabby pelisses, bedraggled bonnets, spectacles, reticules bulging with papers and tracts. Miss Gatherall wondered if there could not be some way of temporarily whitewashing the negroes, furnishing them with wigs, and thus boldly walking them over the border. Miss Purse recounted the plot of her next novel. The gaslight flickered, the bonnets nodded. Lanice, detached and contemplative in spite of her excitement, watched them dubiously. They were such kind, good women. There sat old little Amy Spence in her demoralizing Zouave bloomers and ankle-length skirt, her forehead bulged like a baby's.

'Miss Bardeen' — she looked up with her soft childish gaze — 'I think this is one of the greatest, if not *the* greatest moment of my life. Why, I do not suppose so many intellectual, high-minded women have ever before been gathered in one room. Why, there will be a marker here like the one on Bunker Hill some day, my dear, and you'll live to see it. Why, *you'll* live to cast the vote. You'll see women set free from the slavery of their clothes. Look at me. I haven't the strength to drag enormous skirts about on the ground, you know, getting in and out of those horse-cars as I do, but just because they're up three inches, rude little boys call attention to my nether limbs, and sermons have been preached against them. Dear Miss Bardeen, you'll live to walk without hoops. Dear me! If my great-niece — dear good girl she is, too, but spiritually in slavery — has my laying-out, I'll go to my grave with skirts to the floor, and . . .'

She chuckled and blinked at Lanice, who could not

[49]

resist leaning over and putting the dingy little bonnet straight on the grandmotherly head. A wonderful old soldier this venerable woman was! There was no shade of bitterness in her voice as she referred to the vulgar little boys and her unemancipated great-niece. When she lay in her coffin with her skirts 'to the floor,' one could imagine her dowdy old spirit looking down and chuckling that at last the joke had been on her.

And it was true. Clothes, the great hoopskirts, the heavy shawls took so much strength to carry. Lanice bent her body inside of all her wrappings. There it was, a thin white sliver as supple as a willow twig. Why, indeed, should it be burdened and bound? Suddenly the long rings she wore in her ears dragged upon her.

Pauline found some difficulty in calling the meeting to order, but finally rapped so loudly with her improvised gavel that every one jumped and subsided guiltily into her chair.

'Ladies, and you few, kind, generous gentlemen. We have gathered here to-night . . .'

Pauline was already breathless, but the meeting was off. Lanice, sitting alone in the crimson-curtained bow window at the back of the improvised hall, felt again a generous impulse to help. The women seemed pitiful, and yet so frankly ugly. Why was it necessary to wear such hideous clothes? Their feet, too, their awkward hands, vaguely irritated her collectively, although individually so many were kind and admirable, like dear old Miss Spence.

All through Miss Gatherall's speech Lanice considered the subject. Women as a whole suddenly hurt her, and she wished she could do something for them, but hardly knew what. 'I think,' she thought, 'I'd study medicine and find out the way to keep them young and beautiful. They wear out so quickly as a rule, poor things. And wear isn't becoming to them as it often is to men. You hardly care how battered and worn a heavy old walking-boot may be, but a white kid slipper must be fresh. Women are the slippers — now. Perhaps not always. I don't know. Perhaps always.' She thought of Mamma and was proud of her youthful prettiness.

Late arrivals straggled in; now it seemed no more would come. The maid who attended the door had gone below to the kitchen to help with the refreshments. There was a vigorous pull at the bell. Lanice waited a moment until it was repeated, and then tiptoed into the vestibule and opened the door cautiously. She was amazed to find herself face to face with Captain Poggy's intimate and publisher, Mr. Fox. Lanice had often seen him and had always liked him, but had never talked with him before. He looked surprisingly young for his forty-five years, his figure slight, compact, and graceful; the narrow face resembled the animal who once was the totem of his ancestors.

'Oh, Mr. Fox! I don't think you want to come in, really!'

'Why not? Murder? Smallpox? A wedding? A baby?'

'No,' she laughed nervously, 'but Captain Poggy is in New York.'

Mr. Fox peered through the sidelights. 'I see — it's a party. Of course I do not wish to intrude.'

'Come inside for a moment,' she whispered, with the instincts of cordiality, but conscious of betrayal.

Mr. Fox would not sympathize. He was an earthly man. He whispered:

'They're Miss Pauline's females out for their rights! Is that it? And Captain Poggy is in New York.' Then added out loud, 'Oh, my God! Well, all I want is a glass of the Captain's Nautilus Madeira. I'm planning to read his "Salem Witchcraft" to-night and must strengthen myself for the endeavor.'

'Shhh. Can't you hear Mrs. Morgan talking about women's work in temperance? "We must demand," said a throaty voice, "the closing of the saloon; my sisters, if we must we can fight, and the Demon King, Alcohol, will need all of our fighting to dethrone him, to cast him down, each working in her own way, all working together, but the beginning of the end — is it now?"'

'Can men go to this thing?' asked Mr. Fox, his prominent brown eyes agog with interest.

'Yes, but —'

'Trust me.'

He seated himself on the wide window-sill and gestured her to join him. The crimson curtains of the bay window partially cut them off from the rest of the room.

Until Miss Meminta Purse began to speak, he

behaved himself extremely well. The literary Miss Purse, however, was so unfortunate as to tread upon his professional toes. Her opinions irritated Mr. Fox. He cleared his throat, screwed about in his seat, twitched his stock, and cleared his throat again.

'I have never,' he whispered to Lanice, 'taken much stock in toothy women, especially when they have Adam's apples.'

Poor Miss Purse did actually have one of these secondary attributes of the male, and she was very toothy. Mr. Fox blew his nose. Miss Purse made the point that many women have assumed men's names as *noms-de-plume*. Homer, for instance — who knew whether or not Homer might not be some gifted Grecian matron whose husband had caddish objections to seeing his wife gain notoriety? She seized upon any little-known author as a potential lady. He jumped up.

'I like to prevaricate, even lie, as well as any man,' he whispered to Lanice, 'but may I hang if I can sit and listen to this rubbish, ugly as home-made sin.'

Lanice went out with him.

'Wait,' she whispered, 'I'll run down and fetch the Nautilus Madeira.'

He flimsily protested that he had been joking, that he never drank Madeira so late in the evening. But it was at best a half-hearted protest. They went below to the dining-room where the refreshments of oysters, ham, sponge cake, hidden mountain, lemonade, peach supreme, and ice water were spread out. Here Mr. Fox drank her health in the famous Madeira, and to the confusion of all ladies who think. He looked at her suddenly, as if for the first time.

'You don't think?' he asked.

Lanice blushed. 'I'm afraid I do. At least I draw pictures and I read serious works. You know, not merely the "Godey's Book" and "Hearth and Home."' (Mr. Fox was the proprietor of the latter.)

'How splendid!' he exclaimed. 'I'd been saying to myself, this young lady is charming, lovely, generous, but probably she does not think, and now I find you are, beyond any reasonable doubt, a great mind.'

'But do you like ladies to think? I thought you did not.'

'Why do you say that?'

'You just drank to the confusion of all ladies who think.'

'How cruelly you mistake me. Ladies — especially wise ones, and how I admire that type — are never so irresistible as when they are somewhat confused. All this evening I have been saying to myself, "This young lady is charming, lovely, generous — she *thinks*, but nothing can confuse her." Look at yourself now in the glass! Probably you write stories as well as read them. Well, here's to the confusion of all lady authoresses — may they be extensively red.'

And at this atrocious pun the gifted Mr. Fox laughed convulsively. Lanice obliged him by blushing until the tears stood in her eyes. He led the conversation back to herself. It came out, she had had some dozen stories already published, a few even in his own 'Hearth and Home.' Now, however, she was consecrated to her Brush, but she was not at all sure but she would prefer to be an author. She secretly hoped he would ask her to bring in some more of her stories, and was surprised and hurt that he did not remember publishing 'Martha's Side Saddle' two years before (her *nom-de-plume* then had been Myron Kerfew), or 'Pharaoh's Daughter,' which had run for three issues even more recently. Considering the fact that he was nominally the head of this great woman's magazine, he seemed curiously innocent of it. Now that he had started her talking freely about her literary aspirations, they seemed to bore him. He jerked at his stock, and said abruptly:

'Well, that's that.'

Just as he was leaving the front door, he added:

'By the way, "Hearth and Home" needs what we call a captive artist. You know, one who will sketch out the lamp-mats, night-caps, knitted sacks and baby's blankets, occasionally do fashion plates from rough sketches sent us from New York and Paris, or even illustrate stories. Are you interested?'

'I'd love it.'

He answered her enthusiasm cautiously.

'We won't commit ourselves. Come around to my place on School Street, and I can give you a try and you can give me a try. The idea would be for you to stop in, say every other day, and take your work home with you to do. Probably you'll not care for it, but stop in and blush for me, anyway, and I'll show you all the graves in my back yard.'

That night neither Lanice nor Pauline could sleep.
Wide awake one thought of working on a magazine
for a great publisher, the other of women — women
working in the South for the slaves, for temperance in
evil-smelling bar-rooms, for a right to control the
destiny of their children — women in hoops and
laced with whalebone and buckram — who some
time, God help us, should be as free as the envied males.

3

Lanice heard the Park Street Church clock strike
three and then, almost before she realized she had
been to sleep, it struck eight. She leaped out of bed,
flung up the window, and found the day dull and
cold for summer. She rapidly laced and buttoned
herself into her clothes, choosing for the exterior a
moss-green dress lavishly banded with mink. Her
face was pale and the lavender shadows about her
eyes that had haunted her since childhood showed
against the pallor. Mr. Fox would not think her so
charming as he had last night. He would not want her
about, even as a captive artist. Absurd. It was her
skill with a pencil that interested him, not her ladylike graces.

At breakfast Pauline, in 'half corset' and morning
cap, lingered over a pile of correspondence. There
were tumbled yellow ribbons in her cap. Pauline,
who despised finery, often would suddenly indulge
herself and then always overdid it. The bows were
too big, too yellow, and too obviously ripped off a
dress and pinned to the cap.

'Wonderful, wasn't it?' she asked Lanice.

'Oh, yes, Cousin Poggy, and wasn't it *wonderful* that Mr. Fox came and asked me . . .'

'Mr. Fox? Who permitted him? This is insufferable, an intrusion. Mr. *Fox* at *our* meeting! I had no idea . . .'

'I let him in. He wanted some of the Nautilus Madeira, you know, the wine that was sent back in the Nautilus when it carried food to Madeira during their famine. And so . . .'

'He dared to come begging for alcohol at such a time! Oh, if he only could have heard our Mrs. Morgan, that noble woman! Why, her *lowest* plane is as high above Mr. Fox's *highest* as God is higher than the angels! Oh, Cousin Lanice, dear child. It is such men who are our deepest, darkest enemies. They take us for — for toys, *baubles*. To think he begged for alcohol in the very house and the very evening that Mrs. Morgan spoke!'

'He heard her talking; that is why he wanted to come in. He sat in back almost hidden in the Beacon Street window. But Miss Purse angered him by saying that perhaps Homer was a female, and he twisted about so much I took him out and gave him some Madeira.'

'The low, sottish cur, poking into our business.'

'But he isn't low. He is so gifted! And this morning I'm going to see him, and if he likes my sketches he is going to hire me to draw for "Hearth and Home," fashion plates even. I'm overjoyed.'

There was a long, difficult pause. Pauline elaborately went on sorting letters. She cleared her throat.

'Miss Gatherall has had her letters left for her here. I must arrange for them to go to her at Roxbury. She has a lovely soul.'

'But —'

'Now, Lanice, I do not want to discuss Mr. Fox or his degrading magazines. I can't understand how you can turn to such opportunities as he offers. I was educating you to be a great artist, not to draw fashion plates for Mr. Fox.'

'Oh, Pauline, I know, but I'm not an artist, not really. It isn't in me. I realized it all last night. When Mr. Fox asked me to go to work for him, I knew that was as far as I could ever go with my brush. I've never painted anything wonderful; anyway, I'd so much rather write. Perhaps I may really develop talent in that field.'

'Well,' said Pauline, slapping the papers down on the table, 'if you can't decide what you do want to do, I'll tell you now you will never do anything.' From somewhere she produced a dingy reticule and snapped it open and shut viciously. Her eyes narrowed and her voice grew hard and logical. 'If it is writing that you want to do, what good is it to draw fashion plates for Mr. Fox? That's neither art nor literature.'

'Perhaps he will let me write for him, not merely stories for "Hearth and Home," but thoughtful articles to be printed in his "Journal." I might accomplish a world of good. I might . . . '

'Never!' blazed Pauline. 'He would not think a

woman had the intellect. Lanice, he will just scorn you inside.'

'I think I will go to see him, anyway. Of course, Pauline, I realize that if I am not an artist and do not do what you want there is no reason why you should have me live with you. I have some money, you know, Pauline. I'd much prefer to pay. What I have done for your father certainly would not make up for my lovely room and all you have given me. And now his book is done.'

'How can you talk to me like this? You're a hard-hearted girl, Lanice. You haven't any natural affection. You want to go away. I'd *die* rather than take money from you.' Pauline gulped awkwardly, gritted her teeth, gazed fixedly ahead of her, then, bursting into tears, fled from the room.

They had it out together in Pauline's tobacco-brown room, lying together on her tumbled unmade bed. Why could she not love Pauline? She realized humbly that Pauline loved her. 'You had better kiss her,' she thought coldly, and did, but hated herself for this false show of affection.

'If you feel so badly I won't go to Redcliffe & Fox. I'll continue to study at the Dummers' studio. but . . .'

'That's not it; but I don't want you to pay, I . . . I . . .' she gagged.

4

Fifteen minutes later, Pauline, complete master of herself and the situation, superciliously examined

Lanice's appearance. 'You won't have such poor taste as to wear *that* costume! Green, with fur!'

'Oh, but it is very simple. I thought . . .'

'You thought,' jerked out Pauline, 'that it made you look pretty. Well, I don't see why a *caged* artist, or whatever you call such things, needs to look pretty. Mrs. Stowe has done a world of good in the plainest of old alpacas. Do Mrs. Morgan or Miss Gatherall wear green with fur? Do any great intellectual women, except' — she added in a whisper — 'George Sand? Now I'd go up and put on your brown merino. It looks much more like cultured Boston.'

'I don't want to look like cultured Boston. I want to look like myself. And Mamma always insisted that I wear pretty gowns and have hats and gloves to go with everything.'

Pauline, still extraordinarily ugly from her weeping, said in a slow, cutting voice, 'I suppose you would like to look like your mother; act like her too, perhaps.'

This hurt. Lanice sprang to her feet, staring blankly at her cousin and looking surprisingly like a child's stiff doll in her voluminous green gown and tumbled black silk curls. 'Sometimes,' she said, her voice shaking with anger, 'you are horrid, Pauline. You can be horrider than any one else I have ever known. You can't love me or you wouldn't talk to me like that. I think you really hate me, and my dear Mamma.'

Wrangle, wrangle. Her nerves trembled with the confusion and bickering.

At eleven o'clock she crossed the Common, still wearing the uncultured, fascinating green costume. There were horses in gigs and shays tied under the trees along Park Street, but one slim saddle horse was tied upon the Common itself. This she knew was Mr. Redcliffe's own mount. He, the senior partner, was of a more tempestuous nature than the suave Mr. Fox. He kept this fast horse always ready so that when it was necessary for him to direct the printing at the Cambridge press he might throw himself out of his office on School Street, run the two blocks to the Common, fall upon his nervous mount, and disappear in a cloud of dust up Park Street and so out upon the Mill Dam along Beacon Street. Lanice had often seen Mr. Redcliffe dash past on his fleet Zephyr. Captain Poggy would say, 'There goes Redcliffe on his way to the Press,' and if Mr. Fox were sitting beside Captain Poggy he'd make some amusing remark that would make haste seem ridiculous. Mr. Fox could make haste himself if there were need, but he made haste slowly.

Lanice stopped and chirruped to the strawberry roan, feeling a new, almost proprietorial interest in him. He had been rubbing his bits against his ankle, and without raising his head he pricked his ears and gazed at her with wild shining eyes gleaming through his long forelock.

On the ground floor of the old brick building occupied by Messrs. Redcliffe & Fox was a bookshop where Lanice had often made purchases. She knew that here and in the publishers' rooms above, the

[61]

greatest of Boston's literary men were apt to gather, talk, smoke, and enjoy their own and each other's wit and wisdom. Here Thackeray and Dickens had both held informal salons, and Whittier with his quaint 'thees' and 'thous,' Emerson, Longfellow, and Hawthorne all were habitués.

She entered by a narrow door crowded in beside the shop, and ascended to the editorial rooms. Extraordinary clutter! Files of magazines, their own and those of their rivals, piles of bound books, and books in 'sheets,' proofs, filing devices, and an odd assortment of intelligent-looking human beings gave the place a professional and literary appearance, confusing to the lay mind.

From the main room (once, Lanice judged, the dining-room of the mansion) cubby-holes and staircases radiated in all directions. On the walls were original drawings framed and unframed, autographs, maps, colored reproductions, and even hand-tinted fashion plates from 'Hearth and Home.' Lovely mincing things, exquisitely engraved and colored by hand. A very big little boy with a double chin swaggered forward to meet her.

'Miss Bardeen, I suppose? Mr. Fox expects you. He'll be free in a moment. Dr. Holmes is with him just now.' She caught a glimpse of the rare soul's little back slipping down a back stairway.

Mr. Fox graciously came to meet her.

'You are not, I see, merely a pleasant hallucination brought on by Mrs. Morgan's speech and the Captain's Madeira, but an actual young lady looking for pictures to draw. Well, come with me and all in good time we will see about the pictures.'

Three steps up, an unexpected twist past other desks where clerks and editors labored, and she was led into an old square room overlooking the King's Chapel Burying Ground. The disordered stones were tumbled about like jackstraws and the ripe grasses grew high among them.

'Hester Prynne is buried out there,' said Mr. Fox, seeming to remember that he had promised to show her the graves in his back yard. Perhaps he sensed her excitement and confusion, for he turned from her and stood gazing out the window. 'Or at least her prototype. There are *that* many people at least,' he said with satisfaction, 'who will never more submit a manuscript.'

Lanice got a vivid and unforgettable impression of the man as he stood half turned away from her, his shapely head silhouetted against the eternal melancholy of the graveyard.

'First of all' — he turned back to her — 'remove whatever of your costume it is customary to remove under these circumstances, and be seated. Then we will talk things over. You didn't bring any paintings with you? That's good. Artists staggering in with their portfolios always are a pathetic and therefore irritating sight. Poets with rolls of poems are bad enough, but they are on the whole less docile and not so touching. You do draw, don't you?'

'I've been with Mrs. Dummer for the last eight months and I have always had the best instruction obtainable since I was a child.' She noticed he had some bound volumes of 'Hearth and Home' on the desk before him.

'Yes,' he confessed, 'I have been looking up those wonderful stories you said that you had written for us. They are pleasing — well adapted to this particular magazine. Perhaps as well as furnishing us with pictures you will occasionally do us a story. Probably you have a hatbox full of them hidden away somewhere in the Poggy house.'

Seeing an eager look in the young lady's eyes, he quickly put on the brakes. 'When you've worked with us for a couple of months and know our requirements, you might trot some in and we'll go over them.'

Obviously she was not to 'trot them in' immediately. 'Well,' he continued, 'turning to the case in hand . . . ' He excused himself and soon returned with a manila envelope containing crude sketches and a letter.

'By the way, you tat, knit, crochet, stitch, sew, and so forth?'

'Yes.'

'Very well. Here in this envelope are directions for making articles for a "Fancy Fair." Our correspondent has done her best to draw pictures of the things she describes, but you are to re-render them in the more elegant manner of Mrs. Dummer. Select five of these objects, make me drawings of them several times larger than the finished cuts should be, and come back day after to-morrow.'

As Lanice started to thank him, he dismissed her abruptly with a 'That's that,' and almost showed her the door as if he was afraid he had given her the inch and she would take the ell.

5

She opened the bulky envelope alone in her airy, yellow chamber. Thank Heaven, Pauline had gone to Roxbury to deliver Miss Gatherall's mail. By the time Pauline returned, much cheered by a day with Mrs. Morgan and Miss Gatherall, five sketches were satisfactorily completed. They represented a crocheted basket of white glass beads and crimson wool, a watch-case in chenille, a 'Bosom Friend' or 'Sontag' (a knitted chest protector), and a billowy lamp-mat made in the shape of a doughnut. Pauline chatted eagerly, seeming to fear a pause less Lanice tell her of her engagement with Messrs. Redcliffe & Fox.

Before the drawings were finally submitted to Mr. Fox, she showed them to Mrs. Dummer. She was not enthusiastic, her eyeglasses glittered with emotion as she told her that there were 'more wonderful things in this lovely world of ours' to interpret than lamp-mats. But Mr. Fox was elated. He called one after another of his large staff and insisted that they admire the Bosom Friend or Sontag, a garment which seemed to have fascinated his restless mind. Through his admiration Lanice was secretly sure that he was laughing at it and at her. He next proposed a 'purgatorial' three weeks. At the end of this time, if she continued to show ability, she could

[65]

consider herself 'Hearth and Home's' captive artist.

He introduced her to a number of his associates,
Miss Bigley, a vast and dowdy lady who lived on
West Cedar Street, and who, under Mr. Fox's su-
pervision, was largely responsible for 'Hearth and
Home's' prodigious success. Her complacent size did
not save her from excessive nervousness. Mr. Trelawney, a tall, thin man with a dark, gypsyish face,
and a suggestion of potential tragedy about him.
There was also Mr. Poindexter who preached Sundays
in a large church and during the week served as
editor-in-chief of 'Church News,' a religious monthly.
He was strongly Congregational and keenly interested in abolition. She wished she might have a desk
in this interesting place and stay intimately with
these charming people. No one else seemed to have
thought of such a thing. Even Miss Bigley spent
most of her time modestly in her father's house.
While necessarily in the office, she kept her bonnet
tied to her head and a shawl laid about her shoulders,
symbols that she had not gone 'out into the world.'
During the first meeting she told Lanice that she
always considered a woman's first duty to be towards
her family, and stared hard at her new assistant out
of swimming blue eyes.

The antagonism which she instantly felt between
herself and Miss Bigley was partially explained by
Mr. Fox, who told her, as they strolled together
across the Common, each on the way home to dinner,
that the lady editoress had always done the odds and

ends of drawing herself. She often worked until after midnight. She was a 'convulsive worker' who had broken down a number of times and yet never seemed able to do less than all. Mr. Fox stopped abruptly to watch the ducks pushing about in the dirty water of the Frog Pond like tiny submersible tugboats. 'I wish she'd learn from them,' he said; 'they take life so agreeably. But if she were one of those ducks — say that white one' — he indicated a portly individual with a yellow bill — 'instead of swimming about and being thankful for scum, she would make herself sick trying to eat it all up and get the place clean.'

Although Mr. Fox assured her that he himself always kept an eye on 'Hearth and Home,' he was especially concerned with his own 'Fox's Journal,' a weekly. This was stronger food than was fed out to 'elegant womanhood' and reflected to some extent the diverse, diverting, and sophisticated personality of Mr. Fox. He had run it for years in New York before old Mr. Redcliffe one day had come raging into his office and persuaded him into partnership. Then he removed his headquarters from the vulgar capital of fashion to that of culture and gained the benefit of a closer union with the celebrated Concord, Cambridge, and Boston literary men who were in those days sprouting up like mushrooms, but branching out like oaks. He boasted of the fact that he had never written one word for 'Hearth and Home,' except when he had first come, and was very much afraid of Miss Bigley, he had been left late in the office to finish the proof. A caption for one of the illustrations was missing and he was forced to select it. The picture represented an amazing garment — sort of an upside petticoat — which he, a bachelor, was sure personally never to have seen. Therefore it must be of an intimate, hidden nature. He indicated that the cut should be reversed and wrote below, 'This fashionable undergarment is ingeniously constructed of black velvet and pink tulle,' and let it go at that. Miss Bigley, home superintending the cleaning of her house, never forgave him. It was a black net cuff with a tight wristband. Lady correspondents and dressmakers wrote in buzzing with curiosity. The mistake did take, as Miss Bigley told Mr. Fox, 'a great deal of my valuable time.'

6

After Lanice's third or fourth visit to School Street, she found to her disappointment that it was to Miss Bigley she was to report, and not to Mr. Fox. Often she ran errands for her superior, usually back to the tidy swept house on West Cedar Street, where the rather rickety but cheerful progenitor of the mighty editoress could be found sitting in his armchair just as his daughter had left him, with newspapers spread beneath him to catch the dropping ashes of his pipe. Lanice liked this gnome-like little man, who always greeted her with a warm 'So *you're* here, are you?' and felt sorry for him because Miss Bigley kept him on newspapers as if he and his pipe were unclean foreign objects in her spotless house.

Miss Bigley 'put her whole heart,' as she said, in her uplifting articles, but also wrote poems. Among the titles were 'Wilt Thou Love Me When I'm Old,' 'The Maniac,' 'The Last Night at Home.' She wrote poetry only when there was a space to fill and no free contribution lying about her desk. This was also her attitude towards stories. They all pointed a moral, and Mr. Fox himself assured Lanice that Miss Bigley had a genius for this particular type of 'literary butter.' Lanice found that she, too, could write poems and stories of any length, at any time, and on any known subject. She learned the mechanical trick of starting in the middle of a scene.

'"Look here, Emma, isn't this the sweetest little pencil you ever saw?" said a young and beautiful girl to a companion as she danced lightly in at the open door one pleasant summer afternoon, holding the object of her remark at the same time before her friend's admiring gaze.' That was the way you did it!

She learned, from Miss Bigley, new elegancies of speech and was highly commended when she said the heart of the beautiful heroine was known to be as 'lovely as its earthly casket.'

Mr. Fox snorted over this and called up his myrmidons to admire, much as he had forced their attention to the 'Bosom Friend' or 'Sontag.' He repeated it with relish to Captain Poggy. 'You can't imagine what a monkey-see-monkey-do-of-a-girl your ex-amanuensis is. Why, she bigleys about like an old hand. Frankly she has a genius for writing the most unmitigated rot.'

[69]

'And you're not doing anything to help her? Really, Fox, you would sell not only your own soul, but that of my young cousin as well. Can't you point out to her the cheapness of the "Hearth and Home" literature? She has so much ability.'

'Oh, if she has any talent she'll see through herself pretty soon.' Mr. Fox remarked airily. 'But if she didn't write these things, what would she write about? She isn't very experienced in life. I'll admit the work she did on your witchcraft book is brilliant, quite free from all the trite elegancies of Miss Bigley's popular style.'

The great 'Historical Study of Salem Witchcraft' was published at last, and Lanice was almost moved to tears as she read Chapter Three, which was entirely the result of her studies and skill. Mr. Fox found her so engaged, noticed the chapter number, and slyly asked if she were reading her favorite author.

'I have always known that you wrote that chapter, and of course every one is one's own favorite author. It is well up to the standards of the "Journal."' Catching sight of Miss Bigley's bulk moving behind the packing-boxes he said, 'Miss Bigley, what if I take your "Hearth and Home" author-artist and shape her up for my "Journal"?'

Miss Bigley appeared, her dirty hands pushing her bonnet straight. 'Of course, if you feel the need, but personally *I* feel that the scope of "Hearth and Home" is much more appropriate to a young lady than the deeper waters and further shores of the

[70]

"Journal." Why should not Miss Bardeen be satisfied to write tales and articles that will serve and inspire her own sex and teach Christian morality and domestic virtue to countless numbers? The young people to-day need help as never before in the history of the world. Indeed, we are losing track of the simple virtues . . .'

'Well,' interrupted Mr. Fox, who was obviously very bored, 'that's that.' And he swung off, looking completely satisfied to leave Lanice writing stories of pure hearts in lovely earthly caskets and quite content with the morals of the younger generation.

CHAPTER IV

AND ANTHONY JONES

1

SHE saw fall come to Boston. The elms grew yellow and early relinquished their leaves, as if, thought Lanice, they were proud of their shapely trunks and limbs and so put on a clothing of leaves late in the spring and laid them aside early in the fall. Unlike the oak, which clings to its rough coating of leaves as long as possible, the elms have no ugly twists or growths to cover.

Ladies of fashion, for such there were in Boston, although Lanice never saw them either in the offices of Redcliffe & Fox nor at Pauline's meetings and institutes, swept up the leaves that fell upon the Great Mall and the Little Mall with their fine, full skirts. That year their dresses were the colors of autumn leaves — burnt orange, dull crimson, russet, and a bright, light green, the shade of the winter rye which Lanice knew in country places was rising fiercely out of the ground. The beautiful Paisley shawls, which they carried more than actually wore, were also of the colors of the dying year. That fall the hoops were enormous, and if two met in a doorway, one must stand back, and there was started an agitation requiring the horse-car companies to enlarge the entrances and exits of their vehicles. Now and then in Philadelphia or New York, and sometimes nearer home, one of these fine ladies would catch fire. The yards and yards of material spread upon the hoops burned like tinder. The lady was instantly enveloped in a rising curtain of fire, and no adoring elegant beau in plaid waistcoat and pantaloons could save her. Lanice knew that once your skirt brushed across the lighted hearth you were doomed to die cruelly. Yet like the other ladies she accepted the danger and inconvenience, and like them she walked a little stiffly and consciously. She was conscious not only of her billowing clothes but of the burden of her ladyhood, and she carried herself as she might some rare and fragile thing, almost too precious to trust to its own feet. But sometimes she was more conscious of the gross skeleton beneath the transient elegancies of her toilette, the satin skin and delicately modeled flesh. He (for to her all skeletons were male) waited within and knew that some time all else would be gone and then he would come forth, grinning. As her fingers felt for him, she grew afraid and resentful, and turned with timid desperation to other more cheerful thoughts.

In spite of the burden of her own ladyhood and Miss Bigley's ideals, she at last asked Mr. Fox for a corner of her own in the warren of Redcliffe & Fox. All the younger gentlemen laid off their tight coats and helped move the two ceiling-high bookcases that were to cut off a small cubby-hole for the 'captive artist.' Mr. Fox insisted that the backs of the bookcases, which made two of Lanice's walls, should be painted soft green to match her portièred entrance.

When the paint was dry he helped her tack up some hundred colored plates from 'Hearth and Home.'

The Rockingham water-cooler, with a pewter cup chained to it, was next moved into her room. It pleased Mr. Fox to say that it was the cleanest spot in the place and therefore should hold the water-supply. Most of Lanice's impressions of her associates were gained by seeing them stand by the water-cooler with the chained pewter mug in their hands, chatting with her as they sipped. Only 'Old Blow-hard,' as the senior and most serious partner was generally called, never stopped for a word. He was a choleric, rather handsome old fellow whose tumbled white whiskers always seemed to be blowing in the whirlwind of his personality. Mr. Trelawney came and drank. His leanness and square chops made him slightly resemble a thin black tom cat. His eyes, almost as dark as Lanice's own, were far more romantic. As he drank he would chat a little about the oddities of literature which interested him intensely. It was from him that she first heard of the Decameron. Although the kindest of men, he thought it was good for young ladies to be shocked. In fact, he thought anything was better than being a 'lady' in Lanice's sense of the word.

Sometimes gentle Whittier would be led in for a drink, or the philosopher Emerson, who, although he listened with a saintly courtesy, seemed by the very force of his wisdom to impose silence upon others. She spoke once to Mr. Fox about this barrier which stood between Mr. Emerson and the world. 'He feels it himself, too, poor soul,' said Mr. Fox. 'The wise ones on earth pay a terrible price for their wisdom.' Occasionally little Dr. Holmes would come frisking in; he was as merry as a cricket and bubbling over with stories about his medical students at Harvard where he said he did not have a 'chair,' merely a 'settee.' Professor Longfellow at first disappointed her. She had expected a tall man, and thought his large, beautiful head misplaced on his smallish body. Later she, like every one else, thought him the handsomest of men.

2

All that fall, as the yellow leaves dropped from the elm trees on the Common and the chill in the air at last forced the ladies to assume their Paisley shawls, Lanice heard continually of a new and spectacular star that had risen in England. This wonder had the commonplace name of Anthony Jones. The man had been a captain in India, and had, six years before, been sent North into Arabia to buy breeding-stock for the Indian cavalry. Instead he, and the regiment's money, had remained in Arabia. Something in the man, no one knew quite what, had appealed to the Bedouin tribes and he had mastered their language, for he was a born linguist. He had become a Mohammedan and some sort of a prince. His translations from the brutish but beautiful Arab poetry, 'Garden of the Jin,' had made a name for him in eclectic literary circles and the stamina and courage the man had shown in forcing his wild tribesmen to support England in a series of small crises had won him his young Queen's gratitude. In England his lectures had been sensational, although the Queen, who had granted him certain public honors, refused to meet him socially.

Mr. Fox, working through Sears Ripley, whose interest in Oriental literature had brought him into contact with Jones, and the English publishers, Clapyard & Dunster, persuaded him to come to America on a lecture tour. Redcliffe & Fox would publish the American edition of his great book, 'Sands of Araby.' Ripley and Jones had corresponded for years over details of Arabic. Once they had met for a few days in Smyrna. There was a bond between the two men, and they were, strangely enough, friends. The conservative, steady Harvard professor secretly admired the wild young Englishman whom, however, he never felt he could 'quite trust.' Jones had a rather simple nature and liked Ripley largely because he knew that this distinguished scholar liked him.

'Miss Bardeen,' said Sears Ripley, 'you must meet Anthony Jones.' He was sitting in the largest of her two red leather chairs and sharpening her drawing-pencils with exquisite nicety into the waste-basket he had drawn between his knees. Lanice considered Jones 'unprincipled' and 'loose,' and did not like the way the men gloated over the fact he was a professed believer in polygamy and kept women 'in their place.' She continued sketching at her desk, presenting a stiff, uncompromising back to Professor Ripley.

'I am sure we will have nothing in common,' she replied.

'I know, but that is why you should meet him. You say you want to be a novelist, and if so, some time, you may want to put in some such gallant rascal as our friend Jones. Yet you are afraid to meet him.'

'Even you, who are his friend, call him a rascal.'

'Yes, he considers himself one. The fellow is a born advertiser. He knows that being a Mohammedan, with a reputation for . . . adventure, is good business. Miss Bardeen, I believe you are the only lady in Boston who is not languishing to meet him. This is certainly a case of casting the swine before the pearl.' Both laughed and Lanice swung about. She tipped back her head a little, and for some reason suddenly looked pretty.

'Bring him in, by all means. "Hearth and Home" might run a series of articles about how they make bread and bring up children and marry in Arabia.'

'Everything that is fit for a lady to know about Arabia.'

'That's what I don't like about the man and his nasty country,' said Lanice rather hotly. 'Mr. Fox and Mr. Trelawney, you, every one, are always suggesting that there is so much that a lady shouldn't know, I think I'd rather know nothing. But bring him in. It will be, after all, but a business meeting.'

3

Three days later, her sage-green portières were pushed aside. Sears Ripley and a strange young man

stood side by side before her. Any one to have seen
the two would have selected the Bostonian, with his
height and width, dark beard and small, wise eyes, as
the great traveller linguist, and master of men. In
comparison Jones looked boyish and shy. He was
only an inch or two taller than Lanice and as slender
as the Arabs whom he had led. The set of his shoulders, however, suggested army training. His mouth
drooped slightly and was too short for the blunt,
broad cast of his features. In comparison to the expressive eyes, mournful and intelligent as a hound's,
the mouth seemed inarticulate. Before Sears Ripley
had begun the introduction, she put her hand out
timidly towards him. 'Captain Jones,' she said, and
flushed when she felt his hard hand, small for a man,
close over hers. Sears Ripley murmured a belated
introduction and suddenly hated to see Jones's hand
upon the girl's. The Englishman hesitated before he
spoke, almost as though he once had had an impedi-
ment in his speech to laboriously overcome, then
said:

'You are the young lady who is going to write
things up . . .' he paused — 'for a female magazine.
Ripley thinks you may even . . . invent an "Anthony
Jones antimacassar" for your readers to knit. I am
delighted.'

Professor Ripley laughed and looked at his inexplicable friend with proprietorial eyes, and then
glanced at Lanice as if to say, 'Isn't this a fine fellow,
if one does not take him too seriously?'

'We've only five minutes now,' he said, 'before we

all go over to the Parker House to eat some of the famous oysters.' He stopped to tell of Thackeray's visit to the same hostelry a few years before, and how the oysters were so large he insisted they looked like the High Priest's ear which Peter had cut off, and when he finally got one down, said he felt as if he had swallowed a baby. Captain Jones's face lighted up almost merrily and his mouth, which in repose looked as if it could never smile, widened.

'I must indeed . . . have some of these gigantic ears to eat.'

While Sears Ripley went about the building gathering together the diners, the lady editoress talked with Jones. To find herself alone with him and responsible for his amusement frightened her. Her heart raced a little and she felt secret excitement. What an unprincipled, loose young man! She had expected to hate him, but he was disarmingly without Byronic poses. Why did every one say he was such an advertiser and liked to make capital of his ill-spent life? She thought his wide-open grey eyes the frankest and in a way the most innocent she had ever seen in the head of a mature man.

He spoke to her in his suave, hesitating way, asking what she had in mind and whether the material he was willing to give her for her female magazine could not be used in such a way as to increase the sales of 'Sands of Araby.'

'I must make the thing sell. I need . . . the money to support myself as I am accustomed to living in Arabia. That is why I am lecturing . . . so exten-

[79]

sively. And in native costume. People must say' —
he mimicked slightly the clipped speech of fashionable
English society — '"he is *so* picturesque, and have
your read his utterly . . . devastating book?" That is
why,' said Mr. Jones, 'I let people over here call me
"Sir Anthony." . . . I couldn't do that in England,
they'd know. But in New York, why, I say don't call
me "Captain," call me "Jones." And they come
back with "Sir." By the time I reach Pittsburgh I
will be . . . a lord. And I'll not go to Cincinnati,
whatever that may be, for less than . . . a belted
earl.' He watched her attentively and when she
smiled a very little, he smiled too. She made some
remarks about 'Hearth and Home.' His eyes maintained their look of sadness and faithfulness. He let
her finish and then asked her abruptly about herself.
Did she like office life? Was she a Boston girl? Did
she write stories and draw pictures herself? Lanice
answered his gentle cross-questioning rather fully.
Shy herself, the great traveller's hesitating speech
made her feel poised and sophisticated. She was quite
sure that she liked him and could not understand why
even his friend, Professor Ripley, considered him a
rascal.

'Did any one ever tell you,' he asked, 'that you
are much the type of certain Persian princesses . . .
often painted by artists of the Mughal School . . . a
type . . . which, if it ever did exist, does not exist
now?' He did not tell her how his restless eyes had
roved over the earth looking for this evasive beauty
in the flesh.

[80]

Sears Ripley's manly head appeared between the portières. It was time the gentlemen assumed their capes and ate their midday oysters. Lanice said quickly, in a very low voice, 'The daughter of an old East India merchant gave me a miniature ... Hindoo, I think. She said it looked like me.'

'May I see it?'

'I'll bring it in.'

'No, no. I will call.'

The girl looked up at him out of meek, frightened eyes.

'I'd so much rather bring it in.'

'Of course,' he said, 'do what you want and don't let me bully you.'

He smiled, and his smile was devastating and joyous, an incredible performance for his sombre face. Sears Ripley saw their eyes meet, and in some way lock together. He saw Miss Bardeen's sleek, shapely head settle back slightly upon the neck which swelled and took on curious beauty. He realized for the first time in his life that the girl could at mysterious moments assume an almost wanton loveliness, and his curiosity was deeply stirred. He looked at Captain Jones. He, too, had discovered the girl's fleeting but haunting beauty. Then, quite without warning, she put on the expression of a perfect lady. The look irritated Captain Jones. She was probably a most banal young lady, and a female editor at that, a foul bluestocking! It seemed to him unfortunate that she of all the women in the world should possess at moments the look of a Mughal princess. Well, as his

American publisher, Mr. Fox, would say, 'that was that.'

4

It was Sears Ripley who could not eat his oysters. He was sorry that he had introduced these two friends, and that their eyes had locked together. Late in the afternoon he restlessly crossed and re-crossed the Common between the Poggy mansion and the publishing house. He noticed that at last the trees were quite bare of leaves and that small crystals of ice were forming on the Frog Pond. Stepping down the long walk, cheerful, amused, and wide awake to all the world, was Dr. Holmes in his little brown gaiters.

At last Lanice came towards him dressed in a short, bottle-green jacket trimmed with bright green fringes. She carried a little muff of the same materials. The man, his high beaver hat in his hand, joined her. She noticed that he always wore square dark blue clothes almost like a sailor's, as if he was proud of his nautical blood.

'You cannot tell me, Miss Bardeen,' he said after a dozen steps and a few words about the weather, 'that you found the great Mr. Jones as repellent as you expected.'

'Oh, it's always Captain Jones! I'm tired of him already. Is he not quite an insignificant-looking man to have had such an interesting life? But, of course, you are his friend . . .'

'Oh, that's all right, say what you please. I think in

a way I understand and like the man. Criticisms will not make any difference.'

'Then you will not mind if I say that I . . .' she paused, and a dark wave of anger seemed to rise up from below . . . 'that I dislike him. I thought at least he would have a romantic exterior, like Byron, but . . .' she bent her head and pressed her muff against her mouth. 'If a man must be a Don Juan, he should look the part.'

Sears Ripley looked at her quizzically. A man of no moods himself, he had a gift for understanding the most changeable and moody of people, especially women.

'Was he in this afternoon?' he asked curiously.

'I don't know; I didn't see him.' The showman in him was sorry that Lanice had not appreciated Anthony Jones. But all the rest of him was glad. He could not understand the violent aversion which she evidently felt. His curiosity was intensely piqued. For the first time since the death of his wife, Prunella, he found himself thinking continuously of a woman.

Late in the evening he and Captain Jones sat in the library of Professor Ripley's Concord house drinking port and eating cake. The old mahogany table was spread with manuscripts in Arabic and with dictionaries. Ripley grew sleepy and twice suggested bed. Jones was as alive as a cat and his wide eyes glittered when the firelight caught in them. There was a delicate sense of excitement about him which, tired as Professor Ripley was, he found contagious.

Finally, without warning, the Englishman abruptly announced, 'I've an idea that Redcliffe & Fox's intellectual young lady may really be a perfect fool.'

'That's because you think all ladies fools.'

'Oh, no. I think the Arab women very wise.'

'Oh, shut up, Jones. You are not talking to scandalize the newspapers.'

They sipped their port, and Jones ate his third piece of tipsy cake.

'Rather liked her.'

Ripley's heart contracted and sank. He was not sure he had understood. 'You what?'

'Liked her.'

The professor was conscious that all the waves of excitement he had felt emanating from Jones had Lanice Bardeen as their source. He felt very tired and rather worn and middle-aged. He said wearily, 'How flattering to Miss Bardeen.'

'What did you say her name was?'

'Miss Bardeen.'

'And her first name?'

'I am afraid I do not know,' Sears Ripley lied coldly.

The two men looked at each other. Jones smiled in a faint but friendly fashion.

'I don't want to ever see her again. There is something about her, a primness, a what you'd call a "virtue" that I find irritating. I can think of her as I saw her one moment and say truthfully she attracts me, but if I knew her everything would be spoiled.'

[84]

5

On the evening of Captain Jones's Boston lecture the snow fell, the first snow of all the deep snows of that famous winter. It came without wind in great tattered flakes. In an hour it had padded the city with inches of silence. Runners replaced wheels and the cold music of the sleigh bells jingled in the crystalline air.

'I always forget snow is so thrilling,' said Mr. Fox, as he and Lanice, with their faces pressed against the panes, watched the whitening of the graveyard and the obliteration of the stones. Miss Bigley hurried in shaking the drifts out of her vast dolman and off her bonnet.

'I assure you, Miss Bardeen, the other ladies that serve as ushers are already gathered at my house to put on their costumes. Dear Mr. Jones, tired as he is, is assisting. Such brocades and gauzes and jewels were never before seen in this city.'

It had fallen upon Miss Bigley to select five girls of social eminence and sufficient beauty to usher at Mr. Jones's lecture. Mr. Jones himself had selected the sixth. Miss Bigley could not understand why he should choose one who was neither a belle nor an heiress, a mere stranger in Boston from Amherst. Lanice hurried into her wraps, tied down her bonnet, and fled to the hack waiting outside. Miss Bigley, talking breathlessly as they swished along over the snow, did not tell her that Mr. Jones, evidently scenting the social difference between Miss Bardeen from Amherst and the Boston-born Endicotts,

Scollays, Lowells, and Sears, had put aside for her a dull heap of ancient garments, whose rosy copper and emerald green could not compare with the pink and blue gauzes of the other girls.

Jones was elsewhere and the other girls were dressed. Their glibness and intimacy with each other embarrassed Lanice and made her feel the outsider that she was. Miss Bigley flattered them and rolled her prominent blue eyes in admiration. Lanice, unassisted, found a small chamber where she could divest herself of her hoops and crinoline and pull on the odd straight garments. There were at least five layers, and they had been so folded, presumably by Miss Bigley and Mr. Jones's Hindoo servant that she could not mistake the order. Saffron first, then ivory, then cherry stuck all over with gold stars. White gauze next, and over it a reptilian coppery thing that suddenly gave out cold blue lights. Everything was exquisitely made, sewn with gold and seed pearls. About her waist she twisted a sash of purple and green.

A rap on the door. Miss Bigley coming at last to help her. 'Come in.'

Captain Jones, swathed in white like an Arab, and banded with gold, but with his characteristically European head uncovered and his hair looking tumbled and boyish, opened the door.

'That's it,' he said. 'You've got . . . the right order and this . . . old rag goes on top.' He stared at her with frank, innocent eyes. Only think, if he had come five minutes earlier! Lanice blushed at the thought.

[86]

Mr. Jones had the same thought, but did not blush. He laid an armful of fluent gold across the chair. The girl had never guessed that such things existed. Fairy-land seemed possible. She put on a shapeless thing of metal cloth, embroidered all over with trailing Persian flowers and fruits, springing birds and leaping antelopes. It wrapped her closely as though its weight came from water, not gold.

Dazed and shy, she stole back to the parlor where the Captain, Miss Bigley, and the five enchanting girls chatted and waited until the time of departure. Miss Bigley rushed out breathless to meet her, and exclaimed over the number and the intricacy of the garments. Lanice read in her protruding eyes that the sumptuous golden overdress was inappropriate for an unpretentious editoress.

'Now, Miss Quincy, with all her wealth of golden hair . . . now really so much gold makes you look quite pale, Miss Bardeen, and Miss Quincy's costume is overplain, is it not?' Miss Quincy wore the four-hundred-year coat and Captain Jones evinced not the slightest interest in this change. Lanice wondered why he had given her this treasure. She guessed that her costume, so lifeless in a heap and so vital upon the body, was more precious than the modern hangings of the other young ladies. Now she was dressed as he had wished, but he only cast upon her a careless, roving glance and was entirely absorbed in the Scollay girls. Their father and handsome young uncle Lanice knew had made much of him.

There was a subtle manœuvring among the ladies,

even Miss Bigley not being too dignified to hope she
might ride in the closed sleigh with the dashing
Captain. The two Scollays succeeded. They were
pretty girls who seemed to have no jealousies towards
each other. Lanice found them attractive and wished
that she could know them. In the end Lanice and
Miss Bigley rode to the lecture with Professor Ripley,
who was second in command under Miss Bigley.
Lanice withdrew to a dark corner of the hack and felt
sad. Miss Bigley began to chatter about the duties
of woman and the sanctity of the home. Sears
Ripley, almost invisible, relaxed into sadness, but
the occasional contact with his knees subtly comforted the younger woman. So they drove to Tremont Temple.

6

All during the evening, when Lanice had finished
her rather nominal duties as usher, Ripley devoted
himself to her. His eyes caressed her in a friendly
fashion. Boston had accepted the occasion as one of
distinction, meriting best black silks, real laces, and,
in the case of the younger and more frivolous women,
of voluminous flower-colored evening dresses trimmed
with garlands of velvet and silver gauze flowers.
The ten daily newspapers on the following morning
referred to the lecture as a great social event un-
rivalled since the pure and lovely Jenny Lind had
sung to Boston. The ushers were pronounced to be
'enchanting,' 'the loveliest of houris,' who combined
the charms of the desert and of Boston. 'Many and

many a night has passed since the commodious Temple has witnessed such a scene. Sir Anthony Jones, the bright star whose rising upon our firmament has been anxiously looked for by the fashionable astronomers since its transit across the ocean was announced, shone forth in all its brilliancy this evening. He was attended by some score of Boston nymphs who served as ushers in Asiatic dress and were pronounced the Brightest of Constellations.'

To all who had met Captain Jones in European garb and in the daily walks of life, his appearance on the rostrum was sensational. Lanice could not believe that this young man, who entered, swathed in white and banded with gold, aloof, speaking with the dignity and beauty of a prophet, could ever seem ill at ease or boyish. Now it was possible that he was a leader among savage men and that his courage, justice, and intelligence had taught them to respect the English nation. His face looked ruddy beneath the drooping white headgear bound about by rolls of camels' hair. His gestures were few and expressive. Sears Ripley explained to her in a whisper that he had that gift, rare among Englishmen, of listening for hours without speaking, as well as the commoner Anglo-Saxon quality of unflinching and, if necessary, cruel courage. She was very conscious of Ripley's generous admiration.

Jones told of his travels, mostly through the Great Red Desert in North Araby, and of the fine, lawless people that he found there. He did not tell by what means he became emir of five thousand tents, of thirty

[89]

thousand people, nor from what source he drew the vast amount of gold pounds which it was evident he had spent. Lanice became more interested in him than in his smoothly flowing words. Behind him stretched the desert, a thing of infinite size and horror. Across it moved the white-shrouded fierce lancers of the desert, the red and blue tassels forming silken skirts before their horses' knees. She saw these men at daybreak, when the first clear rays stood level from the horizon, turn towards the sun and, without the prostrations and ablutions of the true Mohammedan, go through their own ancient rites until the orb was clear above the desert's edge. 'For they were Sun-worshippers before Mohammed came,' said Jones, 'and such they really are to-day. Their prophets have warned them that it is evil to salute the rising sun because at this time the Devil's horns appear. Nothing can change them. They know nothing of the pilgrimage to Mecca except how to plunder the pilgrims and are indifferent to the feast of Ramadan. They still sacrifice sheep and camels at the tombs of their ancestors.'

He spoke of the lakes of mirage, rising before one on all sides, quivering in the heat, nodding their phantom palm trees. 'Dreary land of death ... little dried-up lizards looking as though they had never had one drop of water upon their ugly bodies.' And once travelling out from the Wells of Wokba he and his caravan had all but perished of thirst. For days fifteen or eighteen hours out of the twenty-four were spent on the camels crawling like flies on the black surface of the desert. Then, at midnight, three hours of tantalizing sleep broken so soon by the wise old guide standing in the door of the tent crying, 'Oh, master, if we linger we shall die.'

Oases with camels lying about, looking from a distance like 'teapots.' Tall, speechless women of the Badaweens, shrouded like ghosts standing sometimes six feet in their sandals. Patriarchs such as these solitary places have always bred since the days of Abraham.

He stood before her, clothed in the glory of his strange, bold life. The infinite spaces stretched behind him and the awful power of life and death was in his hard, square hands. In the sadness of his eyes and the silent disillusionment of his mouth was a philosophy older and deeper than taught by Mr. Emerson, who sat but three seats away. Under the compulsion of the smooth, low voice she felt little by little the moorings of her soul breaking and leaving her free to float off down some dreadful and beautiful river.

She was frightened by her own absorption, and tried to pull herself back. She said to herself desperately, 'If I fall in love with him it will kill me. I can't! I can't!' — and stared at him rather grimly. He was only a young Englishman in what she contemptuously called 'fancy dress,' advertising his new book and making money to go back to a country which, after all, seemed to be a travelling pigsty where no Christian 'man of principles' would want to live. She decided that all that was attractive about him was Arabia, and that Arabia was filthy. Its romance, of which Mr. Jones had nothing to say, was exaggerated. They were a lot of dirty people, black as Africans, and suffering from skin diseases, who wrote horrid poems, ate flour paste, rancid butter, and smelled of decay. And if this was all of Mr. Jones's charm, it was little enough. She whispered to Sears Ripley, 'He must have spoken for more than an hour and a half.' He looked slightly hurt, as one would if a member of one's own family had out-talked his welcome, and surreptitiously glanced at his Gorham watch.

'I think he feels so sure of his audience that he is talking a little overtime.'

'The people who live in Cambridge will miss the last horse-car.'

'Better that than Arabia.'

The voice went on. She felt stifled and was suddenly desperately anxious to leave the hall. If she did he might notice it and guess that she was bored. It might even hurt him. But, of course, he was so conceited nothing could do that. Professor Ripley moved slightly and his thick, navy-blue shoulder pressed against her silken one. He whispered to her gravely that the reason Jones was smooth-shaven except for an inch or so before either ear was the distaste the Arabs felt for a yellow beard.

No one except Mamma had ever hurt Lanice so much. She could not tell whether she liked him or hated him, but she knew he had the power to move her deeply, a power Augustus never had had, and temperate, friendly men like this nice Mr. Ripley could know nothing of. She struggled against the hold she felt he had upon her, and her natural egoism resented it. The instinct to submit to him warred bitterly against the desire for liberty and self-assertion. If she could have respected him, as for instance she respected Emerson, the battle would not have been so cruel. Sears Ripley felt her moving restlessly beside him. Never restless himself, he was patient and forgiving with her. He tried to encourage her with the information that the lecture must be nearly over because he now was talking about the French project of building a canal from Port Said to Suez. The best-informed in the audience, realizing the French and English rivalry at Suez, guessed without Jones's saying it that here was the real reason for his five years of freebooting through Arabia. Undoubtedly England had supported him as some sort of super-private agent and was the source of the gold which he had spent so freely.

The applause, muffled by the gloved hands of the gentlemen as well as the ladies, subsided, and Lanice was impatient to be gone. Miss Bigley was running back and forth throughout the audience striving vainly to herd together her ushers and get them into the two sleighs hired for the occasion, and back to her house, and so into their own clothes. The enchanting girls wished to stay for the impromptu reception that followed.

'Will you stop a minute, Miss Bardeen?' said Professor Ripley. 'I see a number of people whom I think you would enjoy.'

[93]

'I'd rather go to the hack and wait for the others,' she replied.

He did not urge her, but silently found the right sleigh, tucked her up with bear robes, and bowing, left her.

7

Alone in the dark she tried to forget the strange moment when she had felt the moorings begin to break within her and the fear that she might come to love this man had terrified her. Absurd, of course. There was no reason why she should love him more than another one. And her code did not permit a lady to love a man previous to his 'declaration.'

It seemed hours later that quite suddenly and softly the door opened, and not Miss Bigley, but Captain Jones himself entered, shaking the snow that still fell in tatters from his white headgear. He turned towards a bevy of young dandies who escorted him. 'Yes, good-night,' he called, and, 'Yes, interesting country ... oh, no, not too difficult ... thank you, yes.' The coachman cracked the whip, the frozen runners held against the first pull of the horses, then broke loose with a jerk. Slowly and casually he turned to his companion. She was humiliated to think that he might believe she was intentionally lying in wait for him, and instantly and rather ungraciously began to explain that she had understood that this was the sleigh reserved for the ushers.

'Yes,' he said, 'but I travel with the ushers, you know.'

'Should we not wait for the others?'

'No. Miss Bigley got them off all piled up in the other sleigh half an hour ago. Ripley told me he had put you in here. I thought you would be so kind as to wait for me.'

'Oh, of course,' she said quickly.

'And I've told the driver to make a turn up Washington Street. I do hope I am not inconveniencing you.'

'Oh, no. No.'

A dark, inscrutable silence lapsed between them which perhaps he did not care to break and which Lanice could not. Her heart had unaccountably sunken when she had seen Jones bow his head and enter the hack, shaking the snowflakes from him. Now it was beating fast and high up within her, and she was afraid he might hear it. Tardily she remembered that she had not said one word about the lecture, but found it hard to express what she felt. The words sounded stilted and labored. He accepted her praise good-naturedly, but as if it meant nothing to him, and again the darkness and the silence pressed upon them. Once he drew the bear rugs up about her and, leaning towards her, frankly inhaled with delight the rosy fragrance of her garments. The strong, odd perfume had puzzled and slightly embarrassed the New England girl. She murmured an apology.

'Good God!' he exclaimed, almost with irritation and none of his usual diffidence, 'that perfume is one of the wonders of the world. Not Arab, of course — there's nothing subtle about the Arab nose — but

[95]

Persian. It's what our mutual friend, Mr. Ripley, would call decadent, but even . . . from my lecture platform, I could see his nostrils quiver like the wings of a butterfly about to light.'

Lanice visibly offended drew back. Anthony relaxed sullenly. She forgot that she had been afraid she might love him. He had almost forgotten that at a few odd moments she could be cruelly beautiful. Nothing but a rascal, as Mr. Ripley had said. Only another of these ridiculous high-minded 'civilized' women, and an editoress at that!

Mr. Jones had his own latchkey and let himself into the Bigley house. Inside, his unacclimated shivering Hindoo, an affectation he had procured for himself in London, was packing up the discarded costumes of the ushers and setting out coffee for his master. So the dismal waiting in the cold hack had really been almost as long as it had seemed. The others had come and gone, and Miss Bigley, so the servant said, and her venerable father had gone to bed. Later Lanice heard that Miss Bigley 'understood' that Miss Bardeen had felt ill and had gone home immediately after the lecture.

Jones showed his teeth and spoke in a foreign language. He pointed to the hearth. The Hindoo busied himself until the orange flames leaped up and colored the room. He and his master drew the big sofa close to the fire. The horsehair upholstery displeased Jones, who ordered an India shawl to be spread upon it.

Lanice wished to leave, but did not know how to go

about it. To take his priceless Persian garments home
with her even for the night seemed an imposition, but
she could not find a way to retire to her dressing-
room. The coffee was served, a thick, delicious syrup
in tiny cups of gold and turquoise. Jones grew warm.
He threw back his headgear that during the lecture
had drooped so becomingly about his sturdy face and
with a careless gesture pushed back the layers of
cloth upon his throat and chest.

'Are you warmer, Lanice?' How had he learned
her name. How dared he use it?

'The fire,' she said primly, 'is very vigorous.'

'Yes.'

Conversation sickened, but there was a false under-
tone to its weakness that suggested a strategic retreat
before attack. The girl had disappointed Jones. In
the Persian dress she seemed almost wholly the
editoress disguised as an ancient princess, while in
hoops and plaid taffeta the disguise had seemed the
other way around. The ruddy fire distorted shadows
and burned orange in the folds of his white wool
wrappings. It glittered on his chest which lay for
some inches bare to the heat. The spectacle of so
much firm clean skin revolted her, who was trained
to believe that the body is in itself evil. Such a lack of
collar, cravat, and waistcoat was disgusting. As she
turned, and as the fire leaped, cruel blue lights,
bright rosy copper flamed in her robes. The man
could have laughed as he noticed the mincing kid
shoe with elastic inserts below the robes of an oda-
lesque.

[97]

He stared at her face, and she turned it towards him, the light catching in her lacquered black eyes.

'It must be really very late, I fear. May I not send you these garments to-morrow?'

He started to reply, but his eye fell upon her earrings. They were filigree pitchers and struck him as ugly, inappropriate, and quite inadequate for her voluptuous clothing. He said, 'I know what is wrong, it is those earrings.'

Calling his servant he addressed him again in jargon.

'Indeed, I must go.'

'No, no, not yet.'

He smiled delicately.

'I will not call you "Lanice" again. I only did it to see if I could either anger or embarrass you, but you merely retreated and left me. Ah, here we are. Please remove those golden gewgaws in your ears.'

The salaaming servant laid a crystal and silver box upon his master's knees. Anthony opened it and took out, wrapped in crimson cloth scrawled in gold mottoes, a pair of earrings, the jewelled fringes of which would hang down upon the wearer's breast. They were of a massive, savage beauty set with rubies and turquoises. The man caressed them lovingly. He knew that they were old enough and fine enough to have once hung in the ears of Scheherazade herself.

'Put them on, Miss Bardeen.'

'Oh, I couldn't. You see, the hooks are much too large for my ears. In civilized countries the ear is

[98]

pierced only with a small needle. How could any one have worn them?'

She gathered them up and turned them towards the fire. Her face burned with a childish wonder and the light from the hearth glittered over her sleek, blue-black hair. Once again she created the illusion of ancient Persia. A demon stirred within Jones's chest. He bit his lower lip and smiled, partly at the idea that there was a civilized way of cutting holes in flesh for the suspension of baubles, partly in recognition of her brightening beauty.

'Nonsense!'

He pressed close to her. The thick perfume assaulted his nostrils. 'I'll . . . put them in for you.'

She struggled, cried out twice in agony. The pain was much greater than the original piercing. A drop of blood welled from each lobe and slid upon her neck. She sprang from him and, whirling about, faced him utterly bewildered, pressing her hands to her cruelly burdened ears.

'Why did you do that?' she cried out hotly, all the emotional turmoil of the evening suddenly trembling in her voice.

He stood away from her, his dark face almost angry.

'Now you will never forget me,' he promised.

'Why should I remember *you?*'

'Because there is a bond between us, Lanice. You feel it as strongly as I, but your training has been so damnable and, Heaven help you, you are such a lady, you will not recognize the fact.'

[99]

She turned her head away from him and her body drooped wearily. 'What bond?'

He said defiantly, 'What you would consider an "evil" bond.'

'*You* are evil.'

'As life itself.'

She began to cry, and this sign of weakness irritated him, who had been intoxicated when she had first turned upon him and asked 'Why did you do that?'

'Weep,' he said, unsympathetically, and kicked the fire with his red leather boot.

'I want to go home!' she cried. Her voice was anticlimactic. She gathered her draperies together, wrapping herself in a mist of copper gold and fragrance. The cruel, bloody earrings hung to her breast. They faced each other for a long moment, questioning the future.

'Come,' he said, 'let's part friends' — and bent his face towards her. She leaped back in maidenly terror, and, wordless, fled from the room. In the hall she found her mink pelisse which she did not stop to put on. The door slammed after her. She plunged through snow to her knees and flung herself into the waiting hack. The pain in her ears tormented her, and sobbing a little she managed to unhook the earrings. 'Why did you do that?' she cried over and over in her mind. Wave after wave of emotion raced over her, leaving her hot and cold. With closed eyes she could believe that Jones himself still sat beside her in the hack, that in a moment she would feel him against her. She wanted to cry 'Don't, don't!' to the spectre, for her fear of him was very real. Then she would shut her eyes again, and again feel painfully conscious of his devastating presence.

8

'Don't scold so, Ellen,' said my grandmother mildly as I very reluctantly commenced the mending of a pair of hose. 'What would Fred Graham say if he could see your dimples lost in such a cloud?... Lost in such a fog ... lost in such ... lost ...' The words beneath the lady editoress's pen jumbled into Arabic. Abracadabra. What she wrote stared back at her. Anthony Jones, Sir Anthony, Lord Jones. Jones the Belted Earl. She glanced at the hundred painted plates from 'Hearth and Home' tacked upon her movable wall. Their perfect little faces mowed at her and they seemed to rustle their belling skirts. She pressed her hands to her ears. They no longer hurt her and she vaguely regretted their complete recovery. 'If I am in love with Anthony Jones,' she thought, 'why can't I feel the way ladies do in stories?' She inked her pen.

'I did not care what Fred Graham would think. I was an exception, truly! I had no doubt that every one of the girls was glad that it rained so that we could not go on the picnic only that they might stay at home to enjoy the exquisite felicity of darning old hose. Oh, of course! How delightful! And I began to cry.'

Miss Bigley wanted a good, stiff moral lesson.

Something that would drive home economy. So Grandmamma in the story must tell an improving tale as 'I' darn and pout. 'You have often seen your cousin Mary, Edward's wife, and expressed your surprise that a man so handsome and so nobly gifted could marry a lady that was so unmistakably plain, one, too, that admired beauty so intensely as he did. Let me gratify your curiosity. Once upon a time, years ago, when he was much handsomer than now and a rising young lawyer, he loved Caroline Willoughby; she was extremely beautiful, accomplished, fascinating, and a great belle. He worshipped her with all the enthusiasm of his gifted nature. One summer evening they were riding down the shady road in silence. He had determined to tell her of his devotion, but could find no words. The horse shyed unexpectedly and she fell; he was at her side in an instant, pale with fright. He conveyed her to the nearest house and sent a servant for a physician. He came, and fearing that her limb was fractured, signed to a servant to remove her stocking. Off came the dainty little boot that Edward had held so tenderly as she mounted, and revealed a tattered stocking. The physician smiled, assured him that no bones were broken, and sent a carriage to convey them home. Neither spoke. Entering the house, he briefly explained to her mother the circumstances, expressed his regrets, and turned to leave; then suddenly pausing he added in a moment of hurry, "I had almost forgotten it . . . Miss Willoughby's stocking." And bowing, placed it on the table. The poor girl fainted and was sick for some time after. She really loved, and it was a great blow to her. She married old Goldthwaite, the millionaire.'

The story was coming just right. It sounded exactly like Miss Bigley. She wriggled her toes guiltily and found the small hole in her left stocking. Dear, dear, if Anthony knew she had deliberately put on a tattered hose, he would . . . no, he wouldn't. He'd hardly care. There couldn't be girls that looked like Persian miniatures in Cincinnati; why probably there was hardly a 'lady' in that frontier town. But Anthony had obviously thought the Scollay girls fascinating, they with their brisk, gold hair and sweet-pea faces, but in Cincinnati. . . . Ah, the Park Street clock. Eleven. Miss Bigley wanted this story by noon. Well, here goes!

'As for Edward, this cold bath of his imagination cured his love. He avoided ladies' society and rapidly rose to eminence in his profession. It was six years after this when he met your cousin Mary. Her self-sacrificing care of her invalid mother, her warm heart and native sense interested him deeply; still, his former experience had made him distrustful. Accident decided him. Mary's former governess was living in very destitute circumstances in an obscure part of town. And one wet day she went to see her. The carriage not returning, she set out for home alone and met Edward. He offered his services and at a muddy crossing her light slipper was left in the mud. He stooped to fit it on; there was no one in sight and she timidly advanced a dainty foot with the cleanest of

[103]

stockings and one of the neatest of little darns. He could resist no longer, and when he told me the story he showed me the identical hose.'

Now the thing's done. Except for an ending bringing 'me' and Fred Graham together over a basket of darning.

They didn't wear stockings in Arabia or stays or hoops or trousers, really. She gathered all her pencils together and, leaning almost at right angles over the waste-basket, began to sharpen them meticulously. Mr. Fox sauntered in, whistling, and as he drank from the Rockingham cooler he watched. Miss Bardeen's exactitude in the matter interested him. Not a sliver fell to the floor. Each point was perfection.

'Another story for "Hearth and Home"?' he asked, glancing at her desk.

'Yes.'

'What do you think of the stories we publish in that magazine?'

'Oh, some are very skilful. And I'm sure, as Miss Bigley says, they must do a world of good.'

'What ones have you enjoyed?'

She shot him a quick, birdlike glance. 'I liked "Mrs. Troubles' Twins" and "The Hands of Martha."'

'Did you like "This I Have Promised"?'

'But that was in your "Journal." Yes, it was stupendous.'

'The thing coagulates like life. Do you think "The Hands of Martha" is like life?'

'Why, yes.'

'If women are patient and self-sacrificing they find love, wealth, and happiness. They always do in your stories, you know. Do they in life?'

'I think,' she said with an abominable smugness, 'we usually get what we deserve in this world, no — not always.' She recalled Eliza Hornblower, a good, gentle creature blessed with all the virtues and cursed with a wretched complexion. In stories, when you call girls 'plain' you are never specific. If Eliza had been wicked, unchaste, would she have been more cruelly punished? Mamma was the happiest person she had ever known. She humbly asked the oracle, 'Shouldn't a story be better than life, in a way truer?'

'Should it?'

'Teach a lesson?'

'Shouldn't it? One has to work these things out for one's self. You haven't read or lived very widely yet.'

'Mr. Trelawney wants me to try Gautier and George Sand, but I've always heard the French masters are so sadly immoral.'

'Well, if you want always to write for "H. and H.," keep away from them. Keep on rolling sugar-coated moral lessons for ladies of delicate digestive tracts, intellectually speaking.'

The girl thought guiltily of the dreadful books she had read with furtive eagerness at the Athenæum, all about witchcraft. Of course, not even the wicked French could possibly be as bad as that, but then why tell all one knows? She went on sharpening pencils exquisitely, after Mr. Fox had gone. She thought of life and how unlike a story it was.

Life was a patchwork of all things. Things ugly and beautiful, sordid, pathetic, wonderful. You never could make things in stories as wonderful as in life because the stories were just the heads of flowers pulled off without any stems or leaves, and surely no hidden roots with black mud caking them. And no dead flowers withering into new seed or decaying noisomely. Just the pretty heads pulled off and arranged in geometric design. In a story you could never tell the truth of Mr. Matthews's lewd embrace, or the fact that it was intended for her mother, or that she had afterwards retired to her room and been actually sick, in the English sense of the word.

Nor could you put into the story that one terrible moment in Miss Bigley's house when Anthony Jones had held her and hurt her very much, and for some diabolical reason the whole little room had flamed up with emotion ruddier than the firelight on the walls, and she, at once degraded and magnified, fled the room.

In stories you never put in what you really think of men. How once on a country road you had let an ox-team boy fold a blanket on one of his team and seat you on it, nor how he held your hand in his big red mitten and pressed his forehead a minute against your thigh. (The scene returned vividly, the boy's sturdy face framed in his wool cap looked helmeted and Roman.) Men — so strange. Other men a long way off, men walking in the spring with reins about their necks following in the furrow a plough. Lumbermen in winter with upturned sheepskin collars, heavy figures wrapped in frozen breath. Sweating men in midsummer, hoeing corn, loading hay wains, men early in the morning crying 'Co' boss' to the cows. She did not think of Augustus or the other students. Only of the men she had never known. The bestial but eyeless bronze boxer in the stereoscope suddenly leaped out of the blackness at her. All his bulging muscles seen in perspective. And suddenly she thought of Anthony Jones and a warm tide rose somewhere within her, swept up and almost drowned her. Anthony was at once all the men whom she had ever seen walking far off calling to their beasts. If this is love, if this ghastly feeling of suffocation . . . Her sigh quavered and broke. She wanted to cry. But the story was not quite done, and there by the portière was her friend, Sears Ripley. Why did he come in to see her so often? Of course he had to finish the arrangements with Mr. Fox for Anthony's great book, but he always stopped in her office and looked at her consideringly. Perhaps he had known that she would fall in love with Captain Jones, if that was really what she had done. She felt no shame in his presence. She could have told him all about the brief scene in Miss Bigley's parlor after the lecture. Suddenly she realized that if she ever wanted to she could even tell him how, long, long ago, Mr. Matthews of New York had mistaken her for her mother.

CHAPTER V

SHE SEES THE SUNLIGHT ON THE SNOW

1

THE snow was still deep on the frozen ground when Anthony Jones came back.

Old Mr. Bigley must go South for his health, and his formidable daughter, who prided herself on being a woman first, flung down her editorial duties with a martyr's frantic haste. Mr. Fox must understand that dearly as she loved 'Hearth and Home,' she must always think first of her venerable parent, and hers and Papa's own hearth and home. For days she worked twenty out of the twenty-four hours and became so irascible that no one dared speak to her. Almost in a collapse she got herself and the ancient gentleman off for the South, and doubtfully left Mr. Fox and Lanice to struggle with the April issue of 'Hearth and Home.' Mr. Fox, whose agreeable motto was 'Work with pleasure, for yourself, Miss Bardeen, the office force, and the public,' was very little interested in this profitable magazine's April number. It seemed to offer him great opportunities for remarks about the fair sex in general and for various absurd misunderstanding of their social and sartorial problems. He wandered about Lanice's small office restlessly and occasionally offered her hard candies as well as literary advice and wit.

Captain Jones, his lecture tour over, wrote that he

intended to stay in Boston long enough to read the proofs of his first volume, complete the manuscript of his second, make up indexes, give captions to the illustrations, and superintend the map-making. Would Mr. Fox find him a small house? What could be more opportune than Miss Bigley's evacuation of her estimable dwelling! Mr. Jones must have for part time at least a trained amanuensis, and Mr. Fox, knowing Lanice's scholarly achievements for Captain Poggy, volunteered her services. She protested. Miss Bigley was gone. What now would happen to 'Hearth and Home'? Every day there were scores of letters to write, letters about fashions, needlework, etiquette. 'Oh, Trelawney and I will start some new style. We will say that, due to Anthony Jones's triumph, all clothes this spring shall be Arabic. Why, before you and Miss Bigley are back, we'll get the ladies in face veils and bloomers. And as for social usage, we'll introduce polygamy. But it won't take you more than a couple of hours a day to help him out.'

Realizing that he had perhaps overstepped his rights in offering her services to Jones, he reconsidered the matter a few days later. Lanice's prejudice against Jones was absurd, but, after all, if she didn't want to work for him, she should not.

'I just met that pair of pretty Scollays trotting down the Tremont Mall, cheek by cheek like two little prize ponies. They can talk of nothing but the adorable Captain Jones's return, and are languishing, in fact Miss Lydia said "yearning," to be his private secretary, and . . .'

'Oh, I've decided I'll have time to do it, Mr. Fox.' Her voice had a slight edge to it. She assumed an almost sullen manner to cover her excitement.

2

They met daily in the office, Lanice with averted eyes, Anthony scarcely glancing at her. She decided that she had never admired his type, and that his hesitating, gentle speech was, indeed, an affectation. But as she began to read his manuscript, she came to admire him as a workman. He wrote glowing, ringing pages, smelling strongly of camels, sann and musk. There was a vigorous saplike push to his work unlike anything else she had ever read. His drawings, about which she had heard nothing, impressed her trained eye more than they had Mr. Fox. He drew exquisitely in lead pencil and only in outline. His odd technique was self-taught and his sense of proportion so perfect he could draw in complete figures beginning with the head and working down without once lifting his pencil or making a correction. When he found that his drawing pleased Lanice, he was grateful for her praise, and often worked at her desk and used her fastidious pencils.

She told herself now, with assurance, that of course she did not love him, and whatever had flamed up so violently in Miss Bigley's small parlor had been some other emotion. Behind his back she criticized him rather curtly, arguing with Mr. Fox about his genius, telling Mr. Trelawney that she doubted if he had been in Arabia more than four years. Oh, no, he was hardly handsome, his short drooping mouth was stubborn rather than strong; but once when she tried to tell Ripley that Captain Jones was not a man to appeal to the affections of elegant young American females, her voice broke suddenly. Mr. Jones himself seemed to have completely forgotten the odd incident of the earrings. He was often reported playing a guitar in the Scollays' drawing-room.

It was easy to work for Jones, as easy as for Captain Poggy or the gallant and sweet-tempered Mr. Fox. She suggested rearrangement of material. The great traveller was entirely amenable. She copied, in her neat, fine-lady hand, chapter after chapter of his green-growing, living narrative, and indicated where she thought his illustrations should be placed. He humbly, even gratefully, agreed to everything, and told her again how little he knew of books. It seemed he had read but little. That was why, perhaps, his style was so undecorated with the elegant words and fastidious euphemisms that Lanice herself so much affected. The story of his five years in Arabia grew up out of the sun-baked country itself. There was the mark of Eastern magic upon it and ever the Jinn and the houri in his talk. This rather ignorant young man, as he always seemed to Lanice, was an authority on such things as the Thousand and One Nights, and the poems of Antar, Khayyam, and Yazid Ebn Moamia.

It was more convenient that Lanice should spend her mornings in the West Cedar Street house. The first time she went, a respectable cleaning woman fulfilled the duties of chaperon, but after that no pretence was made. It did not seem strange to the girl who had worked so many hours with Captain Poggy. The sunlight filled the second-story morning room which Captain Jones had selected for his study. There were always fresh flowers from the Scollay conservatory and an easy, exotic atmosphere.

The third time she rang the bell she heard the shuffling bare feet of the Hindoo servant. Jones himself, lazily puffing his cigarette, met her at the head of the stairs. He looked sleepy and tumbled, yawned often, and once scratched his head so hard as to embarrass his well-bred amanuensis. In private life there was hardly a trace of Captain Jones the lecturer. In spite of his wandering wits they managed to work for an hour.

'I can't get anything done.'

He lay in the sunlight on a small chaise-longue that was quiet beneath his weight, although Lanice had often heard it creak beneath Miss Bigley. He flung out his arms, arched his chest, and looked at the girl speculatively as if wondering what she could do to relieve his boredom, then fell to playing with his seals and looked away. Lanice in her turn studied him slyly. The sunlight gilded Mr. Jones, and she noticed how it coarsened the skin of his face and showed every pore on his nose. It gilded his hair, too, which was like dark, half-pulled molasses. The two inches of beard before either ear was rough and metallic in comparison. Towards the eyes beyond the sweep of the razor was a delicate fruit-like down, almost white.

This carnal discovery shocked her, and she blushed at her own powers of observation. Surely no woman before had ever examined a man with such morbid care. Evidently, however, his own observations of her had been of an even less delicate nature.

'Miss Bardeen, I don't know whether or not we can work this into the book, but I must admit that women's clothes in this country and Europe really shock me.'

'Shock *you?*'

'Why the emphasis? Surely. It is true . . . just immorality can hurt me . . . no more. . . . I am not afraid of passion, even in women, but unnatural things in action or clothing depress me, and, yes, shock me.'

'You find our clothes unnatural?'

'Oh, very. Now the Arab costume, which you think merely a shapeless sack, still gives more the impression of . . . a real woman than does your elegant armor of plain taffeta and whalebone. Don't you see, as I look at you . . . I've no idea what is you and what is . . . corsets and, pardon the word . . . bustles. The figure of a civilized woman fascinates me only from the point of view of a guessing game. Frankly, it would be more decent to come out in the open and wear no clothes.'

'Captain Jones!'

'Or just wrappings like the Arab women.' He got restlessly to his feet and pulled a chair up to her table.

'Take even their veiled faces. At least you really

see their eyes, while, pardon my rudeness, I find among American and English women such ridiculous bonnets and claptrap. I cannot see even the eyes. The Arab obliterates her charms, but they're there all the same, fairly burning holes through the clothes. European women disfigure ... or even ... deform them. Now frankly, as two grown people ... two artists, let us consider the divine form. Look.'

He took up a pencil and began to sketch in his exquisite way the nude figure of a woman. Lanice, fascinated and incredulous, watched his quick fingers moving confidently over the beautiful little creature to whom they gave existence.

'There! That might "launch a thousand ships." See what civilization does!'

His pencil took large bites out of the waist, converting it into the customary hour-glass. 'But this substantial flesh must go *somewhere*. Of course, the hoops conceal the distortion of hips and abdomen, but the corset pushes up the breast, which is ugly for the slender and hideous for the stout.'

Lanice began to blush slowly, furiously, until tears of mortification stood in her downcast eyes. She was suddenly, overwhelmingly conscious of Mr. Jones's physical presence. The back of his hand touched her wrist.

'Lovely hands,' he said quietly, 'and neck and face. I've never seen another face that could ... at odd moments ... move me more. How can the rest be only whalebone and buckram? Lanice, you could be a ... beauty, and love as women loved a thousand

[114]

years ago. You prefer to be a dressmaker's dummy and a lady editoress. Oh, by the eyelids of the prophet!'

He brushed the cheek that she had so carefully studied against her hair and she felt herself melt within and her arms grow heavy.

'Captain Jones!' she protested feebly.

'Yes,' he purred, and rubbed his face against her like a cat.

She stood up. 'This is not the conduct of a gentleman towards a lady whom he employs.'

'No,' said Jones, and smiled, 'but I don't employ you. Mr. Fox does, and lends you to me.'

Suddenly she felt homesick for Mr. Fox and his courtesies, and, forgetting the weakness that enveloped her at his touch, she turned on the handsome Englishman. He thrilled to see that her hands, which seemed to him delicately carved from ivory, were clenched. A smile lighted his face, and he looked at her expectantly as a dog does that hopes some one will throw him a stick.

'I shall go now and I shall never return.'

'Now I am standing in the door and you cannot go.'

'How ridiculous. . . .' She turned from him, but as she turned she started the hoops swaying in the flower-like way that she had learned from her mother.

'By the time I have packed up my reticule and assumed my shawl and my bonnet, I shall expect to leave, and I will.' She was breathless.

'Lanice . . . you shall not . . . be so cruel to your-self and to me.'

He took her in his arms with a hardihood that pre-cluded struggle. If he had made the little furtive ad-vances of Augustus, she would have known how to re-tire modestly, but her flimsy code went down before the novelty of this situation and the onslaught of this grasping animal that a few minutes before had been what she would have described as 'one of our authors.'

The sun, intensified by the snow outside, splashed down over the chaise-longue and gleamed on the brassy yellow of Mr. Jones's tumbled hair and the sleek black of the girl's head.

'Captain Jones, don't, don't, don't! . . . Oh, let me go! Dear God, help me!'

'No, no,' he protested; then after a long, pregnant pause, 'never.'

3

That night she dreamed that the bronze boxer Mamma had sent her got out of the stereoscope and, still maintaining his exquisite and almost painful per-spective, chased her over great desert spaces. She woke at dawn, feverish and aching; lay awake, cried a little, thought what clothes she would take with her to Arabia, and wondered if Captain Jones really could prefer her own sleek charm to the sweet-pea prettiness of the Scollay girls.

For two weeks she went daily to the small red house that stood on the lower side of West Cedar

Street, three doors from Chestnut. She had no conventions for unconventional conduct, and came and went with greater freedom than a Paris demi-mondaine would have dared. She came to care passionately for Anthony Jones, to care so much that when he held her her veins seemed turned to thin wires pulled tight through her body. If she as much as breathed, she was afraid they might pierce her through. But if they talked, words pushed them apart, he from her, and she from him.

Once, seated before the fire in the morning room sipping their coffee and eating Eastern preserves, Jones tried futilely to tell her all he had suffered from childhood at the hands of women. He told her of the grey-eyed, lipless governess that cajoled, flouted, and obsessed him before he was ten; of health-burdened English girls with raw skins and honey hair; of the pallid wives of Anglo-Indian colonels, and of voluptuous Arab women with hips which, in the language of the poet, Anu Ebn Kultan, 'were so round and heavy that they were tired.' The Boston girl listened coldly. It seemed to her it was not Jones who had suffered, but the women. However, to hear of the undeviating devotion he had always borne for the Persian princesses of the Mughal Court, dead for centuries, quickened her blood. Her New England conscience could not be reconciled to spending in his arms the time which should be spent in writing 'Sands of Araby,' and she would insist, with a high seriousness that amused him, that the book must always come first.

'Now a ten-minute rest from Araby.'

[117]

'Not more than five.'

'My watch is run down.'

'There's Miss Bigley's timepiece on the mantel.'

It was strange to think that this was Miss Bigley's house, her clock, her chair, her chaise-longue, her table, her chintzes, and that through her well-scrubbed panes the radiant sun smiled in upon them. Lanice always had the feeling that the formidable editoress was but in the next room or on the stairs, and that at any moment she would look up and see her blue swimming eyes widening as they gazed upon her and the affectionate Mr. Jones.

She could not understand how Jones could brazenly continue his love-making in the presence of his servant, who came and went seemingly on velvet paws. If Anthony's words often chilled her, to an almost greater degree did hers irritate him, but still there was a piquancy in never knowing whether you held in your arms an editoress or the reincarnation of a Persian princess. He realized this affair would end when the book was completed, and he would return to England, and he was afraid that perhaps her naïveté had led her to think they were to marry. Women always thought anything, everything, led to marriage. Before he left, he would break the news to her very gently, and in the meantime he believed he was doing her good rather than harm, getting her out of her emotional shroud of New England ice. He would find another woman, and Lanice — well, she would marry Ripley. Ripley was always dropping veiled hints about this girl, and even urged him not to play

[118]

'fast and loose' with her. He wondered if he suspected how desperately involved they were. He was the only one who ever presumed so far as to call upon Anthony Jones in the morning. Once he came up and had coffee with them.

The same day, unknown to Jones, Ripley had called upon Lanice rather formally in the Poggy drawing-room and indulged in an evasive discussion of varying moral codes. So he showed how what is right in the Old Testament is not right in the New, why polygamy may be countenanced in Arabia and not in America, not even when headed by Mr. Young and Mr. Smith. He diverged into the interesting story of the Mormon westward exodus, then taking place. Lanice, always as alive as an Athenian to new wonders, drank in his description of Mr. Young and the late Mr. Smith, and tried to remember carefully so she might tell Anthony.

The conversation swung back to Arabia and the undeniable fact that Captain Jones was as much a Mohammedan as anything, but perhaps a fire-worshipper like the most primitive of Arabs.

'You mean he has several Arabian wives?'

'None, I think. I believe he has only what the Koran would sanction as concubines.'

That was something Solomon had had. She did not know that they existed at the present day, even in Arabia, nor the exact duties of a concubine. After the storm and excitement of Anthony Jones, who never cared to understand and whose emotional power over her hurt and alarmed her, Professor Ripley seemed

compassionate and comprehending. On his departure
they shook hands warmly. 'Captain Jones,' he said,
'is an extraordinary man, something like Arabian
literature itself, from which one may take either harm
or good. I beg of you, Miss Bardeen, take only the
good, but . . .' their eyes locked together . . . 'if every
. . . if anything . . . if this business relation you are
enjoying with Mr. Jones should . . . if you want advice . . .' He cleared his throat and amazed her after
the fashion of a widowed man by assuring her he had
loved his wife Prunella very dearly. Then he continued to beg her at any time to come to him for anything. She naïvely thought he referred to a possibility
of the adventurous Mr. Jones leaving the country
without paying off his secretary.

4

'It is zero weather, Cousin Lanice. Surely you will
not be so foolish as to risk a lung inflammation in an
open sleigh.'

'I have my mink pelisse, Cousin Poggy.'

'If you must go, do put goose-grease on your chest.'

'Oh, no.' (Had she not under her basque secreted
the minute gold vial of attar of rose?)

'Surely, if you insist, you had best take Snowball
and Favorite, with our sleigh. There is no reason why
Captain Jones should be at the expense of a hired conveyance. I assure you these livery hacks raised out
West in Ohio are never safe in the cities.'

'But he knows how to handle horses.'

'The fair sex, too, from what I hear.'

To which there could be no answer. Pauline nervously began to pick up and set down the ivory and jade ornaments on the drawing-room table; her knuckly fingers trembled.

'I had hoped so much from you, Lanice, and now you are ready to leave all and go off with this fast young man in a sleigh.'

'But why not? Of course I'll be back before it is really dark. Surely it is of no consequence.'

She tried to speak lightly, but her voice vibrated. Pauline muttered something about a symbol. The silence in the Poggy drawing-room became ominous. Lanice went to the grate and mended the fire. Pauline hunched over the table like a moulting bird, stopped her exploration of its *objets de virtu*, and fumbled about her face.

'Lanice,' she said coldly, 'I am in a sense your natural protector. It is my right to know whether you intend matrimony with this young man.'

Instantly realizing that it was not her right and that she was approaching the subject clumsily, she changed her style and swooped over to Lanice, patting one pale hand and murmuring, 'I think I know just what you are going through, my love. Now let us talk things over perfectly calmly and sensibly. Jones is so *fascinating*. Sometimes men who have sown their wild oats make the steadiest husbands. There, there, I did not mean to upset you.'

'Pauline,' gasped Lanice, 'he's going away next week ... England. I don't know whether or not I am supposed to go with him. I know he loves me ...'

'You have not, I hope, Lanice, ever let him so much as lay the weight of his hand upon you?'

Gathering affirmation from the girl's lovesick, tear-filled eyes and parted lips, she again abruptly changed her rôle from mentor to confidante. 'Why, of course, I understand, dear.' She almost winked at Lanice, as if she too could tell tales of embraces and feverish stolen kisses, as if Jones had often held her close to him on Miss Bigley's sun-drenched chaise-longue.

'But you see, Pauline, to-day I must go with him and find out what he intends of me.'

'Perhaps,' sighed Pauline almost hopefully, 'he is a wanton destroyer of female virtue.'

The younger girl went quite white. She gave a whimpering sigh like the ghost of a lost lady in a haunted chamber, and looked at Pauline in a way that would have wrung the heart of Sears Ripley.

'Let us talk calmly together.'

'No, no, not now. He'll be here in half an hour.' She wanted to get away from Pauline and her almost contagious ugliness. With her lace-edged handkerchief fluttering in her fingers, she fled the room.

5

Pauline, half hidden by the crimson curtains of the bow window, lay in wait for Jones. He came at last in a great glitter and jingle. Red Russian sleigh, silver bells, black satin horses. She drew a dirty fascinator over her head and hurried to the door.

'She will be out in a minute, Captain,' she said, and looked with more curiosity than distaste at the great

[122]

Mr. Jones's ruddy face, innocent grey eyes and black bear coat.

The horses pawed impatiently and snuffed the air. No livery stable hacks these flashing cat-like creatures. Then she remembered hearing her father say that Mr. Scollay had recently bought a pair of black Morgans, the handsomest horses ever seen in Boston. So this lost and wanton man had borrowed from the family of one young lady the wherewithal to dazzle another — sly dog! And these unfeeling, sinful, even lustful brutes are not only our equals but our masters, forsooth. Would, under different circumstances, dear little Miss Spence effect a like perfidy? Would Miss Gatherall stoop to borrow the horses of one man that she might play fast and loose with another? The jet buttons strained at their moorings.

Lanice came belling down the stairs, her fetching new brown velvet frock filling the narrow hall. With it she wore her mink pelisse, furred Russian boots of green leather, a cinnamon-brown bonnet with coral-colored roses to match her coral breastpin, earrings, and bracelet. The girl was hardly an heiress. Sinful to care so deeply what one puts on one's back, and the heathen running naked!

'Good-bye, dear Pauline.' She kissed her with a new-learned fervor which left Pauline shaking her head, rubbing her chin, and squinting between the heavy curtains at the red sleigh glistening on the blinding snow, at silver bells shaking on satin horses.

'Lanice, we shall go for miles . . . far out in the

country. I wish it were still before Christmas and we'd get evergreens for wreaths.'

He gentled and soothed his plunging pair, forcing them to take the bridge to Cambridge at a walk lest they exhaust their first freshness pulling the sleigh over the boards, which had already blown bare. Below, the tide was full and blocks of gray salt ice heaved on black water. The sunlight on the new-fallen snow was dazzling, the smell of cold like wine to the heart. The heavy folds of the Buffalo robes and Mr. Jones's own bodily heat flooded his guest with languorous warmth.

From the bank before them, from the bank that they had left, the elfin music of sleigh bells tinkled in the bright metallic air. A countryman with a sweating tandem, the leader of which carried a cow bell, passed them on the bridge. Jones pursed his lips, craned his neck about to be sure they were not observed, then turned his head quickly and brushed the girl's cold cheek with the teasing promise of a kiss. Both laughed and looked at each other with brightening color. The cold lashed their faces. Cheeks and noses reddened and Lanice's breath froze upon her lace veil.

The bridge crossed, the runners gave no resistance to the packed snow. The black Morgans pointed their dainty ears, held their tails high, and flashed into a twelve-mile trot. Other runners creaked on the hard snow, but the red Russian sleigh skimmed along with a swishing sound. The horses grew a little warm and the not unpleasant scent of their sweat mingled in the icy air with the faint attar of rose in the girl's breast, the tobacco of the man, and the pungent warm smell of the buffalo robe.

Neither cared to talk. Evidently Jones was finding great pleasure in merely handling the beautiful Vermont horses. The girl was sunk in the consciousness of her lover's nearness, the intoxicating backward rush of snow beneath the runners, and the oncoming and disappearing snow-burdened landscape. Through the length of Cambridge professors stopped to gaze with admiration at this elegant equipage. Tired intellectual ladies seated in bow windows put down their books and raised their glasses. Children making snowmen cried, 'Look-it, look-it.' A royal progress! Some recognized Sir Anthony Jones. At least two knew the girl to be one of Mr. Fox's female assistants.

Out on a willow-bordered road, flashing up and down endless hills. Hoofs and snow flying before, the world in its whitening slipping past. Blood racing within, and feet, thanks to Russian boots, buffalo robes, and a stove-like quality in Mr. Jones, deliciously warm. So into Weston, and beyond. So into Wayland, passed before realized. The Morgans had found their perfect stride. Jones exclaimed over them as all but equal in speed and quality to the desert horses, although he believed them inferior in beauty and courage. Lanice, swimming in delight, no longer worried about Mr. Jones's intentions, disengaged her mind from the pleasant process of merely living and asked him more about these famous steeds. He drew the Morgans to a restless walk and told her about the Arab horse, how it has one less vertebra than the European, and therefore an extraordinarily short back and high tail. He told her that its muzzle is so delicate it can drink out of a china teacup, and then laughed and said he had never seen one do so. He told her that the cruel Arab bit can break a horse's jaw and how the animals live in terror of it. This gives them a characteristic mincing walk, pointing their noses, rearing and arching back their necks in constant fear of its punishment, and he described the beautiful 'listening' horses and a lovely war-mare who had died under him in battle and whose death he had cruelly avenged. Recalling Professor Ripley's lecture on moral codes throughout the world, she tentatively drew the conversation from horses to manners. And from manners Mr. Jones himself led to morals. It took him less than half an hour to show the girl that morals, as she understood the word, he had none.

Was the man she was pledged to marry . . . if she were so pledged . . . ?

But why did he only tell her that he loved and wanted her? Why did he not ask her to marry him? Mr. Fox, even Professor Ripley, could have told her why.

Surely no man could be so sinful as to declare himself to a woman and then go off . . . forget . . .

Yet what else was he trying to tell her but that love came and went and came again and went again. That love, as she cherished the word in her maidenly heart, did not exist. There was only, so said Mr.

Jones, something brief and explosive that gripped you one moment, bent you to its uses, then left you to snap back, if you could, to your original state. Most married people, he said, were like cats tied together by their tails and thrown over a clothes line, clawing at each other's vitals. Marriage, he said, if congenial, reduces the erstwhile lovers to a brother and sister relationship which makes desire seem incestuous. Desire, he said, goes readily towards the strange and balks at the habitual. Love, he said, 'Hearth and Home' love, mawkish love, possibly existed in New England, but it was a thing of which he knew nothing. Finding his companion's hand in the layers of furs, he pressed it.

The girl grew cold with a chill that came from within and worked out to meet the icy air whistling against the buffalo robes. What had he said? In her heart she had always known that he wanted no more of her love than this. She had always really known that he had no desire to marry her, nor any woman. 'I must go back,' she thought.

Then, feeling his warm body pressed against her side, a flood of heat followed the chill and she was devastated with the desire to be kissed and caressed by this man who had no morals and who did not understand love. Nor did she herself love him as she had expected some day to love a man. The bonds which held her to him were at once more primitive, more binding, and lighter.

She told herself passionately to look at him again and see for herself that he had no greater charm than other men. He did not think nor dream nor hope as she did. Why, then, did his hands and mouth, sad grey eyes and halting voice rock her senses? This cannot be love. Oh, God help me, this is not love . . . and she thought guiltily of Mamma and Mr. Matthews. Is there, then, something stronger, more terrible than love? Something wicked, against which clergymen had preached when she had been a sleepy child in church, against which prophets major and prophets minor had raised their voices? Augustus had feared that she might have inherited her mother's wantonness . . . and she thought piteously of that lovely woman. Jones's arm stole around her just as she was on the point of begging him either to love her more or less, to take her with him to Arabia or to let her go now.

The copper-pink sun rolled from the icy sky towards the horizon. A long, glittering path spilled from it to the red sleigh across the white enamel fields.

'Captain Jones, we have driven too far. You forget we yet have the return journey to make. We must have come over ten miles.'

'Twenty-odd. Look.' He pointed with the whip and the horses crouched and sprang against their collars.

'Nam, nam, nam,' he called to them in Arabic fashion, and 'Look,' he said again to Lanice. 'There's the Red Horse Inn.'

Up the slope, behind great oaks, was the portly, gambrel-roofed hostelry.

'You have never been there?'

'No, I . . . I thought it was not frequented by ladies.'

'Oh, to the contrary, quite correct. Washington himself stopped there. They have his great state coach in the coach house still.'

'But did Mrs. Washington stop, too?' she asked, and laughed.

'Oh, indeed, she must have. And Professor Long-fellow and your Mr. Fox are habitués. In fact, Long-fellow is intending to write a series of poetic legends, fancies, and such things, and the scene of the telling shall be this old inn. He calls it "The Wayside Inn." They have a living-room reserved for them here, where they tell each other stories, translate Italian and German, and discuss the nobility of so wretched a thing as life and the power of so puling an art as lit-erature. I grow sleepy, I yawn, scratch my head, and take another drink. Frankly, I don't like most of the literary men of Boston.'

He drew the horses into the driveway.

'Captain Jones, I feel, really I believe, it is wisest *not* to stop.'

'My dear girl, I cannot drive the little horses all the way back without giving them any rest. Come, Lanice, I've ordered dinner, and have arranged things so cleverly we can be sure of a private dining-room. In the evening, in the moonlight, we'll drive back again, I assure you.'

The landlord bustled out to meet them, calling over his shoulder for a stable boy to care for the animals, but Jones, having left Lanice at the door, would go himself to see that the pair were rubbed down and fed and watered. A kindly woman with bobbing grey curls and robin's-egg blue eyes led the stiffened young lady to the big fire in the taproom.

'Now that's the most comfortable rocker in the house,' she volunteered. 'Get down, Toddy,' she suggested to the black cat curled on its cushions.

Lanice picked the creature up and held it purring hoarsely in her lap as she rocked and warmed herself before the fire. It looked up at her with its beautiful diabolical green eyes.

'It's a grand night for a party, Miss,' the landlady continued. 'And everything, the ducks, the wine, the puddings, and the port are just as Sir Anthony ordered.'

'A party?'

'Six guests in all, three ladies and three gentlemen. But the others, I fancy, will not arrive until later.'

Something within Lanice, perhaps a soul, a conscience, lifted its head and reported danger. Why had Anthony not told her? But it was, she believed, the last time they would ever be together, the last time ... the last time.

He had divested himself of his bearskin coat and fur cap by the time he joined her before the taproom fire. The landlady brought pewter mugs of mulled cider. The barmaid frankly smirked at the sober young Englishman, who, in turn, gazed at Lanice and the fire. He leaned over and stroked the cat.

'I like them,' he said, 'because to me they always

[130]

seem baleful, the principle of evil. They are ardent and musical in their love, beastly in their killing, and their kittens smell sweet as incense.'

The landlady reported progress of the dinner, her face rosy and shining from bending over the stove.

'The others will come together, Sir Jones?' she asked.

'Yes, any time now. We'll go to the dining-room. Will you be so kind as to send the others up when they arrive?'

'Who will they be, Sir Jones?'

Lanice saw his eyes grow puzzled.

'Oh, Professor Longfellow — and — er — the two ladies and the gentleman who come with him.'

He was lying. She could not imagine that Jones would ask Professor Longfellow or that he would accept if asked. Evidently the name had a respectable sound and so he had used it. He knew the room prepared for him, and the two went upstairs and entered it. A faultless table was set for six. The heavy goblets were alive with firelight, the white wainscotting pink with it. The two young people stood with their heads close to the low beams.

'This would be considered a good inn, even in England,' said Mr. Jones enthusiastically, and shut the door into the cold hall.

'Come, Lanice, we've no time to waste.'

She felt again the now familiar, sultry upward flame of passion, and resigned herself to his devastating love-making, but part of her mind remained for at least a moment oddly aloof, and noted the fact that

[131]

such conduct was evil. They heard the landlady creaking on the stair, but when she entered, followed by a maid, Captain Jones was mending the fire and the brown velvet lady was looking out of the window at the gathering darkness.

'Dear, dear, young people aren't what they used to be. Fancy being bored like that, and Sir Jones so handsome and the young lady, whoever she may be, so genteel and elegant.'

She chatted as she worked over the table, hoping to break the ice for two who obviously ought to be lovers. Then suddenly she caught the glitter in Sir Jones's eye and noticed his hard, stubborn mouth. She changed her opinion abruptly.

'My land, it's hardly respectable to feel like that in public. My land, he could fairly eat the young lady, and she so cruel and cold.'

An hour went by, and the fictitious guests did not come. Another hour, and the ducks burned and the kitchen was thrown into confusion, and Jones and the girl lingered in the candlelit, fire-bright room locked in each other's arms, conscious only of the necessities of their nature and the duty of keeping a close ear for approaching steps on the stairs. Each knew it was the last time, and in each was pain and the dull anger that only the other one could assuage. The girl was weeping silently, and the joy of love was lost in its pain. The man bit his lips and broke off occasionally to pace the room. Once she saw him standing by the fire, his eyes shut, his lips parted as if asking help from some dark god of his, Pan or Priapus. She

[132]

seemed to him the most elusive woman he had ever known. To herself she seemed nothing — seaweed floating in ocean currents, or a tree bending before wind.

'Will you always love me, always, Anthony?'

He lifted her hand from the heap of brown velvet and kissed the fingers.

'No, not always.'

'Anthony!'

'Now you are flower leaves and silk, and now I love you, not ten years or twenty years when you are grey and I am palsied ... darling ...'

Time, he told her, had made her, had taken twenty-five years for her perfecting, but time would as surely destroy her. Her pulses throbbed. He flung himself against her, his voice broke. At that moment she was for him all the women that time had ever made only to confound. She was the symbol of the thing that had obsessed him from youth.

'Lanice,' he begged, 'don't love me too much! Don't love me too long! But for God's sake love me now!'

At last dinner was served. 'We'll wait no longer for the others.' At last the port was drunk, the candles guttered, and the big hearth log fell to embers. Then Jones left the girl and went soberly to the horses. He did not go back to the inn until they were harnessed. Then he found Lanice, white and heavy-eyed, huddled in her furs as an owl huddles in his feathers, holding the black cat in her lap. The great moon on the snow made a new and colder day. The

shadow of trees lay like black lace. Mr. Jones drove
with his left hand; with his right arm he clasped the
long, delicate body of the sleeping girl. He hoped she
would not be too hard to forget; he hoped he could
some time forgive himself for his treatment of her.
Nothing hurts for long, thank God.

It was still, and even colder, and in a few hours it
would be morning, and in a few days he would be
gone. The girl's head fell back on his arm. She
smiled in her sleep, but the cheek turned away from
his warmth froze in the Arctic air.

CHAPTER VI

SHE FEELS THE SHADOW

1

THEY came and went through her office on heavy feet that struck brutally through her consciousness. They talked and their voices were as unreal as voices heard through fever. She could not write the story Miss Bigley had ordered by mail, a story to show once again virtue triumphant. Even the little faces of her fashion plates looked peakedly back at her under her pen. Luckily, Mr. Fox, with his shrewd feminine intuition, was in New York with Professor Ripley. They had seen Jones sail. Mr. Trelawney, finding her white and speechless, brooded over her and tried to interest her in medieval thought. She began a poem to fill a four-inch space in 'Hearth and Home,' three stanzas of four verses each. It was so easy to do things like this, she found. She could write her poem with no more effort than sharpening a pencil. 'Lines,' she wrote for a title, and then, with the idea of deception added, 'to my absent wife.'

> 'Earth no music for me gives;
> Lone my heart without thee lives.
> Symphonies, though sweet, are drear,
> Unless thou, my love, are near.'

One verse, and she read it over with impersonal interest as though it were the work of some other person. A sudden sense almost of nausea surged over her. She couldn't finish it. She couldn't ever write things like that again. If Paul saw his Saviour in a great light walking towards him on the road to Damascus, so surely was Lanice struck a miraculous blow and saw once and for all the falseness of her false art. She tore the paper to pieces. She would not work on 'Hearth and Home.' She would ask Mr. Fox for a position with the 'Journal,' and if he would not have her . . . All that she had previously written was an insult to the mad and glorious process of living; she had pulled off the flowers and arranged them in ugly patterns, yet flowers lose their beauty without leaves and stems.

Her green portières were brushed aside and she looked up to meet the eyes of an almost stranger. One of the Scollay girls stood in the doorway; she did not know whether it was Lydia, the pretty one, or Elpsie, the very pretty one.

'Miss Scollay?'

'Yes, and really I don't know your name. But won't you pardon my coming? I know I'm intruding.'

'I'm glad you came,' and after the words were spoken Lanice was surprised to see that they were the truth.

'You see,' said Lydia holding her head with the slightly defiant manner so at variance with her sweet nature, 'I've just gone through it all with Elpsie and I couldn't help but think of you almost all alone here in Boston and how you were the one Anthony really cared the most about. And I thought . . . well, I couldn't stay away, and I thought perhaps you were going through the same thing as Elpsie. Of course, he liked you much the best. I guessed when he borrowed the black pair from Papa they were for you, and then my Uncle Smith saw you drive through Cambridge. Elpsie was up almost all night listening to hear the horses come back. You'll think I have been spying upon you' — Lydia pushed back her dark furs. In the excitement her pink face was approaching cerise. 'I was just going by. I couldn't help running in to see you because, although he looked so romantic, Anthony Jones was really' — her teeth snapped together — 'a skunk,' she finished with engaging vulgarity.

The two young women looked at each other and an instantaneous understanding was established. Lanice resented neither the spying into her affairs nor the idea that her lover was merely a skunk.

'This morning,' Miss Lydia continued in the rapid voice of a child who has learned to speak a piece, 'Papa had an answer to a letter he wrote a friend in England weeks ago. It was such a comfort to Elpsie; I mean, she now *hates* Anthony Jones, and of course it is almost fun to hate a man in comparison to loving him when he doesn't really care for you.'

'Do sit down. What was in the letter?'

'I can't sit down, but all the time, years before he went to Arabia, or even out to India, he was married to an English girl.'

'*Married!*' Lanice had become reconciled to the ir-

[137]

regularities of his Oriental life, but was unprepared for an Occidental wife.

'No,' she smiled, a bland and terrible smile, 'it doesn't make me hate him.'

'Now that Elpsie hates him she feels so much better.'

'No,' Lanice heard a strange voice miles away saying through the darkness, 'no, it doesn't make me hate him.'

'Oh, my dear, you are so white! Do sit down; I'm afraid you are ill.'

'No, not ill.' She could not see the tumbler that Lydia pressed to her lips, but the water revived her. The mists rolled away and there was Lydia Scollay with her exquisite flushed face bending over her, tears beading her honey-colored lashes.

'I was in love once myself,' said Lydia abruptly. 'I know how you can suffer. It's terrible — but I hope I'll fall in love again sometime. If you don't you miss it and that's worse than being unhappy.'

'Far worse.'

'Sometime we'll go for a drive — you and I and Elpsie.'

'But your sister Elpsie . . .'

'A rival? Nonsense. He didn't care for Elpsie — not really.'

'Nor for any one really.'

Lydia smiled bewitchingly. 'You and Elpsie will have so much in common.' And then, fearing that her joke was in poor taste, kissed the sleek hair of her new friend.

2

All day long in the office Lanice had one recurrent thought. Pauline and her father were both away, and after four days of the most desperate self-control she could go home and be alone and cry. She could let the unreal, vacant grimace that had settled down over her since Anthony's departure slough off and show the real face set with the lines of human woe like a tragic mask. For four days in the office she had automatically attended to her work. Almost at regular intervals desolation would rise up through her body, running like little hounds upon her arms and legs, but when it came to her throat she could tie something in a strangling knot and refuse to let it pass. Tears would scald her eyes, and she who had cried copiously over the 'Wide, Wide World' and 'The Dying Dove' defied her nature and did not let them fall.

Then Mr. Trelawney would say, 'Miss Bardeen, here's a letter from the New York office suggesting some sort of prize contest. Why not start one? Best lamp-mat design, or way to prepare mutton, or poem on a deceased infant . . .'

'Thank you, Mr. Trelawney.'

Ten minutes later, and again the terrible upward pressure.

'Miss Bardeen, have you any more letters to be mailed?' And she would shake her head and smile sadly at the big little office boy.

That week she had slept in Pauline's dressing-room because her own bedroom was at last being repapered. Pauline was always chatting about slavery, male

[139]

tyranny or drink, but even after her 'Good-Night' Lanice would listen for any sound from the bedroom, listen for hours sometimes until her cousin's breathing had lengthened and hoarsened. Then she would pull the bedclothes over her head, and, writhing in this hot and suffocating tent, she would wet the pillows with the tears of her remorse and soak her nightgown with the sweat of her anguish. Neither Anthony's departure nor his duplicity had the power to hurt her as did the memory of the response she had made to his light and violent passions. It was her fault. All was her fault. Again and again she told herself that she never should have let him as much as touch her. And he had kissed her and held her! And she had loved him, and he was gone!

But this evening she would go home to find the house all but empty and she could cry for hours and hours freed from the oppressive presence of Pauline and with Mrs. Andrews, remote in her subterranean cell, too far away to hear her. Church bells and sleigh bells. Lights twinkling across the Common. The air sparkled with bells and lights. She stood with one hand on the key in the lock, her back pressed against the door, and looked at the stars swarming in the tree-tops of the Common and thought of God high up in the windy darkness. She said to herself, 'Nothing really matters. In fifty years I will probably be dead.'

Mrs. Andrews had left one lamp burning in the hall. To light the beautiful chandelier when such a large proportion of the family was away would have seemed to her thrifty nature wasteful. Lanice leaned

[140]

over the staircase leading to Mrs. Andrews's domain and called, in the loud, falsely cheerful voice which the heartbroken can summon for emergencies, that she had already had her tea, thank you, and would go immediately to bed. Mrs. Andrews had thought Lanice was going to Hopkinton with Pauline; she began to protest that her room, although papered, was not yet put in order.

'I'll do that. Don't come up,' urged Lanice. For the moment it seemed to her the most important thing in life to keep Mrs. Andrews in her own confines. Nothing should now balk Lanice in her sorrow.

She lighted a lamp and set it on the bureau. The tight nosegays on the new paper pleased her and she immediately began to plan curtains and chintz covers. The presence of the paper-hangers was evident. A stepladder shrouded in the big cloth with which Mrs. Andrews had protected the furniture loomed ghostly by the washstand. The room smelled of damp plaster and of paste, slightly of tobacco, too. Lanice looked at herself questioningly in the familiar glass. Had Anthony Jones marked her face as surely as her soul? She looked tired and years older than she had ever seen herself before. Sighing, she turned to her bed and folded back the covers and opened the lavender-scented linen sheets. She had longed for this room for four days, hoping that she might be alone and permitted to cry unrestrainedly. Now she listlessly drew off her clothes, slipped into bed, and, sighing, fell asleep.

The Park Street Church clock struck two and

Lanice started up as though it had been in the room with her. Her heart was beating fast and brokenly. She was conscious of having been awakened to keep some tryst. Usually a lamp burned lowly in the hall outside her door; now that she missed its faint crack of light upon her doorsill she was disturbed and lonely. No one in the house but grim Mrs. Andrews in the basement. With the fear of dark there also came a cruel spurt of emotion that welled up in her like a fountain.

She sat down shaking on the edge of her bed and said distinctly, but with a catch in her voice, 'Well, cry if you want to.' Then she began. Terrible tears that scalded her face, sobs that twisted her body, and drove her nails into the flesh of her palms. She called herself without mercy all the ugly names that she had ever read in Shakespeare, in tracts about dissolute women, and in the Bible. Then there was a lull and she lay exhausted, and thought over what she had been saying to herself and judiciously repudiated the most unpleasant of the epithets.

Then again an agonizing torrent of grief. The darkness, the disordered bedclothes, her long hair unbraided and now sweat-dampened and tangled about her, upwelling flood of bitterness within. She listened and heard herself moan. Anthony Jones was relatively unimportant. She did not blame him or call him names. This was a thing between herself and life. Life she blamed, and Nature, for making her what she was. Most bitterly of all she blamed herself. It was an inborn craving for something — something

[142]

beautiful that had led her on. For the beauty music sometimes promised, for the wild delight that a flick of Anthony's eye and the radiance of his rare smile had suggested. Mystery and loveliness.

She began to laugh, for she believed she had been cheated, and this, mixed with her spasmodic moaning, made an uncouth sound that frightened her. She couldn't stop. The spasms of hysterics took her breath. She started up in the blackness thinking there were choking hands on her throat. She tried to tell herself in a peremptory way that she must stop. The ghastly sound continued and she was terrified. 'You must stop or you'll go crazy.' There was no stopping. She got to her feet. A doctor could end this terrible gasping and laughing. But when she stumbled to the head of the stairs to call down to Mrs. Andrews, she realized that she could not summon enough voice to make herself heard, and she would be ashamed that any one should see her in this state. Better die.

Groping, she felt her way back to her room. The stepladder in its white shroud suddenly seemed to lunge out of the darkness. She cried out, then recognized what it was and flung herself down upon the floor. She dashed her head against the bureau and chair legs, rolled over on her back and sank her teeth into her forearm and wrist, but the hysterical sobbing continued. She decided to take out the silk shawls that Anthony had given her and burn them all in the grate. Beautiful, cruel things. But, even as she decided to do this, some portion of her brain must have retained its sense. Through the suffocation of all her unhappiness she realized that sometime she would not feel like this and then she would wish she had not burned his shawls. Perhaps there was something in the bathroom — smelling-salts, cologne, anything that would stop this strangling and sobbing. She felt her way in and lighted a candle. As her fingers ran over the bottles in the cabinet they happened on one with the red label of danger. Laudanum! She realized that if she drank the contents of this one bottle she would be through, not only with remorse, but with life. She drew out the stopper, but the smell sickened her and she threw the bottle into the tub. By dashing cold water over herself and letting the faucet run on her wrists she managed to get her nerves under control.

The clock struck four, and she was quiet again, lying on the bed in Pauline's dressing-room. Never again in her life could she smell a newly papered room without stifling and a sense of nausea. Odd, she thought. She had had enough sense not to burn up the shawls, and yet she *might* have drunk the laudanum. As if the miserable night had been a penance, she felt at peace again with herself and the world. Her sorrow, her remorse, and her disappointments had mysteriously passed out of her life. Almost! They were still there in the shadowy background, like dogs that had broken loose in the night and nearly throttled her before she could order them back to their kennels. Now they would lie and through the years occasionally look at her and growl a little, or whine, or sleep. And sometimes, through the years, she would look

[144]

at them not unkindly and they would wag their tails.

3

Captain Poggy advised an ocean trip, perhaps to the West Indies. Mrs. Andrews recommended a cod-liver oil diet. Pauline thought the best way out of a decline was to cease wasting one's time with Messrs. Redcliffe & Fox and give one's self, heart and soul, to a great absorbing Cause. Mr. Fox advised more out-door air and less work. 'You might come in late for the next week or two until you get some color back, and then you can easily make it up,' he said, 'by leaving early.' Mr. Trelawney could only offer 'Leaves of Grass.' Professor Ripley gave her the compassion and understanding of his eyes, and urged her to study. At her age Margaret Fuller could read Hebrew, and Abigail Adams composed in Greek. He had, she found, a contempt for all fiction. Why should she not write a history of Spanish literature, or something erudite and worth-while?

True to the formula of her own stories, she faded rather like a flower, but if her heart was broken no one except Professor Ripley and Lydia Scollay knew it. She discovered, however, that one can break one's heart and live. At first it seemed to be a mere exist-ence, but months later she wondered if she were not better off than before. The expression of human faces, the antics of animals, the fresh spring air grop-ing over muddy streets and fingering the naked trees, the richness of weather change, the heat of sun, the beat of rain; these things she had always seen, but now she was identified with them. One thing was certain. She could write no more stories or poems such as she had previously written for 'Hearth and Home.' She stood humbly before life and could not desecrate it because as never before she understood and wistfully worshipped it. Athough she felt an equal contempt for the large canvases that she had accomplished under Mrs. Dummers's flattering eye, she still took pleasure in her portfolio of small things. Under Captain Poggy's inspiration she began to absorb with enthusiasm the art of the Japanese, and admired the skill with which they could carve a rabbit out of fat jade seemingly by a turn of the wrist. She saw how their fishes really swim, and how their improbable coarse ponies are alive while the great Copley shows us General Washington upborne on the back of a dead quadruped.

She still enjoyed her fashion plates because she liked clothes, and they were but diagrams, not art, not life. Believing firmly that love may come but once, and that Anthony was gone forever, she reconciled herself to the thought that her love life was ended. Of all the many regrets she might have had, she really felt but one. She sighed that love for her could not have been diluted a little with the commonplaces of affection. And why had she so bitterly resented Captain Jones? She could remember moments when she had hated him. It was like trying to warm one's self before a bonfire; either you were too hot or too cold. Of course now she would never marry, never. Not even if Lydia's rich young uncle,

Smith Scollay, who had first admired her as she whisked through Harvard Square in the red Russian sleigh, should declare himself, as there was reason to believe he might.

Life, by some alchemy, had melted her softer metals in its retort, and now poured her out again in different mould, tempered perhaps into a more precious substance. She felt calm and assured. Time had thrown down its gage, for she was twenty-five and considered herself no longer young, but she did not shrink from its challenge. Years whirling out of the onrushing space would involve and in the end destroy. She breathed upon her palm to feel the body's heat, and thought how it is the gift of many generations of dead men. And she would be cold some day and the teeth she tapped with her pencil and the hair she sleeked with her hand would be the last things to be left of her, except the skeleton waiting within. It did not matter what happened to the soul; perhaps like Mohammedan women she had none. Perhaps she lost it during the hours so bright, always, with firelight and sunshine, spent with Anthony Jones. But she had a sense of peace, a feeling that whatever happened she could endure. To herself it seemed that she had reached the andante passages in her symphony, after having lived through the scherzo, and she sighed and stretched herself in her new-found peace. Thank God she had some money. She would never be so driven for it as Bronson Alcott's girls out in Concord. Poor Louisa, just her age, washed and baked and sewed all day. She had even hired out as a serv-

[147]

ant and wrote feverishly in odd moments anything that would sell, it hardly mattered what. Lanice had recently gone to see Louisa and the two girls crept to the attic for privacy and seated on the rag-bag exchanged ambitions.

'I must make money. I will teach, act, write stories. Lanice, I'll even sell my one beauty, my hair. I must get some comforts for Marmee. Oh, we've been so poor my soul is all ragged.'

Miss Alcott — Louisa she called her — was the liveliest of all the literary friends she had made through her profession. She liked her boyishness, her candor, her trusty whole-heartedness, and even her gawkiness in the presence of the unsympathetic.

But Lydia, and to a less extent the more mannered Elpsie, she came to love. Pauline despised the pretty girls with their brisk gold hair, their sweet-pea faces, and defiant blue eyes. She flattered them outrageously, but in a way to belittle them. Lydia was clever enough to see through this flattery which favorably impressed her younger sister, especially coming as it did from so high-minded a source as Miss Pauline Poggy. They were much about the Poggy house, sometimes sleeping with Lanice, three in a bed. The three girls, mounted on little round gentle horses that were considered appropriate mounts for females, although their small size and pony backs unfitted them for the cumbersome side-saddles, ambled about the country roads of Brookline or followed the windings of the Charles. A groom followed them wherever they went and gave them the help they must have in mounting and dismounting. Their skirts were so long the hem was faced with leather so it would not wear out against the stones or horses' hoofs. Sometimes their young uncle, Smith Scollay, left his father's counting-house and, mannishly mounted on a big-boned Irish horse, a half taller than the ladies' palfreys, showed them new bridle-paths along the sea or out into the country.

Elpsie, completely cured of her infatuation with the sinful Mr. Jones, wanted to hear everything her dear Lanice could tell her. Lanice herself listened almost without jealousy to Elpsie's repetition of Captain Jones's compliments to her guitar playing and to her charm. When, however, she quoted Mr. Jones as comparing her to flower leaves, a great bubble of rage burst within Lanice, for so on one memorable occasion had Mr. Jones characterized her.

CHAPTER VII

AND HEARS MORE ABOUT MAMMA

1

SHE thought she had seen a ghost. It was Pauline standing in the sad dusk of dawn telling her to quiet herself.

'You mean something terrible has happened? Oh, do be quick! I cannot bear suspense, Pauline.'

'From your Papa.'

'Then he is not dead. Tell me quickly, Pauline.'

'I beg you to relax. I am trying to tell you. A letter to me from your Papa tells me to break the news to you — that . . .' she consulted her letter — 'on the ninth of February in Florence . . . your mamma . . . perished . . . fever . . . very sudden.'

'You mean Mamma is dead?'

'Yes . . . that is, her mortal body . . .'

It seemed as incredible as the diminishment of the sun, or the glutting of the moon. Mamma was so alive, she doubted if anything could subdue her, not even the angel of death. Lanice did not cry. She was too stunned, but her stoniness baffled Pauline, who had stuffed the pocket of her grey wrapper full of handkerchiefs after Mrs. Andrews had given over to her the letter.

'You must not take it too hard.'

'No.'

'I will send up some coffee — tea — chocolate?'

'Oh, no.'

'Will you journey to Amherst?'

'I don't know.'

Her mother was dead in Italy. What good to travel to Amherst? What good that she and Horace Bardeen shut themselves up together and talk of . . . what?

Mamma, who always could hurt her, now pierced her through with love and regret.

'I was such a child, Pauline, when I left home. I did not understand things very well. I thought I could judge Mamma, but . . .'

Pauline, seemingly intent on giving cause for her hoard of handkerchiefs, said bluntly, 'How can one judge such mischievous conduct but in one way? What was evil two years ago still is evil.'

'But now I don't know good from bad.'

'Lanice! To think you can say such a thing at such a moment! Your *mother* is dead!'

Stifled love turned in the girl's heart like a knife. The mocking, pretty face that age could not dim, the alluring mouth, the small, dimpled hands, so unlike Lanice's scholarly ones, the pretty graces. Her thousand distracting tricks that hurt if you loved her more than they gratified. All this treasury of loveliness was cast into the oblivion of earth. She could not bear that Mamma should lie so far from home.

'I am going over, Pauline. I'm going to bring her back, poor, darling Hitty. Oh, how pretty she was!'

'I imagine her . . . this Mr. Cuncliffe has attended to everything.'

'I am going over.'

[151]

'Lanice, her soul is now free from her . . . entangling body. Can you not think of her soul and forget the corruption of the flesh?'

'No.'

2

Lanice had automatically begun to dress and the tears that Pauline had awaited trickled upon her clean linen and splashed upon her ugly brown merino dress. Not until the last button was fastened would Pauline give her the letter. As she read it, she saw her father, and pitied him. How strangely was her life sprung from these two people who of all the world understood her least. Physically she resembled her father. Augustus had thought she might have something of her mother's wantonness and Anthony had proved it. But at least she had a touch, a spark of her father's scholarly tendencies.

'I cannot imagine,' Pauline whipped out, 'where you are going.'

Then Lanice noticed with amazement that she had her bonnet in her hand and had pulled on her heavy walking-boots with elastic sides.

'Oh, just to walk, along the Mill Dam, any-where . . . '

'Nonsense! I'll order breakfast.'

With one of her odd little bursts of tact Pauline suggested consulting an atlas and the two young women pored over it and located Florence, and Pauline led the conversation away from tragic Florence to the congenial subject of European tours.

But Mamma was dead. Lanice could see her grow sleepy in church under the long periods of the Reverend Mr. Goochey, see her yawn behind her palm-leaf fan which was always kept in the pew, and, as she caught her daughter's eye, turn the yawn into a little grimace. She would move restlessly within her fine clothes and try to whisper to Papa, who frowned and looked straight ahead. A lovely, heedless woman. How could she be dead? There had always been a sweet scent to her clothing and a leafy rustle of silk. Why had she run off with Cuncliffe? Who was he? Why had he run off with her?

And now she was dead, and somewhere the foreign soil held her pleasurable body. Perhaps young Cuncliffe wore black upon his arm and on his hat, the way Papa ought to ... or should Papa? What does a widower of his type do? Professor Ripley was also a widower. If it had not been for Mamma there would never have been a drop of bad blood in her to answer when Mr. Jones had cried to it. One drop of bad blood ... Who and what was Mamma? Who was Roger Cuncliffe, and why?

3

'Papa, I want to go to Italy.'

'You always did.'

'But now I must go. I stay awake so much wondering ... about everything ... at the end. I must go. I can't leave her so far away buried in a foreign land. I want her to be buried here in Amherst.'

'She never liked Amherst especially.'

'Would you mind if I went, Papa?'

'No, suit yourself.'

'But you are not in sympathy?'

'Of course not. I even profess to Christianity which, I believe, tells us that the body is not the soul.'

(True of some, but how could it be of Mamma?)

'I have money enough, haven't I?'

'Enough to go around the world.'

'Then if there's nothing more to say, I'll be going back to Boston, Papa.'

'Wait.' He wrote upon the back of a student's translation of an Horatian Ode, and gave it to her. 'Tell *him* that you are coming. You will find him an agreeable and considerate . . . young gentleman.'

'Why, Papa! I don't want to even see him . . . ever.'

'You will find it difficult to move the body without him. And here's another man you must see.'

He took back the paper and wrote again. 'The American Consul in Florence, also a gentleman,' he explained.

'Good-bye, Papa.'

'Good-bye, Lanice. I'll write you details of the financial end.'

'Thank you, and good-bye again, Papa.'

4

'Mr. Fox, I want to go to Italy.'

'I've noticed that something was coming on. So it's Italy, is it? Well, go by all means, and we'll scrape along here in some miserable fashion. Who are you going with and how long will you be gone?'

'I'm going alone, and I'd like to be gone all spring and summer.'

'You are pretty young to travel about Europe, too young. But luckily you know French and Italian enough for food and hot baths, and you have a steady head, haven't you?'

He was surprised that she answered this rhetorical question with a seriously considered 'I really don't know.'

'As for the length of your stay, we'll arrange it some way, and of course when you come back again you will be much more valuable to us. You will have seen Paris, and perhaps at a distance Empress Eugénie, queen of fashion, and that should help you with your fashion plates and make you more respected by the dressmakers who do the designing. You will have seen the wonders of the world.'

He looked at her quizzically for a moment. He knew that she was beginning to feel a distaste for the literary work she did for Miss Bigley and was casting envious eyes towards his 'Journal.' In his own mind he determined that when she came back he would take her as an assistant and release her from all the duties of 'Hearth and Home' except the congenial task of drawing clothes, which she did exquisitely and happily.

'I have a proposition for you. Would you like to call upon all the greatest of the literary celebrities? A letter from Redcliffe & Fox would be sufficient introduction. Then you could write a series of articles about them for the "Journal," half critical and half biographical. You can make them slightly funny if you do it so subtly that no one but you and I know it, and I'd like a careless sketch-book picture of each, or a drawing of the house. They'll treat you very nicely, invite you to have tea, and ask whether or not the Indians are bothersome in your part of the States. You will flatter them sagaciously and listen to their stories, and if they tell you that your land is uncultured, you will not go to the mat with them over it. Of course, you must be well up on their works.'

'Whom shall I see?'

'The Brownings first, if you sail direct to Italy. Perhaps you haven't heard of Mr. Browning. He is Elizabeth Barrett's husband, and a coming man, in his own devious way. Then, of course, England.'

'England!' Her heart stood still, and she thought of Anthony Jones.

'Yes, of course. Tennyson and Dickens, and Harriet Martineau and Maria Champion and Thackeray surely, and a dozen others. We'll pay part of your expenses.'

He laughed at the pleasure he saw awaken in her face that had of late been so thoughtful, perhaps a little sad. It was not her mother's death; though she had evidently felt this keenly, something had happened earlier. For some reason her days of storm and stress had come upon her and because he, in a more passionate decade of his life, had also known these pains, he sympathized with her. Why they had come

[156]

he could not say. He had often seen her with Jones, and it had amused him to notice how indifferent or even slightly contemptuous she was of this handsome animal. He was glad that she had the intelligence not to be fooled by Jones's sweet voice and lingering eyes. Sears Ripley kept his own counsel.

5

A triple hammer beat within her. Her mother's death, the trip abroad, and the ache of Anthony.

To go to Marseilles you sail from New York. She engaged passage on the swift Diana, preferring a white-winged and buoyant sailing ship to the grime of steam. In such had Captain Poggy laced the globe. Through him she got a deck stateroom at half price. He would have gone to New York to see her off, but his bad leg prevented, and so Pauline alone went with her that far. For some hidden reason Pauline, who showed a certain spite towards Hitty now that she was dead, criticized Lanice that she was not in black.

'I'll tell you the true reason,' said Lanice at last. 'Black is too becoming to me. When I wear all black, it is because I feel romantic and I think it makes me look mysterious. I can't wear black now that my mother is dead.'

Pauline's conversation on the train was filled with warnings as to Lanice's conduct.

'I'm twenty-five.'

'Will this Captain Jones, if he really is a captain, will he be in England?'

[157]

'I don't know. I don't care, really.' As she spoke she pressed her face against the window-pane, gazing upon the backward-reeling landscape, and wondered if this were true. Jones had been like celluloid, a spurt of flame and all was over. This was not love, and suddenly her heart ached for it, the love that Anthony had refused her, and had refused to take from her, although she knew herself capable of giving it.

6

Something of love she might have learned from Augustus's anxious face and staring china eyes. He made elaborate pretence of being in New York on business and happening to hear of the ladies' arrival at Mrs. Gower's Fashionable Boarding House, where they would stay for a few days pending the Diana's loading and sailing.

They walked the park all Friday afternoon in the melting sweetness of a premature spring day. He told her how spring, to him, always was personified by a dainty lady with ruffled skirts, silk mits, and flowered bonnet. Instantly before Lanice's eyes came the picture of a gay hoyden with bare, muddy feet, draggled petticoats, tousled hair, roguish eyes, beguiling but slightly vulgar voice. She tried to tell Augustus of this muddy *primavera*, but the idea vaguely hurt him and he began to protest that none of her own qualities more greatly engaged him than her exquisite tidiness. 'Oh, dear,' she thought, 'he's off again,' and smirked at him so he would keep it up.

[158]

She had never smirked at Anthony Jones, except on the first day.

'Lanice, it is so warm. If I spread my ulster upon this bench may we not sit for a little in the sunshine? If you are cold . . .'

'If I am cold I'll fasten up my cloak. Oh, you can *smell* Spring to-day, although it is months away! Oh, delicious!'

'I think,' said Augustus cunningly, 'Spring keeps her handkerchiefs in sachet. That is why the air is so sweet.'

Lanice had not thought about Spring and her handkerchiefs. Perhaps Spring merely snuffled.

'It is not to tell you of Spring, ma'am, that I am come to New York.'

'I know. You are here on pressing business.'

'Indeed, yes. The most important business of a man's life.'

Lanice gazed at him innocently. She had taken off her bonnet and the sunshine reflected on her sleek black head and, as Mr. Trainer noticed, bathed her pure brow.

'Mr. Trainer, I cannot imagine what you mean.'

'Once again I beg of you to consider me as your contracted husband.'

'But you could love any one. I want to be loved for myself. You only love a fancy portrait of me, sir. The truth is, I've had this so-called love of yours for years and never could find any earthly use to put such a thing to. Perhaps I do not want love.'

'I know . . . nothing carnal . . .'

[159]

She squared her light jaw. 'I'd rather have that,' she said with an ungirlish stolidity, 'than the imagined passion that you affect.'

'You would prefer vulgarity?'

'I'd prefer *anything*.'

'My dear young woman, you are so innocent you do not understand how your words strike the cruder masculine ear.'

'But why must you always harp upon my innocence?'

'But that is why I love you. And it is apparent in all your motions, in your modest responses to my kisses. How many times I have pressed my lips to your cheek and met only maidenly shrinking. Come, Lanice . . .' and he endeavored to bend her to his arms.

'You do not kiss me,' she said, 'you have never kissed me, but only pecked at me like a bird at a rotten cherry. When you go courting again, some other girl, remember this.'

She took his face between her hands and pressed her shiny, tight red lips against his dull mouth. Both recoiled like released springs. Jumping to their feet, facing each other, gaping in amazement that a pure young woman could act thus and thus. She stammered —

'I didn't want to kiss you! It was unintentional. Please believe me. How could I kiss *you?*'

'How could you, indeed?'

She saw that he was oddly excited and there was something hateful in his white-lashed eyes.

'Can you teach me some more of these tricks,

[160]

ma'am?' he inquired in a voice of elaborate and dangerous unction.

The girl grew defiant, and her long black eyes snapped.

'Yes.'

'I am much interested.' His thick hands were shaking. 'Lanice, I love you.'

'But it is impossible, considering the way I feel towards you.'

'Would you, would any innocent unmarried woman so kiss one of the opposite sex . . . if she did not love . . . was not swept off her feet?'

'I did it by mistake.'

'Ah, but your innermost heart dictated this action.'

'No. I was simply tired of hearing you call me innocent. Because,' she said, 'I am not, Augustus.'

He looked at her and slowly realized that perhaps she was, as he had sometimes feared, spiritually as well as physically her mother's child.

'Not innocent? Why, that is the quality I have always adored in you.'

'What do you know of me? You've never cared to find out what I think or how I feel.'

'Come, sarcasm is not a woman's weapon, especially the woman who is to become my wife.'

There was a touch of rather crude vitality in the poise of his thick body and a threat in the lowered thrust of his head. She almost could have loved him if he had always been like that. She ceased playing with him, and turned towards him fairly.

'I tried to tell you by actions that I am not, never

[161]

was, and hope I never will be the ambling nun you have always insisted in considering me to be, and I ... and ...' her voice trailed away and she dropped her shining head. He heard her say 'some one else' and something that 'love was not.'

'Some one else, Lanice?'

'Some one else.'

'You mean you love ... you will marry?'

'I can't define love any more, except that it wasn't at all like what I thought it would be. I can't marry him. He is married already, and, anyhow, he didn't really want me. I mean, permanently.'

Her voice wavered ... 'anything ... die for him' he thought she said. She twisted her hands and gazed upon the basket of fingers that she had made. She was pale and sad to look upon.

'Tell me plainly about this rascal. Lanice, you mean you love such a man?'

'Yes, I think so. I would have died for him, if he had asked me. I'd have torn out my throat.'

'And he was married?'

'Yes.'

'Such a wicked philanderer should be boiled in oil.'

'No, he was just made that way. If God had not wanted him to behave as he did, he would have made him differently.'

'And you, ma'am, may I ask how you behaved?'

'Yes.'

'Well, then, how did you?'

'There is nothing in the world I would not have done for him.' Her voice shook.

[162]

'My God!' he cried, the perspiration making his greyed face ugly, 'not that. Oh, Lanice! You are merely concocting lies so as to make me go away and molest you no more. Come, I'll go away without your desecrating yourself to this sinful extent.'

He looked at her through sick, staring eyes.

'I'd rather die than believe your implications. No, no, I cannot.'

'But what if what you believe is the truth?'

'Like your mother. A hussy like your mother. My God! and all this time I have been looking up to you as one too holy to possess, even in wedlock, and you, you have squandered yourself on the first man to make improper advances to you.'

'Yes' — her voice was flat and hard — 'he was, as you say, the first to love me and not offer marriage.'

Augustus flew into a difficult, heart-breaking rage. He mouthed at her, his hands, his lips shook, but without unison. His words fell like blows from dull weapons. Tears rolled unnoticed from his eyes. He was at once grotesque, pitiful, and terrible.

'If I am all that you say, beginning with a slut, and I'm sorry my vocabulary does not take me to the end, I cannot, of course, complain of your disgusting language. But . . .' and her voice broke — 'I wish we might have parted friends.'

'Lanice, darling, darling, forgive me. It was not I that spoke so brutally. I could never speak so to you, my angel. Come. Let me protect you in the future from the lusts common to my own sex, protect you from a certain weakness one might expect from your

[163]

mother's child. Lanice, I will care for you. No temptation or need ever will come near you. We will carry this to God together, on our knees, strength for us both.'

'No.'

'Tell me who it was you loved; I demand it.'

'You can't demand, Augustus. But it was . . .' her quickened breathing choked her words, but her lips formed the name of Anthony Jones.

'May God punish him for robbing a woman of her most precious possession.'

She neither denied nor admitted. 'I cared for him so much, I would have died for him,' she said, and Augustus bending his head, thought he heard her again use the ugly phrase 'tear out my throat.'

'In a moment of foolish passion. No, no, I cannot connect that word with you even in my thoughts. In a moment of weakness you forgot your womanhood. You succumbed. But even so, Lanice, miserable and fallen as you are, I will take you. Abandoned by your wicked seducer. Come, tell me one thing more. Is that the real reason for your trip to Europe? Are you following him abroad?'

'I don't know where he is. He may be in England with his wife, or in Arabia with his concubines.'

'Lanice!'

The silence became ominous. Mr. Trainor leaned heavily upon his cane and the young woman melted down upon the bench. She felt like an actress in a play, reciting a memorized part. Her ears were alert to receive her next cue from the lips of Augustus.

'I would have rather believed,' he said at last, 'that the Virgin Mary was a woman of the streets and our Saviour . . .' he stopped nervously. His temper had cooled a little and his language had grown less interesting. 'I'd rather believe anything,' he continued lamely, 'than that you are the dissolute woman you admit yourself to be.' This was not her cue. Lanice still waited. 'I don't see how I can still love you,' he cried out miserably, 'What is more ridiculous than to love a woman for a chastity that she lacks?' He paused before adding, 'This is a lesson to me. I will never again believe in your sex as I did.'

Lanice looked up.

'I hope you never will. I hope you'll see we are not made of cambric and sawdust, with porcelain heads, but of flesh and blood, Augustus.'

The way she said 'flesh and blood' fired him. He lunged towards her and would have grasped her roughly in his arms. His ideals and his body were at war, and for the moment it was his body that had the ascendancy. His temper was up and his language grew coarse.

'No, no!' she cried out, as once she had cried to Mr. Jones. His sweating face and raging strength frightened her.

'You are not too fine to lie with a notorious rake, ma'am. Are you so delicate as to refuse me a kiss?'

'I am much too delicate,' she replied in a high, angry voice.

'You sneer at me when I propose marriage, as I weakly did a few moments ago. Come! Women, as

[165]

all the world knows, are either good or bad. You choose to league yourself with the latter. Then, for Heaven's sake, act it and give me now some of the kindness you lavish on other men. You've made your bed. God, now you shall lie in it.'

She struck him a cruel blow on the mouth. Her sleek hair was loosened in the brief struggle and fell unruffled about her. From between the folds of this black tent she gazed at him with a look of utter and abysmal hatred. The blow hurt, and Augustus gingerly fingered his swelling lip.

'You might have killed me. If you had had a knife, I believe you would have killed me.'

'I wish I had. Go away.'

'And you the woman I dreamed of . . .'

'Go away. I never wanted your dreams.'

Slowly the anger died from her eyes and her face grew childish and wistful. The man's heart smote him. She was indeed clay-footed, but his idol still.

'Yes, I will leave you. "Go away" as you beg. Lanice, my poor child, my dear child, you may trust me. Your secret shall go no further.'

He wanted to take his leave, but could not manage it. He seemed to have forgotten his lines, and poked at the gravel with his yellow cane as nervous as a tongue-tied actor.

'Forgive what I have said. But it was a heavy blow. I hope God understands you; I cannot. All that I have loved, adieu.'

'Good-bye.'

She sat on the lonely park bench with her black

hair a silk veil about her, and she shivered with the terror she had endured. How vulgar and ugly he had been, this good man who worshipped purity. Anthony, the earthy, sensual animal, had never been either. She cringed from the memory of Augustus. Yet if it had not been for Mamma she would by now have been married to him. She had given, she knew, a death-blow to his idealism. Never again would she listen to his prattle of purity. Her heart hardened against him, but within its adamant was a trembling pain of pity.

CHAPTER VIII

SHE SETS SAIL

1

STRANGE to feel yourself so alone among so many. Forty in the cabin. American tourists and business men flapping about in sodden ulsters, their whiskers blowing about their ears. English people with their careful bad manners, bad grammar too, with their affected 'goin's' and 'ain'ts,' and their ridiculous patter of 'awful clevah' and 'just fawncy.' Very fashionable people, so fashionable the eldest of the women affected ugly, defiant clothes and every one knew that her sister was a duchess. She wore heavy wool equestriennes over her stockings, bulging down over her shoetops. Other English people. Young men sweet and poised compared to the noisier American youths. Their feminine counterparts usually seemed too big and strong for them. Honest-looking girls whose beauty was often marred by meaningless mouths. 'My saddle mare is out of Rosemary and Pichon sired her. I'm goin' to breed her to Splendor as soon as the huntin's over.' They would never see the *nuances* of life, these handsome rational young women, but the young Englishmen would. Lanice pondered because the two sexes did not seem to tally.

She was lonely; the fog pressed close; the Diana spread her skirts like a great lady, so it seemed to the young fashion-plate artist, and walked upon the waters. And the oily sea breathed gigantically with the stirrings of its infinite life. Damp and cold, having no one to talk to, she felt at first a curious sense of unreality. Sky, sea, and between them the ship and the human particles upborne on its wooden decks. 'It will be like this when I am old,' she thought; 'nothing real and nothing matters, and everything floats by, but does not stop to possess you. I see the people and the waves, but they seem to float away from me.' She wrote assiduously, long paragraphs of impressions, and her pencil would droop in her fingers. 'That is Labrador,' she thought, 'but it is lead-colored like the sea and sky and isn't real. I suppose I am lonely and homesick. Gracious, I do hope not seasick!' Phrases stirred feebly through her mind. 'That at least has always been here . . . always. The Northmen liked the sea because it made them feel sad. I like to feel sad. Why do I wake up at night sometimes, so frightened, and think of death and even suicide? But I've liked to live so much. Probably that is why I could not bear to see life turn grey and bitter like this. I'd rather not live than not enjoy. Oh, dear, that is not Christian! That is why I start up at night so afraid. What am I building old age upon? I do not want it. That's what people mean by the necessity of children. But I feel no need. Will I when it is too late? When I sit as I sit to-day with no one to talk to and the whole world grey? And I grey and lonely as the gulls that follow us mewing like cats. I must have loved Anthony, for my face has

[169]

changed in six months, grown sadder, I think. Oh, Anthony, Anthony, why couldn't you have loved me as I could have loved you? Or at least let me love you as I might have done. My dear Anthony ... English people ... Lady Maude does wear the ugliest clothes. Imagine her looking at me through her lorgnette and saying "quite ladylike for a *clark*, fawncy now," and those dreadful horsey daughters of hers. Perhaps I'm really a bit seasick and that's why I'm so depressed. I must take some of Mrs. Andrews's "Travellers' Elixir." The food is so wretched and greasy I hope it doesn't affect my skin.' She went to the hook where her towel was swaying delicately, got her hand mirror, and suspiciously examined the clear skin. Fog rolling in and the distant sound of a fog horn. The coast of Labrador blotted out and the sea oily and tireless, breathing and alive.

'I wish I could really be sick like that plump Mrs. Pontifex, although it was so hard for her to get out from that wall seat in the dining-room. Oh, I can smell them frying fish *again*. They must want to make us sick — we eat less and save them money. I'll lie down and count. Heavens, I am sick! I'm positively congealing around the mouth. Well, if I'm going to be ... if I'm going to be ... One, two, three, four, five, six, seven ... I wonder if poetry would be better? It takes up your mind more. "Oh — gift — of — God — oh — perfect — day — whereon — shall — no — man — work — but — play — whereon — it — is — enough — for — me — not — to — to" ... I've forgotten the rest. What a *tiny* little basin for

such a big ship . . . Well, I ought to feel better *now*.
Heavens! I'll lie down.'

2

The fourth day out was the Sabbath and the Captain courteously suggested that the three travelling
clergymen hold a joint service, but the clergymen kept
to their bunks and their basins, and the Captain himself read to the crew for a few minutes from his heavy
Bible, and the stormy winds blew, and the landlubbers did indeed lie down below.

A shouting and a roaring above her on the deck as
though the Diana were boarded by pirates, and the
boatswain piping above the shrilling of wind in rigging. White-faced and dizzy, Lanice decided to leave
the eleven seasick women with whom she shared a
cabin and go on deck. At least up there it was fresh
and thrilling. She wrapped herself in a seaman's
overcoat that the kindly steward borrowed from
one of the crew, and ventured up.

They were taking in sail, preparing for storm.

'Clew up the to'gallant sails, man the reef-tackle
. . . hawl in the weather brace. Lower away the
yard.'

'Aye, aye, sir,' and the sails came snapping down
with a rattle of cordage and the goblin piping of the
boatswain's pipe. Lanice was seen and ordered back
to her cabin.

Then the storm was over and the passengers humbly
gave praise to their Maker that they yet lived. Shrill
women's voices filled the cabin.

[171]

'Once on the raging seas I rode,
    The ocean yawned, and rudely blowed
    The wind that tossed my foundering bark. . . .'

Winds whipped up from the west, crowding the
Diana's sails. Still like a great lady she swept the
Atlantic, flying forward without tacking or turning.
The passengers mingled freely. Even Lady Maude
was not so bad, and the horsey girls such friendly,
sensible creatures. She could no longer see the 'types'
as she had the first two days, only individuals. At
least one of the young Englishmen was, as she confided to her diary, so noble and gifted. They spent
hours and hours sketching for their portfolios. Lanice
drew everything, diagrams of the sailors' knots and
tattooing, everything from Lady Maude asleep and
snoring to the ship's cat fawning for food. The young
man usually drew his fair companion.

On the second Sabbath all three of the clergymen
wished to preach, but that honor went to the Reverend Mr. Nightingale, and the service was held on the
deck. The ladies, devout and modest, sat near him,
their gentlemen standing about them, the steerage
passengers at a suitable distance. Here and there
an able-seaman fervently 'got religion.' They sang
hymns such as 'Star of Bethlehem,' 'The Voice of
Free Grace,' and 'We'll Praise Him Again When We
Pass Over Jordan.'

On the third Sabbath the breakers crashed upon the
Scilly Isles and the Lizard's Light stared through the
night, and such passengers as would land the next day
in Southampton and not go on to the ship's final port

[172]

of Marseilles prepared to leave. And then, on the next day, the red cliffs and the smell of the rich Devon shore, and the low rain-swollen clouds playfully pelted down the harmless English rain, then broke apart and permitted the sun to shine through and drink up the raindrops on one's ulster. But the night smelled sweeter than the day, and one saw little cottage lights upon the shore. The noble and high-minded young Englishman sang 'A Sailor's Lassie,' in a husky baritone, and when the moon moved out from the clouds and walked upon the water he kissed the lady's finger tips. But a lady travelling alone cannot be too careful and one must stop somewhere, especially when one's heart is broken.

'I must retire, Mr. Cassmondey. A lady must, as the saying is, have some beauty sleep.'

'But not you, Miss Bardeen. Really, greater beauty would be blinding. Really, I swear, Miss Bardeen . . .'

It was splendid fun, and were it not for the fragrance of England, Anthony's England, coming in soft waves to her through the night, she would have been absurdly happy.

In her cabin, the other women tossing and sighing about her, she pondered piteously on Anthony Jones, and finally fell asleep comforted with the conviction that she would be in England within a month herself, and certainly she would see him again. First her mother's death had ordered her to Italy, and the business of Messrs. Redcliffe & Fox made England necessary. Surely the hand of God was leading her again to Anthony Jones.

3

'So that is Marseilles, Captain?'

'Yes, Madam, Marseilles. I think at least one of every race lives here, except Chinamen.'

'Will I see Turks?'

'Why, put your hand down anywhere in Marseilles and scoop up a handful. Greeks, too, sailormen and merchants, low, lying, dirty scoundrels.'

'And Spaniards?'

'Oh, every other man's a don. You can tell them by their high heads and angry walk. Moors, too, and black folk from over in Africa. See their boats now with the red and yellow sails, striped like as not. You never saw ships like that in Boston, nor water so blue it hurt you to stare at it.'

They paused to look and listen. She saw the radiant sky, the blue sea crinkling under the gentle breeze like silk. The prow of the Diana tore through it and it made a ripping sound as though it were silk and the ship a tailor's shears. White limestone mountains were pale and tremulous in the heat, and below them spread upon the water's edge was the great white port, Marseilles.

'I expect a letter in Marseilles.'

'Well, they may send it on board. From Italy is it?'

'Yes.'

'But what's a fine, healthy girl like you doing in Italy? You look as if your lungs were strong.'

'Oh, yes.'

'There are many there who are suffering from consumption, poor souls, a long way from home to die.'

[174]

By sunset the Diana was in her place, one of hundreds of fine ships whose bowsprits lay upon the stone wharf as a dog would lay its nose upon the hearth.

'In the morning, Captain, I shall go to the post office to see if there is a letter.'

'Nay, better than that. This lad says he has a message for you.'

She looked down and behind the bulk of the captain was a hunchbacked dwarf. The creature seemed more ape than man. He stood in humility as if waiting until the first unfavorable impression should wear off. She felt she had seen him before, and then realized it was on the cover of the English 'Punch.' He wore old-fashioned livery and a little cape over his deformity. His expression was sweet and intelligent.

'You have a letter for the lady?'

'Si, Signor,' he said in a big man's voice, and then, bowing low, presented a sealed and folded blue sheet.

DEAR MISS BARDEEN: This is my servant, Gian, who is as good as he is ugly. He understands English, although he will not talk it. Let him help you on your way to Florence, for you will find little else to help except the saints, who in emergencies are always sleeping or hunting. I am,

Sincerely

ROGER CUNCLIFFE

VILLA POPPEA
FIRENZE, TUSCANY

[175]

4

And in the morning she set out with Gian carrying
her boxes and shawl, his dwarfishness increasing the
appearance of her slender height. His thick, dark
face made hers look fair as a goddess. He managed
all the arrangements for train or diligence. He bul-
lied the hotel-keepers, served her at table himself,
slept just outside her door at night, and took her to
some church every day. She found that he had been
raised by monks and had, until his deformity became too marked, hoped to be a priest. But his life
had been interesting. At one time he had been
valet de chambre to a countess and had hooked her
into her dresses and curled her hair. He spoke often
of young Cuncliffe, 'my master,' whom he adored
with a doglike simplicity, less often but very naturally of his master's lovely 'cousin' who, may
saints give her rest, had died that winter, 'oh, the
pretty.'

'Cousin!'

Young Cuncliffe could not have picked a better
ambassador.

By the time Genoa was passed and the road turned
south to Lucca and Florence, Lanice felt towards
Cuncliffe more curiosity than resentment. Of course
she would treat him very formally, and would only
see him in regard to the sad business at hand. She
would bow and not offer her hand. 'Mr. Cuncliffe,
I presume.' But if she had never met Captain Jones,
how different the meeting might be. Then she really
would have hated him.

[176]

'Those lights, like fireflies swarming, are they Florence?'

'Si, Signora.'

'And to-night I shall sleep in Florence?'

'Si, Signora.'

CHAPTER IX

TO ITALY

1

She bowed and did not offer her hand. 'Mr. Cuncliffe, I presume.'

'Yes,' said the young man waiting for her in the candlelight of the pension drawing-room. 'I'm driving back to my own little villa to-night, but first I wished to know that you had arrived safely. And Gian here,' — Gian and he spoke in Italian — 'you have been a good dog?'

'Oh, Gian has done everything.'

'Then watch the servants with the lady's luggage.'

'Gian's a good man,' he said when he was gone, 'and the most religious I have ever known, but he didn't make you go to church every day, did he?'

'Every day.'

'The rascal! I warned him that you were a heretic and would not wish to go to church. Evidently he tried to save your soul.'

'But I liked going to church — at least over here.'

He surprised her by saying, 'It is one of the pleasures of life.'

He was an ardent-looking young man, and in the candlelight she did not notice that he was very sick. He had a magnetism that drew her. She felt at peace with him and could not understand how, under the circumstances, there was no trace of awkwardness in their meeting. She tried to tell herself that this was the man with whom Mamma had run away, and to harden her heart against him. She looked at him curiously and a little inimicably out of her long, secret eyes. He answered the look gently.

'Don't be angry with me, or her. Do not resent me. I have heard a great deal about you, Lanice, and I hope we may be friends.'

And to her amazement she heard herself answer, 'I hope so, too.'

Their hands met at last.

'You will call me Roger?'

'Yes.'

'Very well, then. Good-night, Lanice.'

'Good-night.'

2

'Fair Florence, beautiful Florence. Oh, Enchanted City of the Soul, teach me your wisdom. Lily of the Arno. Fragrant . . .' She put down her pencil and considered. Florence was lovely and romantic, but not exactly fragrant. No city could be that allowed such *dreadful* things to happen. She found she had developed a tendency of late of starting a lovely description with a flourish and not being able to finish it. Her pen had lost its old unfastidious fluency.

She pushed back the lace curtains of the airy pension room and there below the Arno rustled its watery wings and sped forth to the sea. The drivers cracked their whips about their lean horses, and the

rattle of carts and hoof and feet and angry Italian
voices came up to her, from the pavements of the
Lung' Arno. It was Holy Week, and on the next day
would be, so Roger Cuncliffe had told her, the great
religious procession which she must not miss. 'All
winter,' he had said, 'Florentines shiver in their cold
stone houses which there is no way of making comfortable, and the icy mountain winds breathe upon
them. Then spring comes with a bounce. You are
almost mad with the joy of it, if you are a good Flor-
entine. Birds singing, caterpillars crawling, little
tendrils upon the vine, soft air and flowers, you smell
them in church, in your dreams all through the coun-
tryside. That is why the spring religious procession is
so terribly intense and beautiful. Girls go mad with
religion and throw themselves under the feet of the
marching monks. Monks forget their . . . It is heavenly in Florence in Holy Week. One feels the genuine
pagan spirit.'

'But I thought it was a sad religious occasion.'

'Oh, yes, religious, but not exactly sad. They worship the corruption of the body and renewing freshness of life, death and love. If religion cannot explain
these two mysteries to us, what good is religion?'

He was the most charming man she had ever met,
this young Roger Cuncliffe with his black curls, feverish color, narrow face, and cattish walk. No one had
warned her how sick he was. Every day she saw
sauntering through the streets listlessly — and her
heart bled for them — the young men and women
from her country and England sent to Italy to die.

There was one in her pension already too sick to move, and the landlady begrudging this poor woman the bed she was dying upon.

Several times Roger had suggested that they drive to the Protestant cemetery outside the wall where Mamma lay, but she felt she could not go with him and had not the courage to go alone. She had now accepted the fact of her mother's death, the realization of it did not have power to hurt her as did the thought of Roger's quickly approaching end.

A barefooted maid dressed in the contadina costume begged to inform the signorina that the sick gentleman had called for her. Every one in the pension was sorry for Lanice, thinking she had come to Florence to be with her lover until his death, which the landlady, from her experience, judged would take place in the fall. No one knew much about this rich young man, Cuncliffe. A year ago he had taken up his residence among them, and a handsome, slightly older woman had come with him, a cousin, so he said. Cuncliffe, even a year ago, had been too sick to excite scandal, and, after all, if he said she was his cousin, why might she not be?

Lanice found this gentle wraith awaiting her in the damp lower hall, where, after his pleasing manner, he chatted with the porter. The boy — for so Lanice had always considered him in spite of the fact that he was older than herself — was engagingly unconscious of class distinctions, and his perfect Italian broke down the barriers of nationality. He had already found out that the man was a wood-cutter from the Mugnone Valley, that a year before his mules had died and he had found work in Florence.

3

He drove a smart little English pony cart, so obviously bought to please Mamma that Lanice could not see it without visualizing her mother sitting upon the seat, smiling and flicking the whip. Now it was Lanice who drove and Roger took a lazy pleasure in her efforts to avoid the swarming beggars and children. She was so like her mother in some ways, yet fundamentally older — born older. She was a fiery thing in her own way, but lacked the careless radiant pagan spirit that had made the college boy turn to Hittie in his desperate need, after he had seen the writing upon the wall. She, disappointed in that Mr. Matthews of New York, and for some reason out of sympathy with this daughter, had been wild to get away from Amherst and that erudite husband of hers. She wanted to go to Italy and live, and he wanted to go there and die. Well, she was in her grave, poor soul, and he, poisoned and listless, tasting with every cough the corruption of his body as though he had rotted at the core. She dead, and he coughing and raising blood every morning. My God, my God! Life hurt with sudden agony as a grass-blade cuts the finger.

'Yes, that's the Badia. We'll go there some day, Lanice. There's little of Arnolfo's thirteenth-century work left, but there's a splendid Filippino Lippi altarpiece and it was here that Boccaccio used to lecture on Dante.

'Yes, your book on Dante would tell you to look this up. We are in the heart of the Dante quarter. I'd love to take you about, on foot some day, when it is a little warmer.'

Hittie had been delicious. She was such an unhurtable creature. This daughter of hers now, she hadn't the hard child's heart, that can see without feeling, and lightly cast off the suffering of another. Hittie had been perfect for a jaunt, which, after all, from the beginning, had been something of a death's-head affair.

They drove up towards the hills and looking back saw the lovely city of Florence swimming in a golden haze.

'I'm going to show you my little Villa Poppea,' he said. 'You won't need to guide Beppo. He has a home-loving spirit.'

Beppo jogged and the cart bounced. Lanice chatted a little and laughed once or twice when Roger politely said something to amuse her. Once he surreptitiously coughed blood. Lanice pretended not to notice.

They drank white wine out of antique Venetian goblets and ate honey cakes. It was a lovely place, small, airy, perfect. Lanice was glad to see that the old woman who with Gian served this young 'milord' loved him. They would do all they could for his comfort. Quite far away now was the magic city of Florence. They looked down at it over the tops of misty silver olives and crude green chestnuts. The city stretched in the sun like a cat.

In the garden was the metallic rustle of water, and

against a broken cypress was a lovely, headless nymph fleeing with outstretched arms. Lanice recognized it as the one of which Mamma had sent a picture for the stereoscope.

'Greek, I think,' said Roger; 'late Greek, but once it belonged to some member of the Medici family. They made that inappropriate rococo base for it and the family crest on it.'

'I wish it had a head,' said Lanice. To a young woman trained as she was trained, it was hard to know where to look at a nude statue if the head was gone.

'Do you know, I believe I'm glad it hasn't. It would have been one of those flat, dish faces with lumpy hair. You can see hundreds of them in museums. Often a curator tries to combine headless bodies and bodiless heads, and fathers archæological monsters. Now the head I see for this nymph is wholly individual and utterly lovely. But come, see my other god, and see what has happened to his head.'

A sturdy, red sandstone Pan of doubtful lineage held up towards his mouth his marsyas pipes, but the head, evidently cut from a separate block, rolled on the gravel and leered up with wicked slit eyes.

'This head fell off when I was in America,' he said. 'I haven't put it back because I used to feel rather unhappy at nights thinking how Pan was alone here with my frightened Greek. His leer was so lewd, and she, poor child, without an inch of clothing, not even a face to turn away from his gaze. So when Nature, or Zeus, or the intensity of his passions finally popped his head off and tumbled it at his feet, I left it where it fell. But I suppose the first thing the next owner will do is to put it back on again. He may even be like a countryman of ours who bought a villa at Cartomondo, and had a white iron petticoat made for each of his garden gods.' He poked at the fallen head with a rather tender boot tip as if he had a secret love for the old reprobate.

'I'll show you the library, your mother's room, everything.'

A high, narrow room lined with books and book-scented — this was his library. 'It is the *Canti a Ballo* that have especially interested me,' he said. 'I have tried to collect Lorenzo de Medici's own compositions in this line. Strange to think how this bank president, corrupt ward boss, and art patron used to garland himself with flowers and march through the streets of his city accompanied with a few light, light ladies and drunken gallants, bellowing these songs. And they are beautiful things, some of them.'

He took up a theorbo from a crimson damask stool and idly began to thrum upon it. Then, pushing back his damp black curls, he sang a part of Lorenzo's 'Bacchus and Ariadne':

> 'Youths and maids enjoy to-day,
>   Naught ye know about to-morrow.
> Fair is youth and void of sorrow,
>   But it hourly flees away. . . .'

The fierce, high beauty of the music shook Lanice. The theorbo and Roger and the old Magnifico, dead these four hundred years in his musty vault, all spoke to her of Anthony Jones, and rekindled the emotions she had experienced through him. But, strangely enough, the music promised even wilder, more incredible joys, 'Oh, happy, happy love.'

'Roger,' she cried rather piteously, 'is there anything in life that *is* all the things music talks about?'

'No,' he answered; 'you see, we live on promises. There is a smell in the air a month before spring comes, and it is more delicious, more intoxicating than spring itself. And sunrise always promises us more than the day brings, and youth more than age, and songs more than life. It is this incessant yearning that makes us poor human animals so sad and so happy.'

The theorbo throbbed an incessant tuneless accompaniment. 'Come, Lanice,' he said, throwing down the instrument, 'we will go to your mother's room and then, this afternoon, drive back to Florence by way of the Protestant Cemetery.'

4

At the end of the spring day they came to the high gate of a cemetery lying outside the city walls. The marble hills of Carrara had grown translucent as moonstones, and assumed liquid beauty. Two tired and playless children held out a wreath of laurel and white violets. Roger bought it, and, carrying the wreath and covered with the children's whispered thanks, they passed under the gate and entered the small cemetery. The day grew pink, and in a whisper Roger told Lanice that under these atmospheric conditions the headless Greek in the garden assumed the tints of life.

'Hittie loved the statue,' he continued. 'She wanted to be buried there in the garden and have it set above her.'

'She knew she was going to die?'

'Not at first. You see, the fever went away once. We thought she was well, but it came back suddenly, in a hurry, the way a man who forgets something races back to his house and turns everything upside down, and finding what he wants runs out again, slamming the door.'

'Roger, did she suffer? I didn't want to hear all at first, but now I do. Was she frightened?'

'She was pretty uncomfortable ... not especially frightened. Let's sit down under this ilex tree, Lanice. You see that white marble shaft with the urn on top? That's her grave.'

They sat for a moment. Then Lanice, brushing away a tear, took the fragrant wreath, crossed to the low mound and the white urn, knelt and prayed beside it. Her prayers trod on each other's heels, pushing formless, almost wordless to her lips. She prayed for her mother's happiness and humbly gave thanks that she, herself, was alive. Anthony Jones and Lorenzo de Medici, the opalescent sunset, the beautiful city, this poor, dying boy sitting beneath the ilex, the tired children at the gate. She rose from her knees and as an answer to her prayer came a passionate realization that life itself is its own great reward and that life runs out like sand in a glass. She went back to Roger. His small-featured face was gaunt with sickness. The color high up under his bright black eyes looked crudely put on with a brush. She could not control herself, and casting her body down beside him and clasping his thin hands she cried out, 'Roger, are you really sick? I mean, very sick?'

'Yes, Lanice,' he smiled, 'very, very.'

She could not bear the thought, shuddered, and covered her face with her hands. He remarked quite casually: 'It is all right, Lanice, about dying. You think now that it isn't. But it is something quite natural to the human race. All our ancestors have always done it — successfully. It is quite part of living. I don't mind, so you must not.'

There was a velvet babble of bells from a near-by church, and she saw the pigeons fly homeward through the clear, yellowing air.

'How did she happen to get the fever?'

'This last year while I was hunting about for my *canti di ballo*, Hittie collected old legends. She wrote down but very little, poor soul. Hers was not the mind of a scholar, nor did she remember very accurately, but it was rousing to hear her tell these old romances. Mr. Browning has told me that since her death he has written out in verse three or four of these dramatic tales of hers. He admired her prodigiously. One of his poems is to be about a lady of the Riccardi who had a bust of herself placed in the window where in life she had watched her lover pass. I think Elizabeth Barrett was almost jealous for her "Roberto mio." Well, there is in the Maremma — you know that interminable, desolate marsh which stretches mile on mile to the Roman hills — an old Ghibelline castello with a moat. It stands alone in its marshes, an unhealthy place.' He paused and looked at Lanice speculatively as if he wanted to say that he had advised against the expedition, but that the woman had insisted, and after all she was so much older than he. 'No one has lived there for four hundred years. But it has its ghost . . . the one thing in the world that Hittie wanted to see, and find out why it, or rather she, walks.'

'So you went to the Maremma?'

'Yes, and spent the night in the castello. We had planned to stay at the inn, and as we knew it would be dirty, we brought our own bedding with us on the coach. But the place was filthy, and Hittie suggested that we sleep in the castello instead. We built a fire in a fireplace that had not been used for centuries, and Gian spread our beds before it. She was very tired and fell asleep instantly. I walked by moonlight through the ruins and listened to the night wind and the dismal croaking of a million frogs. I saw the poisonous miasma steam up from the swamps and finger through the broken windows of the castello, and I feared fever. When I came back to Hittie, a slight change had come over her. I never again saw her quite herself, although it was some days before she came down with her sickness.'

'Why?'

'She had seen the ghost.'

'Oh, but you do not believe that!'

'No, not quite. At least, I think a touch of fever came first, and then the ghost. We huddled up by the fire together, and she told me in whispers how she had dreamed of a delicate, pale lady without hands who came and stood beside her and pleaded for a little heat from the hearth. "I've been dead for four hundred years," she said; "I can't make a fire because my hands have been cut off." Hittie was not afraid of this dream. She was glad to build up the fire, but as the poor, transparent lady bent towards her she smelled a fragrance like lilacs.'

'Was it the season for lilacs?'

'Oh, no. Months away. When she woke up she could still smell the lilacs, and this did bother her a little, and next she saw, quite suddenly out of nothing, the handless lady. But even this did not frighten her very much. It was all too distinct and real to be terrifying. The oddest thing about it was the fact that I, too, could smell lilacs. I did, even after her death.'

Lanice saw his delicate nostrils taste the air.

'This ghost of the Maremma has been seen by almost every one who has tried to look it up. We have records of it as far back as the diary of a lieutenant of Napoleon's, but no one before has ever seen her arms. I've traced out the history of this castello and its great family at the Biblioteca Laurenziana. There really was a woman, a Contessa Bianca, whose husband found her with her lover. "That day they read no more." He had her nailed to the wall with a stiletto through each palm, and set fire to that wing of the castello. Crazy, I suppose. I do not blame the Contessa for preferring another man. The lover came back to her, but was unable to remove the knives which had been driven in by the blacksmith. He hacked off her hands at the wrist. But she died — shock, I suppose, and smoke and loss of blood.'

'Is it a *true* story?'

'It is an old one told of many ladies and lovers But it was necessary to account in some way for the gutted castello and the fair ghost.'

'But if Mamma did not know the story, how did she happen to see the hands?'

'Oh, she had read some similar legend, perhaps about Sordello.'

They went together to the marble slab, and, even as Lanice gazed reverently upon it, she noticed that the age was misstated. If Mamma was indeed as young as that, she would have been but eleven when Lanice was born. She wondered if Roger had ever made any such calculations. He would, she thought, forgive them.

'I think she cared more for you than any one else,' said Roger, and stopped awkwardly, wishing he might presume to ask the girl whether or not she knew of the love Hittie had once lavished upon Mr. Matthews. They paid the ghostly children for tending Beppo before the gate, and got into the cart.

'For me?'

'Yes, of course she didn't care so very much for . . .'

'For any one?'

'No.'

'It was so strange about the ghost.'
'Yes.'
Again his nostrils sniffed the twilight air.

5

With Roger she saw the great religious procession
that comes but once in three years. They sat upon
the iron balcony of a prominent English resident, a
pious woman but lately turned to 'The Church.' She
hoped that through this spectacle faith and hope
might be planted in the hard, irreligious heart of the
young man. The sun had set, and the city was sunk
in night. Christo Morto and Good Friday. Pilate
had washed his hands. Peter had denied his Lord.
Judas had hanged himself, and Christ not yet risen.

First came ancient Roman horsemen, flashing
through the dark, then infantry, a stupendous number of laymen bearing torches, some red and some
green, and boys and priests and marshals. There was
almost a suggestion of blood lust in the rather ugly
insistence upon the symbols of Christ's death, but the
words said during the hours upon the cross, printed
upon silk banners, were moving in their tragedy.
Last was a conclave of priests surrounded by torch-
bearers in so black a black that only their white faces
and bony hands were visible. These preceded and
followed the effigy of the dead Christ which was borne
under a black canopy and on a black litter as the
Brothers of Mercy bear their dead. Then Roger
pointed out the weird corpse-flowers carried delicately
by devout little boys. They were, said Roger, es-

[192]

pecially grown for this purpose in cellars; that is why stems and leaves are white as well as the heavy blossoms. They would be laid away in the Holy Sepulchre. Centuries ago, thousands of years ago, other women had grown the same unwholesome flowers to fill the tomb of the dead Adonis. The Madonna, stylish and complacent in spite of the seven swords at her heart, was carried by, winking and glittering in the torchlight. More priests, monks, marshals, and soldiers brought up the rear. The devout silence that greeted all this tragic glory was broken only by the Latin muttering of the churchmen and the measured strain of ecclesiastical instruments. It seemed a solemn and terrifying thing, mysterious and ominous. The New England girl could not understand Roger's evident enjoyment of anything so 'papish' and 'heathenish,' but never in the white First Congregational Church at Amherst had she been so touched with the Godhead of Christ. There he had been a man, an elder brother. Here he was all God, and she watched the passing of his insignia with awe and reverence.

'Shall we go now?' she whispered to Roger.

'No, wait. I want you to meet the Brownings. They have been standing across the street and our holy hostess has just sent her footman over to beg them to join us.'

So Lanice met the Brownings and was able, on this slight acquaintance and on a subsequent supper at Casa Guidi, to write her brief monograph which was in due time published in 'Fox's Journal,' and which

[193]

was to remain to time the most vivid pen portrait of
Robert and Elizabeth Browning in the earlier days
of their marriage. It was in this that she called Mrs.
Browning 'a soul of fire encased in a shell of pearl.'

6

The next morning her mind still seemed choked
with the corpse-flowers, even as she smelled the fresh
violets that were being hawked beneath her window on
the Lung' Arno. Death — love; love — death. These
were the insoluble mysteries of human necessity.
Roger laughed at her distaste for the corpse-flowers
and promised to drive her far out into the country.
They travelled in a big, old-fashioned berlina drawn
by three stout Austrian horses hired for the occasion.
For miles and miles they followed the rushing, swollen
river through hamlets, past castles and villas and
vineyards and meadows. For every turn and every
village Roger had his story. Yonder by the poplars
and the willows Buonconte died of wounds, crying
the name of Mary, and in the same battle Dante rode
in the light cavalry. 'You know the fifth canto of
"Purgatory"?'

'And you have heard of La Verna, "the harsh
rock"; it was here on a bright September morning before dawn (see where I point) that Saint Francis met
the crucified seraph.

'Popes with their gilded trains; swaggering Con-
dottieri captains with their fine hard men of war,
Englishmen among them; the wanton ladies of Boccaccio stepping delicately in fine silks and speaking

lasciviously; the Medici with their gripping mouths and lusty ambitions; Savonarola calling upon man, calling upon God, half crazed and half deified — all these passed upon this road, Lanice.'

The day went like a dream. At last when they reached a heavenly spot Lanice suggested they rest upon the grass, and Roger ordered the berlina to stop. While the driver refreshed himself at a near-by inn and the three thick grey horses pulled eagerly at the flourishing grass, the two exiles wandered under cypress and ilex trees towards the banks of the swelling river. It was spring, and the valley of the Arno was carpeted with the sweet lily-of-the-valley. A great multitude of tiny flowers looking up eagerly from the lush grass, the poplars twinkling in the rustle of the wind. Never a sky so blue, nor mountain of so pink a porcelain. The south wind, the persuasion of the flowering earth, the drone of insects, and the jubilant calling of the mating birds worked their charm. The man and girl sat upon the ground, Roger with arms clasped about his knees brooding with comprehending, tragically contented eyes on the life-burgeoned landscape. The girl flung herself backwards upon the turf, clutching in either fist handfuls of the heavily scented white violets. The sun beat upon her. Earth-fragrance rose from the bruised flowers and spring-dampened ground. Drugged, she lay in her belling dress of pale lavender striped in deeper pink like a fallen morning-glory. The satin of her face glowed with hidden ecstasy. For the first time she could look at Roger's emaciated face and damp black curls

— know that he must die, and feel no resentment. It is enough, she thought, to come in out of the void to enjoy the sun, the spring, the pleasure of existence and then to pull this bright earth over your head, sleep, and if you must — forget.

'This,' said Roger, indicating the florescent carpet on which they lay, 'is what Fra Angelico — blessed be his name — tried to paint. Did you ever dream of such millions of little flowers all in blossom at once? Could anything be more like the Paradise of the old hymns?'

But there seemed to be nothing more to say. Through the golden silence Lanice felt a miracle working within her like the quickening of a child. It was as if, through suffering and acceptance, Roger had reached a level where neither the vicissitudes of fortune nor the cruelty of man or nature could longer hurt him. If he could have put in words the wisdom he had learned, the young woman heaped beside him like a dropped flower would not have understood, but she could drink from his presence and feed on his inarticulate calm the spirit that Captain Jones had so rudely uprooted. The whole world, as she understood it, had fallen in ruins about her head. Here in this poised and now silent young man was the answer to all the questions she had ever asked of life. They were drawn together in closer bond than Jones's iron arms. The great traveller was after all but an external adventure. He had touched but the surface of her being. Roger enveloped her in a pale gold light. Nothing mattered, neither Hittie's disgrace and tragic death nor her own response to Anthony's passion. They ceased to frighten her — those ghastly white corpse-flowers that girls had grown for thousands of years to put in a dead god's grave.

'Roger.'

'Yes — my dear.'

'Are we immortal — please tell me what you really think?'

He paused, not because he did not know what he thought, but he delicately dreaded taking away a belief when he was powerless to put anything in its place.

'Lots of people wiser than I think we are.'

'But you — what do you think?'

He quoted from the old sundial that stood in the garden back of the Amherst villa, '"Time flies, you say; alas, not so. Time stays; we go."' And as he spoke she saw Mamma flit through the familiar garden, nod, and pass out into utter darkness. 'All that seems important and worthy of immortality goes, I believe, into the grave. But all that is transient, the thoughts and hopes and questions, the delights and pains — these things are immortal. The individual is only a fine instrument adjusted to receive these immortal sensations. Think, Lanice, how many have lain among the spring flowers and wondered about death and immortality, and life and love — just as you do now. Then they have gotten up and gone home and quite forgotten — just as you will. It is like a great wind blowing by,' he said, 'first you feel it blowing upon you — and in a moment it is gone, or rather *you* are gone. The wind of human experience

keeps on blowing. It is Godhood. It gives us in passing something of its own immutability. Love' — he
added after a thoughtful pause — 'there is nothing
like love for making one feel akin to all past lovers and
all unborn lovers to come.'

They looked at each other and both smiled. For
the first time Lanice realized that he might have been
an ardent lover — a year ago. That, curiously, he
was made primarily for love. It would come naturally to him and he had only learned to think since it
had failed him. He was curious about her and wished
she would tell him what burden love had laid upon
her.

7

She said good-bye to Roger with one foot poised on
the step of the diligence that should take her to
Bologna. She had decided, without asking any further
instruction from her father, to let Hittie lie here in
this brighter, clearer land where all the colors are so
distinct, but right and wrong curiously foggy. After
all, it did not matter, and she would not long lie alone,
for soon Roger would lay his cinder of a body beside
his 'cousin.' He would not let Lanice stay in Florence
to care for him.

'I do not need any one now, Lanice. I did a year
ago and *she* was wonderful. But that part's over —
so run along, my dear — and do enjoy yourself. I
shall read your literary articles in "Fox's Journal"
with the most breathless interest. Do a good one on
Tennyson — I mean, don't keep on calling him "The

Bard" the way every one else does, but show him up as a growling old lion who too early got enmeshed in the silken net of "Ladies' Albums."'

'But . . .' began Lanice. The diligence was impatient to be off. The guard was beseeching her, or perhaps cursing her, in Italian. She sprang in. 'And write over your own name,' shouted Roger, bound to the last to keep the parting unsentimental.

'Oh . . . I have already sent off my Browning article over the *nom de plume* of "Tempus Fugit."'

'Rubbish!' called Roger, and the diligence jingled and clattered through the Piazza della Signoria.

Roger looked at his watch, whistled thoughtfully, and went back to his waiting pony cart. He was very fond of this sleek, thin girl who had landed almost unannounced in the middle of his affairs, demanding in one breath the body of her mother and an answer to all the riddles of life. He believed, partly from what she let drop and partly intuitively, that she had recently been through some ordeal. Love, probably. Perhaps this witty Mr. Fox, whom she quoted so assiduously. Perhaps the professor, who he knew had written her several times and would meet her in London. Perhaps Jones — obviously one of those loose young Englishmen that always make a bad name for the white man in hot countries. If he still were in England and were the man whom this girl loved, she would probably seek him out — women have almost a genius for anticlimaxes. She was ambitious, perhaps more so than he realized. Could ambition have so wounded her? 'There's a flash to the girl — a *je ne sais quoi*, that might, if she schooled herself and was humble before her art, take her to the first rank. But she'd never wait. She'd spend it all in a series of foolish love affairs or in some ridiculous boiled dinner of a marriage.'

He called to the beggars to get out of his way and whistled to the bang-tail pony.

CHAPTER X

SEES SOMETHING OF LONDON

1

'IT is most kind of you, Mr. Ripley, to take me to this literary soirée and give me the entrée in London, but who are these people? And why is this George Eliot criticized for living with a Mr. Lewes?'

'Very few know who "George Eliot" is — they only know the rather stark and grim short stories that are published over this name in "Blackwood's." But I, Miss Bardeen, having your critical career well to heart, have ferreted out this dawning wonder and am now taking you to see her.'

'*Her?*'

'Her. The scandal — if any one could so call it — is now self-evident. Her name is Marian Evans, but we shall call her Mrs. Lewes, and the future may very possibly know something of her as George Eliot.'

'And Mr. Lewes? Does she — er — just for fun?'

'No, indeed, the highest principles. You see, his wife ran away once and he took her back. Then she ran away again, but he couldn't divorce her because he had once forgiven her. Such is English law. Then he met this slow-moving, solemn woman of genius, and they agreed to consider themselves married and let the world think of them as it pleases. They need each other. Her sombre cast of mind gives poise to his high-strung nature. She withstrains, ennobles, and purifies him. He wakes her up and gets her out of her dourness. I am afraid,' he added with a sigh, 'that you will like him the better of the two ... And here we are in Blandford Square. Driver! the small brick house; there's a woman selling lavender in front of it.'

She felt a certain pride in arriving on Sears Ripley's arm. He was so poised, so intelligent, and in a very superior way so handsome. She sat upon a low divan at one end of the small, flat drawing-room, and, as she chatted about her journeys upon the Continent with two small Jewish brothers, she watched him engaging the clever and obviously versatile Mr. Lewes in philosophical dispute. Marian Evans, her heavy chin cupped in a white hand dotted with freckles, eagerly leaned her great leonine head towards the dispute. She offered no comment, but nodded wisely, and her deep and expressive eyes glowed with excitement when Lewes began to get the better of his opponent.

Ripley caught her eye, 'Come, Mrs. Lewes, won't you help me out? Your husband is giving me the worst of it.'

She pulled herself together and raised her huge chin, assuming for the moment the posture of a singer about to sing, then drooping with an almost childish artlessness began to talk rapidly in so low a voice even the two men close to her were obliged to bend their heads and Lanice could not hear the tone of her voice.

'And now,' said the littlest and most Hebraic of the

[202]

flaxen brothers 'that you have raced pell-mell all over Italy, the Alps, seen Paris, and arrived in London, do you intend to amuse yourself with us for a while?'

'Yes, for a month at least. I have business to conduct.'

'Business? I thought you said you had bought all your dresses in Paris.'

'I did, although I shall not be able to wear them for at least two years — Paris is always that much ahead of us.'

She told them about the articles she had engaged to do for 'Fox's Journal,' and at the name of Fox an older man in a soiled yellow satin waistcoat hitched his chair nearer. He was blind. Lanice regretted that the prim, pretty young girl who accompanied him, and who she had been told was a country cousin who earned her livelihood leading him about, did not care enough for him to tell him that his waistcoat was dirty.

He said gravely, in a rift in the conversation, 'I have known and admired Mr. Fox for years — wittiest man on two continents — I am Mr. Clapyard — of Clapyard & Dunster, publishers, madam.' He was one of the men in England she had really wished to meet, and they began to gossip about certain books that her house and his had published together.

Then she stopped dead, for suddenly she remembered that Clapyard & Dunster would bring out the English edition of 'Sands of Araby.' Her confusion was so obvious and so inexplicable one of the young Jews asked her if she would not like a glass of wine.

[203]

'It is nothing. I suddenly forgot what I was saying. I do that sometimes' — and she laughed nervously.

'And this fall,' continued Mr. Clapyard when order had been restored to the conversation, 'we both of us will be publishing Captain Jones's big volumes on Araby. I have never brought out a book I felt more pride in than that.'

Lanice, completely at her ease once more, smiled and nodded and told one or two anecdotes about the traveller's great American tour. The tight, poor cousin was gazing at her perhaps with envy, perhaps with suspicion.

'This,' she said fingering a lump of amber tied too closely about her neck, with a red ribbon, '*He* gave me this.'

'Yes,' elaborated Mr. Clapyard, 'Effie saw him daily in our office, and was able to help him a little. It was kind of him to remember her in parting — very courteous of him.' The two young women stared frankly at each other.

'He has left England then?' (How lucky it was that her confusion had come upon her before the actual mention of Anthony's name — a name by which to conjure up women the world over.)

'Yes,' said the unfriendly country cousin.

'No — no,' corrected Mr. Clapyard mildly, 'hardly yet. He leaves England within the month, but he left London three days ago. They say, in recognition of some secret good he did in Araby, he is to be appointed Political Agent at Bagdad with an eye out for the whole of Persia and Arabia.'

Three days ago — and Lanice heard no more. Three days ago — and the rain pelting down through the soot and leaking through the arched roof of the dingy London station where, amid porters and boxes and luggage and tired travellers and patient guards, Sears Ripley had met her as she came up on the boat train. Perhaps if she had turned her head she might instead have seen Anthony. Perhaps he saw her — and chose to walk away. Perhaps their shoulders touched in the crowd and neither knew, and he would go his way to Bagdad and she hers back to Boston. Sears had taken her to a respectable and very female boarding-house which he had considered 'quite safe' for her, and after a dilatory conversation about the Continent had left her. But Anthony — if he had snapped his fingers she would have gone with him to the ends of the earth. She resented unreasonably the kind and friendly man who instead had met her. Clapyard was saying, 'I imagine that he is sailing within the month.' The little cousin was staring at her with stiff, uncompromising eyes. Lanice felt no jealousy towards the English girl. The lump of amber, clumsily shaped, was not the trifle Anthony Jones would select for any one who really amused and pleased him. It had been on the top of his trunk ('box,' he would say) and he was tired of it — and he felt he had to give the girl something, or he may have gone out and bought it; perhaps he had said, 'I'll take *that* — if it's not more than nine shillings.' And he knew she was just the girl to tie it on with a red ribbon, and to tie it too tight. She looked patron-

[205]

izingly at the relative, and the girl opened her little
mouth to speak and changed her mind, and her throat
swelled with the words she had not uttered so that the
amber lump stood out.

Conscious as she was of the vibrating current that
passed between her and this possible rival, Lanice
was just as alive to Sears Ripley's eyes and mood. He
had left Marian Evans and her group and had taken
up his stand slightly behind her divan. He was watching her, out of little friendly triangular eyes, with
burning interest. The thought flashed through her
mind that this man understood her, as no one else
ever had done. He knew everything, except that
part of her nature that Anthony possessed. He
understood everything, except the hours spent with
Anthony Jones. Here he was baffled, and slightly
fascinated. Here was her little private soul that he,
who was so wise, never would see.

She tried to find the courage merely to say,
'Where is Mr. Jones? — I must see him — about the
American edition of his book.' But she knew she
might as well say, 'I love Anthony — if he is in this
country I must see him; if he will have me I will go
with him to Arabia.' Some day she would stop in
at Clapyard & Dunster's and look over the English
proofs and say casually to the old blind gentleman,
'By the way, I do wish I could get in touch with Mr.
Jones — about some captions —'

She was relieved to find that the conversation had
left Jones entirely and was concerned with the names
of English inns. There was, it seemed, a famous

hostelry known as 'Made in Heaven' and Professor Ripley was suggesting that it was originally 'mayde' and referred to the Virgin Mary — the name had some way escaped the Reformation. One had slept in the 'Gold Gallows Tree' and another in the 'Blue Cow's Mouth.'

Marian Evans, the philosophical conversation having ended, joined the group. 'The strangest name for an inn I ever heard,' she said in her gentle voice so at variance with her massive face, 'is the " God-Begot House," in Winchester.' Lanice had never heard this word used in any connection except the Bible and was slightly shocked that so refined a female as this Mrs. Lewes should now admit it to her lips. Then she remembered how much less fastidious she had found the English than her own countrymen and how Lady Maude on the ship coming over had told a long story in a loud voice which hinged entirely upon the presence of a bull at a cricket match.

'And it's a fine old house too,' added Mr. Clapyard. 'I've been there myself — the best beef and ale in England.'

His cousin stared even harder at Lanice.

'There is something this girl knows,' she thought, 'but will not tell me and I will not ask her.'

'Shall we not go into the dining-room?' It was Mr. Lewes who spoke.

She glanced up and her eyes met Sears Ripley's and he looked brave and rather miserable and wise and tolerant. To both of them the glance they exchanged meant much.

[207]

('It is just as well that it was *he* who met me — not Anthony.')

('I suppose if she asks me where he is, I'll tell her; after all she's not a child.')

'Some of the French inns have even odder names,' he said mildly, and taking her upon his arm he marched her into the dining-room.

2

She went far North to Westmoreland and there, in a doll's cottage garlanded with fading roses and laced with bird wings, she saw the figure of Harriet Martineau creep out in the sun to greet her, her ear-trumpet — great as the horn of Gabriel — thrust towards her interviewer.

She went to Yorkshire, and with sweating, panting horses climbed a black moor and came to a stone-cold village where even the roofs were of stones and no flowers brightened. At the head of the one street was a churchyard where the dead lay so close there was scarce room for grass. The dead seemed to push against the living and only a feeble lilac hedge held them back from the parsonage where the genius-stricken Brontës had lived and died. 'If I had come two years ago,' she thought, 'I should have seen them — at least I should have seen Charlotte, but she's gone now like the rest.' And she waited half the day to see a sick old man in clerical gaiters and stock, leaning upon his cane and shaking as he walked. What children he had — this sad old man! And they were gone and he was left. She thought of Emily striding upon the moor, with Heathcliffe and Cathy crying upon her with their inhuman voices, and Patrick drinking himself to death, and Charlotte and the gentle Anne. That house which now stood as one tomb among many had once been full of children — but they had never laughed and played like other children. They had been sad, wistful little creatures with the wings of death above their heads and the grave always open before their feet.

Professor Ripley suggested, on her next return to the spinsterish boarding-house in London, that she should go to the Duchy of Cornwall — quite in the opposite direction — and call upon the Reverend Job Paisley, an ancient, retired clergyman who wrote sketches of his own moors much in the manner of the earlier Gilbert White. Lanice knew that it was a long journey for a small author, but think! the *Duchy* of Cornwall!—and the name of his house was Paradise, Moors End, Liskeard. It was not until after she had assented to go and accepted Mrs. Paisley's invitation that she discovered that Sears Ripley himself, 'by the way,' would be a guest at the same time. 'You mean you yourself will be at Liskeard?' Her voice and the doubtful look she gave him did not presage great things for the future.

It was Ripley himself who met the coach as it distributed its passengers before the local inn, and drove her in the vicar's phaeton with not too well-concealed triumph to Paradise, Moors End, Liskeard, Duchy of Cornwall.

Something, she told herself that night, as she

[209]

crawled in between the sheets deliciously heated by the brass warming-pan, was going to happen. She stayed awake long enough to decide that, if she had read aright the increasing tenderness of Sears Ripley's glances, it would now be a good time to 'have it over with.' He was much too self-contained to make a scene — the old dear. Oh, how she would miss him — when she had given him her 'no' and bade him 'leave her forever.' Since being in London she had come to have a very different feeling towards him than when he had merely been a friend of Anthony Jones, a dark background to the other's radiance. She found out rather to her surprise that he really was a distinguished scholar and one of the few Americans whose ease and distinction of manner could stand comparison with England's best.

The next day was unromantically chill. Fogs lay in counterpanes over the wild land and hid from view the village of Liskeard, and its tall trees and square church tower. The vicar's wife would not let Miss Bardeen walk, even as far as the Fountain of Saint Cleer, without forcing upon her her own stout walking-boots and excessively ugly tweed walking-gown. It was so short Lanice blushed to see that her ankles would have been displayed to public view were it not for the masculine boots. She wore over her head a light-weight black wool shawl in the manner of a country woman. It gave her a perverse pleasure to think how plain and unattractive she would look upon this walk which she believed Professor Ripley had planned for weeks.

They smiled at each other in the lower hall.

'Had I best take an umbrella?'

'Oh, no,' said Lanice, 'I want to get wet. Mrs. Paisley has assured me so many times that this cloth and these boots are impenetrable I want to put them to some test. — Oh, and you have on the vicar's raincoat?'

'Yes — and boots. The English certainly are most hospitable when they really get started. Actually these shoes are too small for me — but they have such a low opinion of American boots, I was really forced into them.'

'And his wife's are too large for me. Do we *dare* go back and get our own?'

'I dare, if you dare.'

'Agreed.'

They met again in the lower hall some five minutes later and again they smiled widely at each other. Lanice did not bother to draw the shawl over her head and the fog soon formed dewdrops on her bright hair. They found the rude stone canopy over the Fountain of Saint Cleer almost too easily.

'Let's try something harder,' suggested Sears Ripley. 'The Hurlers, for instance.'

'What are they?'

'Druid circles, far out on the moor. Dr. Paisley has often written about them in his sketches.'

'But is it safe to go so far out on the moor alone in a fog?'

'Not very,' he admitted, 'but we cannot possibly lose our way for long. Bodmin Moor is not so vast or treacherous as Dartmoor, and then, I have a map Dr. Paisley drew for me a few days ago. I saved it until you should come along and enjoy it too. I understand we shall find paths to follow, and if not, why, we can turn back.'

Soon they left the confines of the village and found themselves floating off over the coarsely carpeted moors in the spreading softness of the fog. The thick banks undulated about them, sometimes lifting and showing wild and fantastic glimpses of a desolate land. Almost everything seemed to be horizontal, but such things as stood perpendicular in this flat world gained a gigantic height. The two human beings looked at each other in amazement that such a tall man and woman existed. It was hard to talk naturally — to avoid whispering.

'I feel,' said Lanice at last, 'that when we get there the druids will climb up out of their tumuli and sacrifice us.'

Professor Ripley was dubiously studying tiny footpaths, trying to orient himself by a non-existent sun.

'If we are now on the right path,' he said, 'we shall come to an ancient cross' — and as he spoke and stared, the fog lifted and a broken, wordless cross, looking forty feet high, seemed to walk towards them like a holy vision.

'I do not think it was here,' said Lanice helplessly, 'before you spoke. Do you believe in magic?'

'Yes — when in Cornwall. I believe in the giant Tregeagle and in Hell Hounds, but most of all in the

[212]

pixies, perhaps we are pixie-led at this very moment. If so, the cross will disappear. Why, Heaven help us! it's gone already. Well, the fog was considerate to lift when it did. At least we know our direction.'

They pushed their way cautiously through heather and gorse and roundabout innumerable ancient mine diggings. But where were the Hurlers? In the fog the rabbits looked as large as ponies, and the ponies they continually mistook for prehistoric stones. Most of the little mares had foals with them and were as wild as deer.

'We must be near to the place,' said Ripley. 'You keep to the footpath and I'll walk beside it through the heather. The stones are said to be at least twenty feet from the path. 'Or,' he added generously, 'would you rather be the explorer?'

He saw by her brightening eye that this would please her, and humbly took up his journey alone upon the footpath and let the young female, inappropriately (as most men would have thought) struggle through the heather and make the actual discovery. They called back and forth through the fog so that Lanice would not be lost. The thick atmosphere absorbed most of their voices. 'Professor Ripley,' she would call, and he would answer 'Miss Bardeen.' A little sparrow voice — 'Professor Ripley,' a far-away rumble, 'Miss Bardeen.'

Once she cried, 'I've found them!' — but the objects she mistook for druid stones swished their tails, snorted and fled upon the moor. Then at last a vague black mass loomed before her and instantly behind it, rank upon rank and shoulder to shoulder, stood the Hurlers. She called to Sears Ripley and groping like a blind man he came to join her. They sat on one overturned giant and still in whispers speculated upon the vanished races. They felt like hunters who have stalked their prey and only after the most prodigious cunning out-manœuvred their victims. Both were glad of the fog. How comparatively prosaic it would have been if they had seen the stone circles for miles and walked straight into them! Lanice tried to describe to him how that first great stone had cut through the fog like the bow of a ship.

They planned the article which Lanice — with Ripley's help — should write for the 'Journal.' 'I shall begin,' she cried, 'with a quotation from Dr. Paisley — in fact the whole article will, in a way, be about *him*, only he will be much in the background, and the druids in the foreground.' He was enthusiastic, and, as he told her exactly where she could get the information about druids, Lanice lapsed into silence and had time to recall the strange, impossible fact, that only last night she had made up her mind to 'let him have it over with' to-day. Obviously she should have felt relieved to find that the Professor had no amorous secrets of which he needs must be delivered. It should have been pleasant for her to think that their beautiful friendship would not be overshadowed by any 'lusts of the body' (as Miss Bigley would have said). Obviously it was destined to remain 'on the higher plane.' She moved restlessly. She wished she knew of what he was really thinking — this large bearded man, sitting almost too close, in a subtly episcopal raincoat and wet American shoes. Was he too true to the memory of his dead wife Prunella, or had perchance Anthony Jones dropped some light remark to his friend that would make a *good* man hesitate before offering marriage? He had strode into the house of her being. He had found doors and opened them. He had wandered down corridors and upstairs and he had found one secret door locked against him. One holy of holies which his wise eyes and kind heart could never penetrate. A little locked room to which he had no key. What thoughts were behind that strong brow?

'Miss Bardeen,' he said rather solemnly, 'the vicar is evidently accustomed to nibbling hard candy during his rainy weather calls. In fact this inner pocket — well in out of the wet — is full of them. Allow me.'

They both rolled the durable sweets about their tongues. Lanice laughed slightly.

'Why do you laugh, Miss Bardeen?'

'I was thinking that you looked rather like Zeus and was expecting you to launch a thunderbolt, and instead of that you were fishing about in your pockets, trying to make up your mind whether or not you dared steal the candy.'

He looked at her with a sweet smile. Schooled as she was to Anthony's furious desires, she could not see anything more than affectionate consideration in his glance. When preparing for an unwanted proposal she had taken an obstinate pleasure in the ugliness of her borrowed clothes. Now, with what the

Professor would have considered a feminine change of heart, she began to encourage the black shawl to fall about her with grace and held it poetically to her breast with a long white hand. When he turned away his head to point out to her a herd of fog-wrapped ponies feeding close to the circle, she quickly seized the opportunity to sleek down her black hair over her ears with her characteristic gesture. She wished she knew whether or not her color had risen with the cool damp of the walk. Without color she never had a high opinion of her appearance. As Ripley turned his eyes to the lady beside him, he indirectly answered her thought.

'The fog, these old grey stones — this vast moor that we cannot see — only feel — certainly becomes you, Miss Bardeen. I can fancy myself pixie-led, you the pixie, and this the rendezvous of your kind.'

She rewarded this sop to her egoism with a side-wise goblin glance.

'Oh,' he said enthusiastically, 'look at me again like that. I could see then just the little girl you were at ten or eleven. Weren't you mischievous and secretive, and, pardon me, quite a *provoking* child? You see, I have children of my own.'

'If I was, no one bothered to slap me much. Papa was too interested in his classics, and Mamma — well, she never grew up enough to take a really *adult* interest in a child. She shook me if I got in her way, and how my long ringlets and my long legs all dangled — just like a little wooden doll!'

The man loved children and Lanice's picture

[216]

attracted him. 'Tell me more about your childhood.'

'Nothing, except I was always punished for the wrong things. I think,' she said rather piteously, 'that this started me all wrong. You see I've never believed in justice or right and wrong — the way other people seem to.'

'What were you punished for?'

'For silly childish mistakes — not for the things that really were *wrong*. It made me slightly — lawless.'

The statement sounded strange coming from such an obviously genteel lady. But the Professor did not laugh at her as another man might have done; he nodded and agreed very seriously.

'Shouldn't a child be punished for what she tried to do?' The man slipped quickly into the fascinating subject of the discipline of childhood. He told her at some length his theories in regard to Mary and Ridgewood, and, having finished with their moral and spiritual welfare, he laid down as well some drastic physiological laws for the young. It seemed that he had much care of his two children in their infancy. His wife had been delicate, so delicate she had rarely left her chamber after the birth of Ridgewood. 'She was far from well when I married her,' he explained sadly. 'I think now I would have hesitated — health means so much in marriage. And I will always feel that I really killed her — giving her my children to bear. But then, of course, I was young and less practical. If I should ever marry again I would not permit myself to love an incurable invalid.' He gave an approv-

[217]

ing glance to his companion, and Lanice knew that, in spite of her thinness and her fits of pallor, he had seen through her and knew her to be beautifully healthy and sound. He edged towards her slightly and she delicately edged away.

'I suppose,' she said demurely, 'marriage can be a very happy state.'

'Oh, my dear Miss Bardeen. It is the *only* one for most of us. There are a few exotic, perverse, and often unhappy creatures who can live best without it. I am sure Anthony Jones never either put anything into his marriage or got anything out.'

The sacred name had been spoken. Lanice tightened invisibly and wondered if she could trust her voice to question further.

'Do steal me another of Dr. Paisley's peppermints.' With this ball to click against her teeth she dared continue.

'The idea of Captain Jones as a family man is indeed a droll one — did *it* occur before or after he left India for Arabia?'

'Two or three years before. She was his colonel's daughter — charming, of course, or she never would have attracted Jones in the first place, but I fear of a very nun-like and cold temperament. I'm afraid Jones really scandalized Henry Longfellow the night we all dined together at the Red Horse Tavern by the frankness with which he protested that our civilization to-day makes women so pure it unfits them for matrimony — and then rather — ah, *caddishly*, referred to his own wife. There is a streak of almost incredible coarseness in the man, amazingly mixed with his fundamental innocence. But of course you never saw anything of the coarse side of his nature?'

Did the slight upward inflection of his voice leave a statement or a question? Lanice preferred to take it as a statement.

'Indeed,' she murmured, 'and where now is — where now is *she?*'

'Back here in England again, poor soul.'

She thought to herself cleverly, 'In a minute I will ask him where Anthony himself is.'

'Professor Ripley,' she began abruptly, 'may there not be something — oh, just a little truth in Captain Jones's indelicate remarks? I mean, isn't there such a thing as too great a purity even for women? After all, we are not merely souls.'

He laughed approvingly. 'You are, as always, almost incredibly right. But of course I knew you'd think that. It is splendid that you dare say it.'

'Why — why did you know — I'd think that?'

'Last night — the delicious absorption you felt while eating your roast beef and Yorkshire pudding, and then the almost seraphic look in your eyes when you see tarts and clotted cream.'

'Oh, Professor Ripley, you are calling me a glutton!'

'Far from it — your appetite is never so broad as.it is deep — if you understand what I mean, and then, do you realize, that when I asked you if you had liked Italy, you *first* told me about the *pastelletti* and *then* about the Uffizi!'

[219]

They both laughed together and Lanice felt kindly towards him.

'I believe,' he said rather seriously, 'that the truth of the matter lies somewhere between Captain Jones and his boasted sensuality and the heroes of "Hearth and Home" romances, who so mawkishly extol the spirit to the entire neglect of the body.'

There was a pause and Lanice, although by no means bored, feared that perhaps her companion was, and quickly suggested that they return to the house called Paradise.

'No, no — I beg of you. We will never be in so strange a place again — never so far removed from all the world. And I may never again have a live pixie for a companion.'

He settled himself rather obstinately on his stone. The conversation drifted to the tin mines of Cornwall and the Phœnicians and how *they* taught the Cornishmen the exquisite arts of clotted cream and saffron cake. He was impersonal enough to be slightly provoking to the young lady, who before she had left London had carelessly checked off this week-end as the one in which he should propose — and be declined. She gave him a tentative goblin look, and he, a mere man after all, edged nearer. The conversation swung back over the centuries and across the Atlantic. Quite without prodding from Lanice they began discussing her own fitness for matrimony. She eagerly denied any such fitness, but was piqued when he all too readily assented. Perhaps the Home was not her *métier*. This unexpected stand on his part threw her conversationally out of her stride. She had often indulged in such discussion with the stronger sex — always vowing that she was destined to the arts, the gentleman protesting that such charms as hers would never be permitted to fade in spinsterhood. Professor Ripley merely sighed: 'It will all depend on what you want of life, Miss Bardeen; if a career, I doubt if it can be very well combined with matrimony. Although Mrs. Stowe and George Eliot and certain others seem to make a success of it.'

Some instinct stirred within her. She drew in her breath suddenly, caught her lower lip between her teeth, shut her eyes.

'Oh, Mr. Ripley, it is suffocating — this fog. I feel dizzy — faint.'

But before the gentleman could offer the appropriate support of his muscular right arm, she had leaped up, swathed herself in her black shawl with an inimitable Spanish gesture, and floated off towards the pathway. Her better nature had reasserted itself before her lower had really landed her in those manly, and seemingly uneager, arms.

Sears Ripley, slightly astonished, strode after. Lanice, casting a backward glance over him, had a sudden flattering conviction that if she had followed her first instinct she would then and there have had the painful duty of giving him her 'no.' Now her pride made her even refuse the assistance of her escort's arm. He was very solicitous. 'But I am quite all right. I think the fog was especially heavy over the Hurlers. Now I feel infinitely well. . . . See!'

And the rash young lady whirled her heavy skirts about her and danced fantastically upon the path. In comparison to her wraith-like grace the man seemed to be shambling like a bear.

So the two moved like strange figures from a fairy story, through the fog and over the moor, following the intricacies of the footpath back to the house called 'Paradise.' Sears Ripley did not, and perhaps never would, 'declare himself.'

3

It was when she was in London that she felt most bitterly the insistence of Anthony Jones. It would be so easy to stop in at Clapyard & Dunster's and so un-embarrassing to ask her question of a blind man who never had seen her face. But she had strength to re-sist until, opening her American mail, her eye caught the final paragraph of Mr. Fox's weekly letter.

'And, by the way, do drop in sometime and ask Mr. Clapyard what arrangements we could make with his printers for the frontispiece of "Sands of Araby." That type of engraving is done so much better over there than here, I have decided to import if I can get reasonable terms. . . .'

The seven elderly spinsters with whom she ate her breakfast, and who instinctively disapproved of this exotic presence among them, sipped their tea and raised their eyebrows. Such absorption could only mean a love letter, and the creature was already seeing far too much of the tall, distinguished gentle-man with the beard.

She looked up from her letter and, although she knew, asked her breakfast companions where the offices of Clapyard & Dunster might be.

'Really, an English lady would hardly try to find it on foot, but then we are not accustomed to mixing in the business world . . .'

She got her cab and went, found Mr. Clapyard still in his pathetically soiled waistcoat, his cousin reading manuscripts out loud to him in her cutting voice. 'She cried to her natural protector "Help help" but there was no help. She leaped upon the rock and gazed upon the abyss yawning below her . . .'

'Ah,' said Mr. Clapyard, smiling indulgently, 'I'm beginning to yawn, too. Try another one, Effie.'

The girl clutched the amber at her throat. 'Would you like a long poem on the death of Wellington?' Then she looked up and saw Lanice looking in. 'Here is an *American*,' she said with rude emphasis. 'I suppose she has business with you.'

'If I may interrupt,' said Lanice gently, 'I'm Miss Bardeen, with a small matter of business from Mr. Fox.'

She took the chair offered her and discussed her errand and answered the publisher's questions about her adventures among the littérateurs. The cousin went to the window and stared out at the rain which had begun to course upon the dingy pane.

'And one more thing,' said Lanice, without glancing at the hostile back. 'I wish I had Captain Jones's address. I want to ask him about some captions.' She had taken the first great step with complete ease.

[223]

'Effie.'

'Yes.'

'Look out Captain Jones's English address for this young lady.'

'Yes, Mr. Clapyard.'

When the interview with Mr. Clapyard was over, the two young women went below to the little book-shop which in spare moments Effie helped to serve. From a drawer in a cluttered desk she drew out a stack of letters holding them so her guest might not see the writing. Jealousy suddenly flamed up in Lanice. Could it be that Anthony Jones, who had never written a line to her, had carried on a volumin-ous correspondence with this horrid little girl? Slowly and with a rude secrecy she read letter after letter, looked up and stared into Lanice's face.

'By now he must have sailed.'

'I am sure that he has not.'

'Why do you say that?'

'I feel that it is true.'

'Oh — of course — woman's intuitions. You are very much interested in Captain Jones?' The Ameri-can girl's eyes flashed and her light jaw settled like steel. There was something reptilian and dangerous in the slight swinging poise of her sleek head, on its long neck.

'Yes,' she said.

'Not a matter of captions?'

'No.'

'What if I refuse to give it to you?'

'I'll go back to Mr. Clapyard.'

[224]

The two young women gazed at each other in a white heat of hatred, jealousy, and suspicion. For a moment Lanice thought of snatching the stack of letters from the girl's hand. A young clerk with a pen over his ear came through the swinging door that led to the publisher's.

'If, ma'am, you'd like it,' he said, 'and intend to call upon the Laureate, Mr. Clapyard will give you a letter to introduce you.'

Lanice turned to go upstairs.

'You will tell Mr. Clapyard?' asked Effie.

'No.'

'Do not dare.'

'No —' and she smiled a very little. So defeated, she turned and again went upstairs.

CHAPTER XI

AND LESS OF JONES

HER ticket was bought for the Isle of Wight. She was going to Farringford to sup with the Poet Laureate, greatest of living poets. It was some five years earlier that Tennyson had written his 'In Memoriam,' had become Poet Laureate, and had, after seventeen years of tepid courtship, married the wistful lady of his choice. They had moved but recently to Farringford, deep in its damp hollow among cedars and chestnuts on the Isle of Wight. There, if anywhere, might the Bard find the solitude so necessary to his genius. But even here autograph collectors and celebrity hunters had sought him out. Countrymen of Lanice, even from Boston, so far forgot their breeding as to climb trees to stare upon him as he played battledore and shuttlecock with his wife. Expectant tourists dotted the downs that he had loved because of their solitude, and turned their opera glasses upon the great, dusty, slouching frame of the Poet.

Lanice came as an invited guest. There had been some correspondence between the Laureate and Clapyard. Then, almost as terrifying as a summons from the Angel of Death, came a little thin wisp of a letter from Mrs. Tennyson. Now a cab waited for her in his great name. A brief jouncy ride shook out of her head all the appropriate platitudes that she had been months in culling. Next Freshwater Bay with cliffs and sunset sea, and the drive to the eighteenth-century Gothic mansion. A giant behind a hedge in spectacles and a great cape trundled a wheelbarrow out from among the rhododendrons. Then the red drawing-room, and gentle, tired little Mrs. Tennyson rising nervously from her sofa. A soft grey gown, a soft, beseeching, wedge-like face, a woman who would give her life to protect the great man entrusted to her keeping, the woman who did more than any one else to build up the vast legend of his name. The two women fluttered towards each other. Lanice managed a few comments on the trip from Yarmouth Pier, a remark or two about the luxuriant verdure of the island.

Mrs. Tennyson expectantly glanced again and again towards the door behind Lanice, through which her giant might materialize. More breaks in the spineless chatter, more glances towards the door. A hush. ('Strange, Mrs. Tennyson seems as much awed by the idea of seeing Tennyson as I am.') And at the threshold stood the dark presence of the Laureate. The silence became awful as he advanced upon his guest. If it were he who had so recently trundled the wheelbarrow, his hands were now washed and his spectacles laid aside. He held in one hand a sprig of laburnum which he had intended to give the young lady as a keepsake, but already had forgotten. His dark, near-sighted eyes screwed her through as he waited Mrs. Tennyson's apprehensive introduction.

'Ah,' he growled amiably, 'you are by no means the first of your nationality to seek me out.'

[227]

Lanice, recalling with shame the tree-climbing opera-glass intrusions of her countrymen, was thrown into confusion. She gazed tongue-tied upon this swarthy, shambling man upon whose brow lay a Stygian darkness extraordinary for an Englishman.

'You have come a long way to see me,' he grumbled. 'Do you find what you expect?'

It was almost impossible to see in her host the author of 'Lady Clare' or 'The Talking Oak,' or even of airy 'Lillian.' The memory, the cadence of Ulysses, yes, this man looked like the author of 'Ulysses'; but not like any of his other poems that she could recall. She murmured some inappropriate thing about supposing him to be very fair, 'like a poet.'

'Oh, no,' he said in his cloudy way, 'we Tennysons are all foreign to look at, black-browed, black-blooded, too. ('Alfred!') Some even think we have gipsy blood, it may be Semitic.' ('Alfred!') The Poet shook his impressive head, half sternly, half playfully, at his wife who, after her two attempts to stop the turgid flow of language, relaxed again, invalid-wise, upon her sofa. A pause ensued which ached throughout the red room; even the Dante mask in plaster seemed to feel the horror of that hiatus and to be endeavoring to think of something to say. Lanice was dampened by an inelegant sweat and rendered inarticulate. The Laureate inquired for his dinner and his wife meekly slid from the room to urge on the servants.

'I have never heard of Mr. Fox,' he said abruptly.

'Emerson, of course, and Poe; and, let me see, there *must* be others, but never of a Mr. Fox of Boston.'

'He is very well known, even over here. I met many in London who . . .' she stopped, afraid that she was sinning against his omnipotence.

The Poet muttered something, probably a doubt as to the man's existence. Lanice tried to turn the conversation from Mr. Fox's seeming obscurity to Mr. Tennyson's own wide reputation. The subject interested her host.

'I gather my verses are very well known in the States? Every day I receive baskets full of requests for autographs.' He gestured towards a very feminine and underdeveloped escritoire where Lanice saw cards with his name in its characteristic heavy scrawl spread out to dry. Suddenly she had a terrible suspicion as to how it was Mrs. Tennyson exhausted herself, while the Poet tended the rhododendrons.

'I am afraid that our admiration for you is sometimes inconvenient.'

'Oh, no,' said the Poet grudgingly.

Dinner was announced, and when once seated before the saddle of mutton the Laureate's mood mellowed. Little tapers of conversation were lit, glimmered a moment, and were quickly blown out by some gruff comment from the Poet. The blackness of the ensuing silence was palpable. Had she been affected with the *mal de mer* crossing the Channel? Mrs. Tennyson finally attempted. Lanice replied with more delicacy than truth in the negative. This stirred the Poet's imagination, and with some pre-

[229]

liminary grunts he launched upon a story of seasick people. His Lincolnshire dialect grew so broad that the New England girl could not follow, but, judging by Mrs. Tennyson's frightened glances and futile attempts to stop him, Lanice decided that she was understanding quite enough for a delicate female. At the end came the Laureate's loud guffaw of approval, and a certain insecure sense of comfort descended.

By eight they were seated again in the drawing-room under the scornful Dante mask. The Poet, with some preliminary comments and a few words of sincere praise for 'my Queen,' at last began to read. Black and tousled and rough he looked, brooding over his clay pipe, sucking heartily at his port. As he read, his vowels lengthened prodigiously, and Lanice noticed his hollow *o*'s and *a*'s and the breadth and drawl of his mighty voice.

'Bury the greaaaat Duke with an Empire's lamen-taaaaation,' he read, 'To the nooise of the moooorning as a mighty naaaation.'

'Now,' he said at last, 'I will read you "Maude." You will never forget it.'

'Oooh, thaaat it were poooosible
After . . .'

The red drawing-room, the delicate lady upon the couch, the scowling grandeur of the Presence, and through it the powerful majestic voice of the Poet and the surging beauty of his lines. 'You will never forget it.'

[230]

But towards the end her pleasure was diminished by the thought that soon he would stop reading and an abyss of silence would open up into which she must throw some appropriate remark. It was well enough to say to other poets 'How tender!' but what can you say to a Tennyson?

'It is betteeeer to fight for the good than to raaaail at the ill;
  I have felt with my native land, I am oone with my kind
  I embrace the purpose of Gawd and the dooom assigned . . .'

The great voice dropped, and Beauty, which had beat her wings like a bird through the spaces of the red drawing-room, sank into silence. Tears gathered on her lashes. She was speechless. Under the excitement of the moment she had done the only right and appropriate thing — made the only comment that could have pleased the Poet. She had 'broken down.'

2

They gave her a big Gothic bed to sleep in. In the morning there was early tea and thin bread-and-butter. It was arranged that she should leave the house in a hired conveyance and catch her boat back before the Tennysons should awake. In the dull early morning she was glad there was no one to whom she must make a courteous and appropriate farewell — only the servants and the gardener's boy who stood by the phaeton and politely offered her a nose-gay of purple verbenas and pink sweet peas. 'And a letter, miss.'

'Not for me!' But she looked and saw her name

[231]

written out in a strange and very English hand. She had a dull presentiment that it might be from Anthony, although she knew his writing and this was not his. The thing was unsigned — ominously anonymous.

'In case it interests you, Mr. Jones has not yet sailed and will not until next Wednesday. He goes out on the Lux Benigna and stops first at the God-Begot House of Winchester.'

And Winchester lay but a few miles away up the Solent beyond Southampton. Winchester, upon its shallow bluish hills. It was very early in the morning and her heart was strong within her.

'I will go anywhere in the world but Winchester,' she said. 'I am not such a fool as to follow this man about. I will not go to London because Mr. Ripley is there — I cannot see him now, not until Anthony is indeed gone. I'll hide in the country and sketch thatched cottages and write a good article on the Tennysons.'

3

The sun was high and her heart was still strong.

'I will stay here in this village with only one street and the cunningest houses I ever have seen. It is best to be alone at times like this. Why did that dreadful girl send me his address? If I only have the courage to wait five days, he will be gone and all will be over. Now, keep up your courage and work — work — work.'

[232]

The sun set over the rolling North Downs and with the diminishing of light something weakened within her. She walked, a tragic figure, over the cobbled alien streets and counted to one hundred and back again and recited poetry so that she might not remember Anthony Jones.

The moon flooded her room. She pushed against the night with feverish, meaningless hands. She prayed to him as to a god. There was no strength left in her.

So it was, strong in the morning, but weakening every hour for three days and nights.

4

The House that Jack Built, and the House that God Begot ... 'that lay in the House that Jack Built.' Rat, rat eat malt, dog, dog bite rat ... to put in the House that Jack Built, and a maiden all forlorn that milked the cow with the crumpled horn. Why, it was only a few years ago Mamma used to read her that story out of the old dirty brown book with the ugly little pictures, and yet she had completely forgotten it.

'And Morab begat Nadab and Nadab begat Abidhu and Abidhu begat Aleazar and Aleazar ... Eleazar and Elezzar and Neleazar, and Neleazar — a weasel' ... she laughed, pleased with her own sacrilege and screwed her mouth up to whistle, but succeeded only in a tuneless blowing. She had definitely decided to go to Winchester and Southampton

[233]

and give herself the tragic pleasure of watching Anthony's ship drop down the Solent to the sea, and so pass forever beyond her. She told herself again and again that she did not want to see him — only his ship; that it was her duty to go to Winchester and learn what legends might still be current about Jane Austen; that the cathedral in Winchester was very fine; that the old city once had been the capital of England; and that here, by the Itchen, Izaak Walton had been accustomed to fish. There was every reason why she should go to Winchester. But already in her mind it had become a secret and delightful trip full of vague promises.

The God-Begot House, Winchester. It was time to start, now, immediately — oh, not a minute to be lost. 'Anthony, I fly, I come.' A dizzy rapture seized her — almost a nausea. Anthony — Anthony — she could see him quite clearly seated before the hearth of a strange inn, his back half towards her, his head thrown back with a pewter tankard of ale pressed to his lips. 'Anthony.' He turned as he heard his name spoken, rose and came to meet her. 'Anthony, I've come thousands of miles just to say good-bye! or, 'What, you! I had no idea that *you* were in England — I thought you were in Arabia.' But the first sentence was the one that came again and again to her lips — 'Anthony, I've come thousands of miles just to say good-bye.' In her day-dreaming she had forgotten that there had been any other motive to her European tour, had forgotten that it was not Anthony, but his ship and his inn, that she had wished

[234]

to see; she was only vibrantly conscious of him as a near physical presence. And Winchester could not be far; England was so silly and little. Her mood varied from extravagant gaiety to tearful melancholy; she cried over her breakfast as she spread the clotted cream upon her bread.

Again and again in the series of coaches and post-chaises that took her to Winchester, Lanice conjured up the scenes of the reunion, 'Anthony — I've come thousands of miles . . .' The back of his head or his profile always seemed so real she could put out her fingers and touch it; the moment before he turned to her at the sound of his name and her voice was as actual as any experience she had had with him; but there everything stopped. The truth bore cruelly in upon her that for some reason her memory had perversely failed her. She could not really *see* his face except from the side. She knew he had grey eyes and a sweetly sullen mouth. She knew how his tawny hair joined the two-inches of beard before either ear. She could have drawn his likeness — but she could not *see* his face. In anguish she realized that for the rest of her life he would never turn his face towards her, but sit in half-profile before a fire. Through the years she would come to know every hair upon the back of his head. She would see the cheek-bone, the curve of the jaw, the square, tight set to the shoulder. She would never — even in her memory — see the silver light of his sad grey eyes or the unsmiling droop of the mouth her mouth had craved. She clenched her hands in their yellow kid gloves, pressed her feet

[235]

against the floor of the coach, gritted her teeth —
shut her eyes until the gold Catherine wheels rolled
through the darkness. She would never again really
see him except in half-profile. Again and again she
went through many meetings with him, and her mind
and finally her body became so inflamed and her
heart so wrecked by her memory's inability to see him
as she wished, that she wrung her hands in the dusty
coach and prayed to God to hasten her and to hold
back the sailing of the Lux Benigna.

What the land was that she passed through or what
the sky or weather she did not know ... 'Anthony,
I've come thousands of miles ... and you will not
turn and look at me.' But the day was crisp and
golden, and the larks, hanging before the door of
Heaven, poured out their bubbling song as though
they were little miraculous pitchers forever emptying
and forever full. From Basingstoke to Steventon,
from Steventon to Stratton. Right now, and the road
turns down and the lights gleam self-righteously in
the cottages of good women — who never have heard
the magic name of Anthony Jones.

She was alone inside the coach, and although she
knew every word of the anonymous letter she must
read it. A change of horses. She leaned out, 'Boy,
boy, your lantern — for a moment.' Staring stupidly
at a woman he considered beautiful, the uncouth lad,
wrapped in an aroma of horse stables, leaned within
and held his lantern so that she might read.

She folded the letter and slipped it back into her
bosom. She sleeked her hair and swallowed.

'And to-day is only Saturday, isn't it?'

The boy smiled. His mouth grew and grew — his eyes diminished.

'Tell me,' she cried in a high voice — 'tell me — this is Saturday.'

'Why, M'lidy,' he said, 'if it weren't Saturday or Wednesday you wouldn't be here. The coach don't stop here any other days of the week. And if it ain't Wednesday — and it ain't — it must be Saturday.'

She gave him a shilling.

'I must see him!' she cried again and again. 'I don't care if it is only for a moment. I must see him! I will! God could not be so cruel as not to let me see him — even if he burns me for a thousand million years.'

From Stratton to Winchester.

'I must see him!' she cried. 'Oh, God — let me see him even if it is only the back of his head . . . and then you may burn me forever.'

And so, unattended by the gentle memories of Jane Austen or of Izaak Walton, she came into Winchester at midnight and drew up at the door of that house which was so strangely begotten. A narrow Tudor house, very venerable and zebra-striped. She beseeched the chambermaid. 'You *must* call me early. I must be in Southampton by noon.' She followed the big country girl up two flights of stairs and into a low blue room, cut by the eaves into the shape of a tent. 'Yes — thank you, and you *must* call me early.' She undressed and threw herself into a dream-racked poisonous sleep.

5

They had not called her and the sun was abroad. She jerked at the cross-stitched bell-pull and heard it jingle far away downstairs. Although unrefreshed by her night's sleep, it had at least quieted her. Soberly enough she set about her dressing, buttoning and buttoning layers of garments, lacing her stays, hooking and hooking, and finally, in the thinnest of dull rose wool and with her India shawl and her bonnet in her hand, she began to look impatiently about the upper hall for the chambermaid. The door opposite stood ajar, and within she heard a giggling and humming suggestive of servant girls. So she knocked, and the door swung open at her touch. There were two maids half-heartedly engaged in tidying up the empty chamber. One was busy about the washstand. The other was hunting between the great canopied bed and the wall.

'He swore to me this morning there was a mousey hole back in here'— and both the girls began to giggle. Then they saw Lanice looking very pale, but in some mysterious way very wealthy, in the door. The big girl who had promised to call her was not here. She could not scold them for the other girl's negligence; instead she said, 'I rang and rang — and no one came.' The girls subsided into a frightened silence. 'But never mind — just find out for me what time it is.' The girl who had been hunting for the mouse-hole, glad to get out of the room, curtsied and ran to do her bidding. The other one said apprehensively, 'Lady, your bell rings on the first floor and we are up here. I hope your lad'ship doesn't think us unmindful ...' deed, your lad'ship ...'

There was a faint and familiar smell about the room. Lanice felt slightly dizzy and sat upon the edge of the broad bed. 'Is there time for me to get to Southampton by noon?'

'Indeed, yes. One gentleman has left for there already — a big ship sailed early.' It would not be the Lux Benigna. She would not go out for three more days.

With a senseless childish cunning Lanice asked — 'Is his name — ah, *Pontifex* — quite a large family — called *Pontifex?* Red face and white whiskers?'

'Indeed, they must have lodged at the George. There are always a certain number for the George. They who don't know Winchester. It's bigger than we are — but 'deed, it's common and the maids are all huzzies — A friend of mine, m'lady ...'

'Or was it ... let me see ... a Mr. Jones?' The maid surprisingly came into life. Her thick bright cheeks eddied into unguessed dimples.

'Oh, Mr. Jones — that man — yes, m'lady. He's been here for five days — and he's always talking to me and Lucy about the mouse-holes under his bed. ... And we always must see to it that his bed is warmed for him — he hates our damp English beds — he says heathen countries have spoiled him for damp.'

'And his ship — when does his ship sail?'

[239]

'Why, she's gone out already, m'lady — they'd never miss the morning tide for a big thing like her. The Captain left by daybreak — seems like you must have heard him.'

Then she felt that she had always known she would not see Anthony again. She murmured incoherently about the Pontifex family — but felt she deceived this servant no more than she had deceived Clap-yard's little cousin — there seemed to be a strange freemasonry between the lovers of Anthony Jones the world over, and they were unable to keep from giving each other the secret sign. She added slowly and with dawning wonder in her voice:

'But I did hear him.' The slam of a door, the clump, clump of boots — these things had come to her in a dream, only realized, never heard. That was why she had dreamed of the bronze boxer Mamma had sent her for the stereoscope, and thought that he was trying to get in the window — clump, clump, clump — his massive metal feet . . .

'M'lady, you have had no tea yet. I'll fetch you some and thin bread-and-butter.'

Lanice thanked the girl and listlessly sat upon the edge of the bed and stared at the round dent in the pillow his head had made.

To her feverish hands it seemed that some of his bodily warmth still lingered in the tumbled linen of his bed. She shut her eyes and rocked her narrow body, opened them and looked again upon the pillow marked by the shape of his head. She stared, striving vainly to conjure up the true and living memory of

[240]

his face. Incredible that this inanimate object that had so recently borne the impression of his being could so quickly forget, yet she — so far from inanimate — had been unable to carry his vision. Delicately — lest she break the mould — she pressed her face into the pillow.

6

'It is nine o'clock, lady,' said the servant, returning. 'No, don't move yourself because of me. Lucy is making you some tea.' The young woman, so fastidiously wrapped in thin wool, sat pale and speechless in an armchair while the maid deftly stripped the upper sheet and blankets from the bed. Lanice cried out in terror.

'That! What is that! Oh, what is it?' The maid laughed and lifted from the foot of the bed a red earthenware jug in the coarse semblance of a pig.

'It's just a bed-warmer. A big bottle filled with hot water — least, it was hot last night when Lucy put it in. The Captain *would* have the damp taken out of his bed. But bed-warmers shaped like pigs indeed are rare.'

The ugly squat red animal drawn from Anthony's bed had for the instant a hypnotic fascination. Lanice, mouth and eyes open, standing upon her feet, shrinking back from the sight, put out her arms automatically to touch and then to hold this water-filled clay idol of an ugly god. The thing gave off a small, stale warmth.

The pig — if so crude a thing could be called a

pig — had little detail or feature to mark its species. The legs were turned in upon the body in an embryonic manner; only the snout and close-curled tail were truly porcine.

Lucy entered with her breakfast tray, and if she were surprised to see a beautiful great lady — perhaps a disguised countess — holding so humble an object she did not show it.

'Will you have your tea, here, m'lady, or in your chamber or down in the drawing-room? And I am to tell you that when you have had your tea, why, there's a gentleman to see you — waiting in the lower hall. A Mr. Ripley he says he is.'

The red pig slipped from the lady's arms. The broken crockery and liquid contents splashed upon the floor. Lanice looked down in amazement to see the leering smile of the snout rolling some six feet away from the curled tail. The tepid water had splashed everything — leaving dark welts upon the lady's elegant gown and soaking the cotton stockings of the maid.

'I'll go down.' Without waiting to dry her flounces or to sleek the hair she had disordered against Anthony's pillow, she fled below to Professor Ripley. The maid, still carrying the tea and the thin bread-and-butter, ran after her like a comic figure in a play.

7

Lanice had not stopped to think either what she should say nor what the temper of this meeting should

[242]

be. Ripley had thought of nothing else for days. The two met only to stare and stammer, to look down and draw apart. The girl found herself first. She drew up haughtily and, holding to the newel post with one hand and clenching the other in the folds of her skirt, she asked abruptly:

'You know why I came?'

The man nodded and piteously turned away his eyes.

'I know why — Lanice.'

Then he in his turn straightened himself and asked the same defiant question — flinging it at the girl's feet, like a token for her either to stamp upon or to pick up.

'And you — you know why *I* came?'

She knew — and the reason humbled and soothed and hurt her. She answered very gently, 'Yes, I know.'

The man's love wrapped about her and strangely at this strange moment seemed more real than Anthony's desires. In spite of all he had not said on Bodmin Moor she knew that he loved her and would die to make her happy. She did not know the anguish or the turmoil of soul and body he had endured during the last four days nor how with the determination to go to Winchester — something — some power of self-control — had broken within him. He turned away from her slightly.

'I cannot any longer pretend to be your friend — Lanice, because I am really your lover — I think I have always been . . . but that can wait. Now is not the time.' He did not expect or receive an answer. She stood and patiently watched him as he twisted the big bone buttons on his dark blue coat. 'I know you look upon me as a friend, and I know that it is easier sometimes to make hate and aversion over into what is popularly called "love" than it is — friendship. Well, Lanice, we will see. There are still a good many years ahead and in the meantime we can continue to be friends — can't we?'

'I hope so — that is, as long as you realize there can be nothing else.'

'At least I will act as though I realized it. Of course the present moment — is hardly the one I would have normally chosen to tell you how much — how very much — I have come to care for you — Lanice, but it's said now and why should I apologize? I hardly realized myself how much you — meant to me — until a chit in Clapyard's office told me that you probably would go straight from the Tennysons' to Winchester. You did, didn't you?'

'No, not straight.'

There was a troubled silence. Lanice broke it by saying, 'I think I had best drink my tea now, and then why couldn't we walk over the town? . . .' She hid the quiver of her lip against the edge of the teacup. 'The town, they say, is most worth while.'

'What would you like to see?' he asked humbly.

He knew that she did not care to see anything really, but admired the brave face she showed the world. Poor child! Most women would have been

[244]

wistful — overcome with grief — prostrated, offended.

She sat upon the lower stair and sipped her cold tea and, as she raised her eyes over the teacup rim, she smiled at him.

'I'd like to see anything that has anything to do with Jane Austen and I want to see the Itchen and the cathedral and the school where they sing "Dulce Domum."'

'We had better start pretty soon if we are going to see all that — hadn't we?'

'I'll get my bonnet and my shawl — and my sketch-book. You'll give me time to make a few sketches, won't you?'

'Why, all you want,' he responded, but his heart bled to see how her eyes, which he had always considered long but not very large, had, through the strange alchemy of grief, grown to be enormous and meltingly tender like a madonna's.

She did not want a carriage, she wanted to walk, and he matched his heavier step to her light one and carried her sketch-book and her copy of 'Pride and Prejudice' and an absurd and delicious parasol, made of black chantilly lace, through which the sun might cast shadows of lace flowers and bow knots. He was versed enough in women's clothes to realize that the thing might be wickedly becoming to Lanice. It vaguely hurt him to think that if she were walking through Winchester on Anthony's arm she would unfurl this delicate weapon of her sex and for him display its coquetry. But he took heart to think she

[245]

cared enough for him to take it with her. As she gravely stared at the cathedral, he as gravely stared at her. In the black and dull rose of her costume the turquoises in her earrings thrilled him with their vivid blueness and he noticed upon her finger a massive gold and turquoise ring that he was sure she must have put on when she went upstairs to get her bonnet.

Would she ever forget Anthony? And like an answer came her words, barely audible from the shadow of her black hat.

'Anthony is gone now — forever. I'm glad I did not get here in time to see him. I tried, and I prayed . . .'

'You mean you did *not* see him?'

'I was too late.'

The man began to laugh and his laughter hurt the girl.

'Why do you laugh?'

'I prayed, too. For once God answered my prayers. But I thought he had answered yours.'

CHAPTER XII

WITCHES AND DEVILS TORMENT HER

1

THE world rang hollow underfoot and the stars that
swarmed by night seemed as near as the people with
whom she talked by day. She found herself alone and
in a void. She ate, slept, but she did not know what
she ate nor why she slept. Her work progressed with
an almost automatic nicety and she felt that her
mind had been clarified and sharpened, but that
everything else was dulled. A dam seemed to have
been thrown across the easy stream of her existence
and back of it the waters were rising and rising . . .
She moved, but she moved under a shadow conscious
always that something soon would happen. What?
Nothing!

Little by little the stack of letters of introduction
grew less and the material forwarded to the 'Journal'
began to assume book proportions. Mr. Fox was
enthusiastic, but why did she not look up Miss
Champion? Her work was so immensely popular in
the States and she seemed to be the last left who
wrote in the Radcliffe tradition of ghosts, dark
castles, rattling chains and werewolves. 'Of course
she is in no sense an artist — just a literary workman,
but you might have fun.'

This rather obscure 'workman' and no artist
proved to be the hardest to reach of all the great

names. It took much correspondence with her London publishers, Messrs. Double & Pepys, to discover
that she made her home with Lady May Bracey,
Square Mount Castle, Porlock Weir, North Devon.
Such an address and the prospects of a castle and a
Lady moved Lanice deeply. Double & Pepys inti-
mated that Miss Champion would see her, and so she
set out.

The train took her only to Bath, and from there, in
whirling post-chaises and coaches, she jingled and
tooted across England. A Roman road shot, like an
arrow, over the Mendip Hills. Barrows and tumuli,
ferns waist-high, stunted trees, sheep, rain, wind, and
little sun; but always the sway of the coach, the smell
of wet bracken, the rumble of wheels, the clatter of
hoofs, the snap of a whip. Dolls' villages, dolls'
churches, twisting dolls' lanes. And so on . . .

After the steep drop down into the Vale of Avalon,
the coaches grew poorer, the horses shaggier and
smaller, and the dialect of the natives almost incom-
prehensible. In spite of difficulties with speech, the
inns, with their sanded floors, red earthen jugs, and
huge beds, were hospitable. Exmoor at last. The
coach ran part of the way in a groove between green
hedges, bristling with life, sometimes rising eighteen
feet above the roadbed. The hedges shut one in.

A broken axle, a mired coach, the heaving, wild-
eyed horses jumping furiously against their collars,
harnesses breaking, and an unexpected night in a
lonely farmhouse, where the owls in a walnut tree
hooted all night, and no one slept.

Then the Severn Sea and across the water the white cliffs of Wales. The coach rolled into Porlock Weir. She stayed at the old Ship Inn. There was a rough shingle beach, where the tides sucked and pounded and above were sea-gulls against a low, leaden sky. A few fishermen's houses, loaded like Easter bonnets with masses of flowers. A cobbled street and the old white plaster inn cozy under its hat of thatch.

A certain number of excursionists, free souls, who liked to tramp, came across the moors carrying knapsacks. They knew this inn well and its famous cider.

2

The long journey, the continual jouncing, and the excitement had tired Lanice. She was glad to lie in her whitewashed room under the eaves deep sunk in her billowy bed which the chambermaid warmed with hot stones. 'I'll stay here,' she decided, 'for weeks — if I want to. I may stay for months.' There was a delicious sense of peace and homely comfort. She would explore this wild romantic country alone and on foot. She would eat her sweet bread and fresh butter, drink her tea before the wide fireplace in the common room below, and sleep the clock around in this huge warm bed.

Her first walk was through the park-like woods along the cliffs to the wee church of Culbane, and so on to Square Mount Castle — no castle at all, only a rambling stone country house almost hidden in beech and oak. The next day she hired the only pair of strictly 'pleasure' horses in the village and in a ridiculous canopied landau she was driven over to present her letter. The sweating 'pleasure' horses pulled up to the doorway and a footman instantly presented himself. Miss Champion — very good, indeed. If the lady would wait, Miss Champion shall be informed. The ancestral clocks struck four and then five. She still waited. A maid came to tell her that Miss Champion could not be disturbed — begged to be excused — nor would she be at liberty the next day. The following week . . . ? Would Miss Bardeen leave her address? A second maid arrived with the message that yes, Miss Champion will see Miss Bardeen — sometime. When that time came she would send for her — possibly the day after to-morrow. Lanice gave the inn as her address and noticed the maids' amazement. 'Fancy,' they would say to each other, 'and she looked a lady.'

'Your tea, Miss,' one of them suggested courteously. 'Have you had your tea as yet?' But Lanice declined. The prettiest of the maids smiled diffidently, 'Don't be put out, Miss, they are all like that — these lady-companions, hard and haughty. I think it's because her has to so bend herself to m'lady — and then her's a great author, too.' Miss Champion sent down another maid — now she would be willing to see the representative of 'Fox's Journal.' Lanice, provoked by the lady's whims, sent back word she could stay no longer.

Lanice settled herself at her inn. She felt a strange sense of waiting during the next few days. Waiting for the clouds to blow away and the sun to pour out over the purple moors and heaving sea; waiting for Miss Champion to send for her; waiting for a letter from Mr. Fox; waiting for the impossible — for the return of Anthony Jones.

Her favorite walk was through Porlock Village up towards Hurlstone Point. The foreland was cut by deep coombes which held their purple shadows like green glass beakers half full of wine. Heather, gorse, ferns, crimson foxgloves. To the south the whole land rolled away into Exmoor. She met sheep and shepherds, but few others. The country was rustling with life — moor ponies, birds, foxes, rabbits, and once she started a stag. She walked every day until her feet, flimsily shod in long black slippers, ached, her voluminous skirts and petticoats were muddied, her hair, caught by the clutching branches of the furze, tumbled down her back. Her face and hands were scratched and her mouth was stained with berries.

3

Once, intoxicated by the first day of sunshine, she went farther to the loneliest place she had ever seen — almost to Minehead. The red, ribby cliffs which she climbed dropped dizzily into the sea. But even here the sheep had been. Her path — if it were a path — stopped before a fortress of furze. She found that the sheep had made a hole through the thicket. Their continual passing had rounded it and each sheep had left toll from his fleece so that it was lined delicately as a bird's nest with the wool from their bodies. Lanice, bending, peeked through this strange tunnel. The sun, which was before her, caught in the fibre of the wool and made it radiant as a halo. She got herself halfway through easily enough, but her big stiff skirts were unmanageable. Torn and dishevelled she struggled through, leaving as her admittance fee threads of her black hair on the thorns that held the sheep's wool.

She looked about her — a secret little bower, a darling fair place — which she knew to be hers — a place she had crossed the Atlantic and pursued the proud Miss Champion to Devonshire to discover. As she lay there in the sun and listened to the waves lapping far below and to the nervous activity of the birds, her mind went back, not to Anthony nor to the articles she had so valiantly written for Mr. Fox — not to Roger with his quietude and his fever — nor to the broad bed and good food waiting for her at Porlock Weir, but to the witch women of Salem. Her mind, with its curious focusing power, suddenly was able actually to see them — the court-room, old Tituba, the frenzied, afflicted children. She could see their familiar spirits, the magic yellow birds, the black man, and the detestable rites of the Black Sabbath — 'Hu-hu-hurahu!' — it was thus that the witches summoned the Devil who was also their lover.

A story came into her head. It was called 'The Tale that is Told.'

In the dusk of dawn Gideon, the grey tomcat, was the first to wake. The mice were still frolicking in the corn crib, the birds had begun to chant. 'Quick,

Gideon — take up your duties as a cat.' A little girl sat up abruptly in her trundle bed. She had been sound asleep the moment before, now she was quiveringly awake. Over on the big red press, pewter plates and platters began to shimmer. The spinning-wheel was a great spider web. Nearer, so near her little hand could reach the valance, loomed the great bed on whose deck were stretched the sleeping bodies of Goody and Goodman Bale. Many times before she had awoken at this weird dawning hour and sat thus unreal in an unreal world staring at objects until they became part of her own enchantment. Strange tiny faces began to twist among the onions knotted in long strings from the hewn rafters — hobgoblin faces grimacing. Sometimes a little claw-like hand no larger than a man's thumb-nail would pick at the knots that held it. A whisper at the door — the blow of leaves, the rustles of a skirt. What skirt is that? Not of this world, surely. What woman taps her fingers on the pane? A hag from Hell. Now the red coals begin their cunning winking. The child sees the salamander sprawled contentedly in the fire . . .

Not frightened — not afraid. They are her people. Mine, mine, mine. And she thinks of her father and mother who burned for their witchcraft in France . . .

Two hundred witches had burned that day. The ashes had fallen upon the clean decks of the English boat at harbor there, and Captain Bale, a kind man, finding this witch's cub hungry and sobbing about the locked door of a cottage, picked her up and carried

her back to his wife who believed the little thing to be
the child of the Devil. And so the little creature came
secretly to think herself. She could remember once
gathering nuts in the woods with her mother and a
fine gentleman, appearing in a great flash of light,
drew marks upon her forehead. Or did she dream it,
or was it a story that her mother had told her? She
believed herself signed to the Devil and that he would
come to her — even in this distant new land. Secretly
and joyously she worshipped her god amidst all the
Puritans of Salem. And at last he came — her god and
her devil. She met him one night in the birch woods
and knew him by a sign that he bore. He was really a
sailor charged with piracy hiding for his life. She
never saw him except at night. When she saw the
tiny monkey which he carried about with him inside
his shirt, she knew he was the Devil himself. This
hobgoblin was 'the sign,' the proof of its master's in-
fernal origin. (Lanice shut her eyes and saw the tiny
creature's head against the broad brown chest. It
peeked out wistfully from the open shirt as a lady
might from between portières. One little hand was
clutched in the coarse hair of the man's chest.) The
whole was a thing remembered. A terrible nightmare.
It gripped her until her body grew rigid and her
clenched hands white. Then there was the terrible
end. The young witch, happy in the knowledge that
she had seen her god, dying on the dirty straw of the
town jail, while Mr. Noyes and Mr. Parris prayed
and exhorted her and the village wives whispered outside, smelt brimstone, saw wonders, and watched for

[254]

the foul fiend to arrive and carry off his misbegotten imp. Horns it would have and little hoofs like a kid, and a bit of a tail with a spike on the end. 'Eh, no wonder the witch girl died; 'twould be a fearsome thing for mortal frame to bear a thing horned and tailed — as if a human body was not bad enough.' They were disappointed, for she died before her strange delivery. The look of beauty on her face after her miserable death mystified them. And Mr. Noyes and Mr. Parris still prayed.

This was 'The Tale that is Told.'

That night she sat wrapped in her bedclothing, bending before the one candle, writing with cramped eager fingers. At three she went to bed and slept heavily until ten, then woke struggling to remember — a dream — or was it a dream! The paper lay scattered about the floor. It could not be much good. She believed that she could only write well (as she had written her literary articles) by writing slowly. The little green house in the furze that you come to through a fleece-illumined halo — it could not have existed. Her eyes ached, her fingers were lame. She turned over and slept again.

4

That afternoon Miss Champion sent the baronial barouche and a coachman and a footman and a courteous note. If Miss Bardeen would return in the equipage Miss Champion would be pleased to see her. Lanice instructed the maid to tell the footman that Miss Bardeen was elsewhere. She began another story. Surprising how well she knew the time and people.

She felt a freedom in moving amongst them, she was too self-conscious to have realized in a story of her own times. All her carefully nurtured niceties, all the 'ideals' that Miss Bigley had taught her — all was gone but the curiously grim stage that she had set herself and something alive and burning that she remembered from Anthony Jones. So completely did she come under the spell of this new art she did not leave the inn for five days, and ate and slept but little. She was dark about the eyes, her face white, drawn, and luminous. The kindly landlady was afraid she was ill. Miss Champion came in person. From her bedroom window Lanice indifferently watched a meagre, hatchet-faced old lady, who twitched her bonnet strings and ruffled her black silks as a turkey cock rustles his burnished feathers.

She never again found the sheep path through the furze, and she never again wrote a story of the Salem witches. For better or worse her four stories were written.

First was 'The Tale that is Told.' It had the precocious genius and weakness of a first-born. Next was 'The Salem Satyr,' pastoral almost, with the winds of spring snapping over the hills like whips, and maple leaves unfolding their tiny hands to you. Then 'The Whisperer' next, a weaker brother of 'The Tale that is Told,' a little saner, a little gentler, without either the faults or grandeur of the first story. Last was 'The Amber Witch,' and her poisonous power over men.

When at the end her feet in their red-heeled shoes swung six feet above the rocks of Gallows Hill, one felt that even if by mistake the judges had done well and that the woman should hang.

Next Lanice began to eat and sleep. Languorously she sank herself into an almost sensuous lassitude. She read any books she found about the inn and did not care how dull they were. Nothing mattered.

But she found that the pent stream of her existence had broken its dam. Now she was as she had always been, and people were nearer to her than the stars, and the world no longer rang hollow. August was well upon her and soon she must go back to Boston.

CHAPTER XIII

SHE KEEPS A GOOD MAN DANGLING, BUT —

1

SHE looked about her little office, grown dusty in her absence, and settled herself before the waste-basket to sharpen pencils. Below her was School Street with its rattle of equipages and beyond was Tremont Street and the Common. The lacing trees were little by little releasing their drying leaves and under them and through the leaves criss-crossing on little walks, stepping positively to and fro — were the Bostonians!

No chair in the world as comfortable as the old red-leather one in which she had once sat for months drawing fashion-plates and writing genteel stories for female consumption. She was glad that they had come out under a *nom-de-plume* — even under many *noms-de-plume*. Of course they were a disgrace, but she felt no personal regret for them. They were written by some one else, who, although she looked and talked like her, had thought other thoughts and had really been quite another person. And that was a year ago.

'I think,' she said to herself, 'it is because I really care so much more for life than I did a year ago — that is why I cannot distort it now. You can't, if you like people well enough. You don't want to make them out different from what they really are.

I don't want heroes and heroines any more — people are quite good enough.' She realized abruptly that if this were true she would probably never again write the ordinary salable story, for which she could be sure of a place in a dozen different magazines. What, then, would she write or would she never write again? Her 'Intimate Sketches' had, she knew, not only been acceptable to Mr. Fox's high standards of taste, but had been the outstanding feature of the 'Journal' for the last six months. Letters came every day addressed to 'Tempus Fugit.' Most of them began, 'Dear Sir,' but there were several 'Dear Mr. Fugit'; and one lady, after some literary discussion, had facetiously addressed the unknown critic as her 'Dear Tempus.' Why she had taken this name she could not say . . . something to do with Roger Cuncliffe. And as she looked out at the Common she saw the sky was beginning to color faintly in the west, far out beyond the Back Bay, the blue hills, and the reaches of the Charles River. She thought of the statues in Roger Cuncliffe's Italian garden, and how in such a light the nymph assumed the tints of life. Who now had the little Villa Poppea, now that Roger lay stretched under the earth he had adored. Had they put the satyr's head back again? Had they dismissed the servants and sold the pony and broken the delicate fine Venetian goblets?

She might study, become a scholar even as Sears Ripley would wish, and give up fiction. But she had not a scholarly nature and she knew it. Well, then — fiction. But not for the 'Godey's Book,' not for

'Hearth and Home.' She thought of Porlock Weir, and the old inn, and the proud Miss Champion. She thought of the wet moors and the sun coming out over the Severn. She thought of the four stories that had come suddenly and flamed across her sky. They had scorched her body with their intensity, and had left her when they were written weak and shaken but sweetly content. Writing them had been extraordinarily like loving Anthony Jones. It burned you and you suffered, but when it was over you knew happiness. And it was over — Anthony Jones was over. He was as much gone as though he had never been. That last terrific flare of passion that had driven her to pursue him to Winchester had burned out. She pressed her hands to her temples . . . 'Suppose I should marry Mr. Ripley?' It was the hundredth time that day she had had that thought.

She never doubted her witch stories were good. Violently colored things — dark and angry in places, but with a fierce bright pagan joy in them, too. 'The Tale that is Told,' with its theme of demon-lover. The miserable death of the young witch on the dirty straw of the town jail . . . it was a terrible story; so were they all. In spite of their fantastic trappings they satisfied her as in some way being true to life as she knew and loved it. Their roots were firmly woven in the rich dark soil of humanity, even if their flowering was exotic. The 'Hearth and Home' stories had been rootless, their flowers had been of paper. But what publisher would care for these dark mysteries? Perhaps Mr. Fox would advise her. 'The Whisperer'

[260]

was the least 'objectionable.' With its wistful child hero it was vaguely reminiscent of Hawthorne. This was, she knew, the weakest of the lot.

She told Mr. Fox an elaborate and clever story — how, while in London a young man who had read Captain Poggy's great historical study of Salem witchcraft, had sought her out and given her a story which he had based upon the book. She looked Mr. Fox straight in the eye and admitted that she had added paragraphs here and there — especially the one about the spring flowers, the little cold hepaticas with their furry leaves and chill blue faces. The dainty anemones — out too early in their muslin frocks. She had also copied it for him. Intelligent in the ways of authors, Mr. Fox all but winked at her. He took 'The Whisperer' home with him, and in the morning reported it was by far the best thing that she had ever done — even better than that splendid chapter in the Poggy history, or the really masterful 'Intimate Sketches.'

'Miss Bardeen,' he said, 'if you can do this, there is no reason why you cannot do anything — including making this story twice as good again. You couldn't have written this a year ago. Did you pray upon the grave of Emily Brontë, or did she send you a bit of the stuff that dreams and "Wuthering Heights" are made of? I don't know what it was made your spiritual wings to sprout — if you were a man I would say, "*Cherchez la femme*" — I can't pretend to guess why you so suddenly burgeoned into life — but if you know, go and thank — him.'

[261]

How readily this wise man put his finger on the truth! Lanice withdrew in confusion. He called her back.

'Now I am going to disappoint you. Although this tale, even as it now stands, is really superior to most of the stories in the "Journal," I cannot offer to undertake it. You put your poor little hero through such a parcel of tricks (actually I sometimes think women are positively cruel), and at the end, although he sees the nymphs in the birch trees on a spring night and has felt the satyr in the wind buffeting the house — in spite of all these wonders he has seen you leave him in such an abnormal state he is really little short of idiocy. In other words, your story is one of disintegration — a study of morbid mentality ending in breakdown.' Then he added kindly: 'But it is rather splendid. I'm glad that you wrote it. It is much better to start out with a runaway Pegasus and then train him down than to straddle a brewer's lumbering dray horse. Even if you can whip the thing up to a gallop, it is not its natural gait. It always has a heavy foot. Go to it, Miss Bardeen. Write like the Devil — even about the Devil if you want to. Go to it, and please always feel free to show me what you do.'

Although she appreciated his kindness and wisdom, she did not show him the other stories. So 'The Amber Witch' and 'The Salem Satyr' and 'The Tale that is Told,' soon joined by 'The Whisperer,' lay in the bottom of her dresser drawer. By Christmas she had almost forgotten them.

2

There was always in her head the refrain, 'Suppose I married Mr. Ripley . . .'

Her 'Sketches,' enlarged from her journal and illustrated by her sketch-book, were published. In a minor way their success was brilliant. The men and women of whom she wrote were amazingly alive. The work was clear and a little hard, sometimes coldly epigrammatical. Ripley, in spite of the sphinx-like silence he had maintained towards all personal matters since that day, months ago in Winchester, expressed himself freely and often on the subject of her book. He saw Lanice almost daily, either in her office or more often in the Poggy drawing-room. It was by his advice that she had discarded the *nom-de-plume* and had written frankly over her own name. But a title-page is an unfeminine and doubtful place for a lady's name. Lanice first realized this in Smith Scollay's agitation.

'If you must write books,' he had said haughtily, 'you might have satisfied yourself with "Tempus Fugit." I cannot see how a ladylike girl like yourself can want the whole world gaping at her name. And then, Lanice, this is a *heavy* book for you to have written. Why were you not content with those pretty romances you used to write? I must confess that that seems to me much more in keeping with your character — and gender. Why, people are saying you were actually sarcastic about the Tennysons.'

'Oh, no, I loved the Tennysons — but he frightened me so much.'

Lydia, who had accompanied her handsome young uncle to the Poggy Mansion, crossed over and kissed Lanice's sleek hair. 'It's a lovely book. I'm proud to see your real name on it. Smith — the old bear — is jealous.'

'No, not jealous,' said Smith, flinging up his spirited head — 'only I was thinking — suppose one *married* a lady authoress, what, then, is the etiquette? Does one's *own* name go on the title-page, predicated by a Mrs., or does she merely ignore one's existence and retain her own name for such purposes? I can't say which idea offends me most.' Lydia whispered in the authoress's ear 'Jealous!' But Lanice knew it was something more fundamental. Although Lydia was, as Mrs. Andrews expressed it, as much 'underfoot' about the Poggy house as ever, Smith Scollay's calls gradually dwindled away and at last ceased. He was, so Lydia told her friend, very restless and he had been drinking too heavily. He had been seen much in New York on certain fast and fashionable occasions.

3

Lanice, shamming a bad cold, stayed in bed, although the Captain had limped off to Sabbath service in King's Chapel, and Pauline, she supposed, had gone early by horse-car to Roxbury to worship there locally with her wonderful Miss Gatherall, freshly returned from her noble work among the Southern negroes. She had her coffee served grimly by Mrs. Andrews and, having submitted to a rather becoming red flannel about her neck, enjoyed the lazy luxury of a morning in bed. But when the sun was high enough to fall across the footboard and half of the ruffled muslin counterpane, Pauline, skimpily dressed in rusty black, made her appearance.

'Oh — why, Pauline, I thought you were in church.'

'No — I think I have a touch of *your* cold.' She looked suspiciously at the luxurious young lady in bed.

'It's hardly a very bad cold, Pauline,' Lanice assured her guiltily; 'I shall be up for dinner.'

'What are you going to do this afternoon?'

'Why, nothing I know of — write letters — perhaps.'

'And to-morrow — and the day after — Lanice, what are you going to do with your life?'

'Oh, I'm going to live it. . . .' Lanice's voice rose either from irritation or from the pleasant prospect of living a life.

'You are now twenty-six. If you live to be seventy, it will be all over before long — then what?'

'Then *I* shall be dead. But I do hope there will be others who will enjoy the same things that I have enjoyed — like the red salamanders in the woods and mice whiskers — and people, and —'

'Men —' added Pauline rudely.

Lanice put her slender arms over her head and laced her long fingers back of her neck. She answered this gibe seriously.

'And men — I don't know why it is that I really love men — and trust them . . . They have never shown any real reason why I should. Some people might think that I had been treated badly by them — but the way I feel towards them is deeper than experience.'

'I know what it is,' blazed Pauline, 'at heart you are a slave-woman — you are the true product of generations of women whom men ruled with a whip! You bow before the tyrant, you kiss the hand that strikes you — yes, and the mouth that tells you you are only a live doll — a plaything for the lords of creation!' Pauline's color rose — either from her anger or at the erotic suggestion of kissing a tyrant's mouth. 'But, Miss, please remember that before the human male so came into ascendancy there was a time when women ruled the world. And when you get down among the spiders and the octopuses the male is hardly visible — and by the time you have reached — I think it is the jellyfish, he is — extinct.'

'How pathetic!' said Lanice — who had not entered very deeply into the spirit of the game.

'But there are women — noble, high-minded women — who, I am sure, are descended, not from the slave-women of history, but from the great free female rulers of an earlier date. . . . So in a few years you will be quite ready to let them put a weeping willow and an urn at your head and write your epitaph.'

'Yes, something like this —

> 'Here lies the body of Lanice Bardeen,
> The recklessest girl that ever was seen.'

'Humph, they will hardly call you a *girl* at seventy-odd. But you have so much ability and yet you are ready . . .' Pauline's hands clenched . . . 'to let it — *rot*. Rot, I say — rot.'

Lanice answered meekly. 'I know I have some ability. Perhaps if I were a man I could do something with it. There is something wrong with women and I can't put my finger on it — only feel it, in myself and in others. It isn't that we haven't the brains — or even the emotional force — but I'm afraid we are too sensible. Frankly, I'd much rather live a comfortable life now — while I am alive — than starve in a garret and be worshipped for centuries. Or suppose success came during my life. What pleasure to me that every one stop and gape when I come into a room or climb trees with opera glasses to spy upon me — the way they do at poor, dour Tennyson? We lack the divine childishness of men that drives them to sacrifice their own health as well as their families for such phantoms as art and fame. I think the great artists never outgrow adolescence — never grow up . . . see things disproportionately, *my* picture, *my* book, *my* immortal four lines.'

'You are a pagan . . . Lanice, shame upon you.'

'Perhaps I am,' she confessed, and thought swiftly and poignantly of Roger Cuncliffe — who was dead. 'Pauline,' she said, without bothering to make the connection between her last sentence and her next, 'I want to tell you something. When Anthony Jones left me, I found he had pulled down everything — my whole house of life. He had moved out all the furniture and left everything strewn about like children's blocks. Then Roger, without saying anything, built the whole thing up again, out of the same blocks. Now the house is *really* done. Some one else'—she thought of Ripley—'might add a few gables or a classic portico, but he couldn't tear it down nor build it up.'

'And yet you have no idea what you want to do with this elegant structure.'

'Live in it. Work in it. I really like to work, and I have not done badly. Mr. Fox now pays me almost as much as Miss Bigley.'

'Money! Bah, is money your standard? If it is, why did you not marry Smith Scollay? You'd have earned more money that way than you ever will with Messrs. Redcliffe & Fox. He seemed to drop you very abruptly, Lanice. I suppose you were vastly disappointed to see such a *good catch* get out of the bag.'

'No, we weren't suited. I opened the bag myself — and let him out.'

'Do you intend to marry?'

'No,' she gave the stereotyped answer convincingly.

'Then why,' blazed Pauline, in a voice that suggested that this was the climax of the whole conversation, 'do you wickedly persist in dragging Professor Ripley, that distinguished scholar, about after you? He is an older man, Lanice, of established reputation. It seems to me that you have kept him dangling long enough.'

'Dangling? He doesn't dangle. I did think for a while that he was interested in me — romantically. That was when I was in England. I ... er ... even gave him a chance to declare himself — out on Bodmin Moor. But he felt no necessity — and later at Winchester. But men are strange — they get excited over one and think they love — and then they cool off and don't. It's very wrong, I think, to take too seriously what they say sometimes, by mistake. And since we've been back in Boston I don't know what to think. He likes me, but . . . he won't marry me. I'm glad I have my work. He always seems to be waiting for something — I don't know what.'

'I imagine he is waiting for you to show sufficiently noble character to dismiss him. Oh, Lanice, why can't I inculcate in you some of those lofty aims, those noble principles which characterize, which should, *must* characterize our sex?'

Lanice had no answer, and Pauline continued: 'But I suppose *you* are unable to see the fine quality of a man like Professor Ripley. *You* like loose-living young rakes like that terrible Jones man or even Smith Scollay. Well, such men seem to drop you quickly enough.'

Lanice waved a graceful hand clad to the wrist in an uncompromising cambric *robe de nuit*. She said in proud pantomime, 'Let them come, let them go.' Then she turned her eyes truthfully towards her cousin.

'You know as well as I that Smith Scollay was nothing to me, and Captain Jones — well, he has *gone* — that is all; as if he were a bright flame that some one blew out. And marrying is a different thing.' She sat up in bed and clasped the tent of her knees and said rather wistfully, 'I have now come to a place many girls reach in life, I believe, and never in stories. Would I rather not marry — or marry some one whom I care ever so much about and who understands me, but doesn't simply carry me off my feet?'

'You are referring, I suppose, to Professor Ripley. But you just said that he did not want to marry you. Are you such a hussy as to use tricks to force him into an unwelcome union? Oh, no wonder men scorn our moral sense!' She added as a triumphal afterthought: 'And then, you told me that you *once* tried to make him declare himself out on some moor last summer. Are you now more skilful, or is he more gullible? You simply have a low feminine desire to force him to propose so that you may' — Pauline waved her rusty arm in imitation of Lanice's graceful genture — 'turn him down, and say with a shrug you can get a better one.'

'No,' said Lanice with a sudden angry defiance, 'there is no better . . . ' She stopped, surprised that she had said so much. 'I think he is the best man in the world. At first I only saw him as a — a background for Anthony. And then in England, and since then in Boston, I've come to like him more and more. Now . . . I like him the best of any man I've ever known . . . I like him so much that I really, in a way, *love* him.'

'Indeed!'

'There are so many different ways of falling in love —'

[270]

'As many ways as there are men?' inquired Pauline with exaggerated courtesy.

Unoffended, Lanice continued: 'You fall in love one way and you think that is all there is to it. And then — some other person . . . and a different way . . . not the same, not the same ever again. Pauline, tell me. I've always wanted to ask, was Captain Jones *really* as handsome and fascinating as I thought he was?'

'The man was a viper. Unfit to undo the latchet of the shoe of a good woman — like Miss Gatherall or Mrs. Mosely. It was an insane infatuation.'

'But he must have been attractive. Even men like Mr. Ripley and Mr. Fox said he was . . . but I can't remember any more . . . he's gone from me, Pauline. I can't even see his face clearly and I've forgotten his voice.'

'One thing I wish you would tell me. Did you or did you not see this Jones man when you went to England?'

Lanice gazed at her cousin with startled, innocent eyes.

'Why, Pauline, of course not. A lady travelling alone cannot be too careful.'

4

'But do let me tell the Captain that you are here, Mr. Ripley. He will be vastly disappointed to wake up and find that I have kept you to myself for over an hour.'

'I would not interfere with the gentleman's Sunday

nap, not for three glasses of his famous Madeira. But how stupid of me! Of course, you are going somewhere and I am keeping you here talking.'

'Oh, I love to talk, and really there is nowhere to go. It doesn't pay not to go to church in the morning, one feels so restless all day.'

'Are you restless?' He asked the question as if it had great meaning for him, and looked at her with his wise little eyes. She had a sudden premonition that if she said she was, the conversation would leave the heights of Transcendentalism, which he had endeavored to elucidate for her, and become purely personal; if she said she was not, they could go on with the interesting philosophical discussion.

'Yes . . . sometimes, dreadfully restless.' She felt a delicate, imperceptible barrier snap between them. He felt it, too, for he moved a little nearer. Her sensitive nostrils caught the faint and delightful aroma of his riding-clothes, for he had come in from Concord on Minerva, his sturdy bay mare. It brought back wave after wave of tender childhood memories. How lovely they had been, Mamma's sleek horses standing in the Amherst stable, their polished haunches towards you, always peeking back so prettily! Ginger and Ruby, the pair; and Alfred, who grew so fat and lazy; Silk and Satin, how black and dangerous they had been, and how big! She could not have been more than five or six when Mamma had bought them in New York and soon afterwards sold them. And once she had had a white donkey called Moses, and once a spotted Western pony named Dizzy. He had broken

[272]

his leg, poor soul . . . oh, a hundred years ago. They were gone, all these lovely creatures.

'It is a good thing for one occasionally to feel restless. It makes you take stock of yourself and the manner of life that you are leading.'

'Oh, Cousin Poggy always keeps track of that for me. Only to-day she asked me what I intended to do with my life.'

'And what did you tell her?' His voice was eager, and again he bent towards her so that again she thought of all the fine horses she had known, and of Moses, the donkey.

'I told her that I intended to — live it.' She looked him squarely in the eye as if challenging him to keep her from this secret expectation of joy.

'Live it?'

'Yes. I want to travel some more and write a great deal; what, I hardly know as yet, but something that will include all of life as I have seen it. I mean *all*. Show how varied and exciting and boring and vulgar and beautiful and funny and serious it is . . .'

'You aim high; Lanice . . . you once let me call you that . . . tell me this, will you be satisfied to go on, always looking back towards a love — I suppose you'd call it — that's gone, never expecting anything from the future?'

She cast down her eyes, partly because she was afraid that he might read there the fact that what he supposed she called love was indeed gone. It hurt her because the pain of the memory was now almost a pleasure. She sat calm and collected close beside

[273]

Sears Ripley and could hardly remember how such proximity to Mr. Jones had made her heart race within her breast.

'Lanice . . .' and yet her feeling for him was deeper, more lasting than it had ever been for the Englishman.

'I said in Winchester, you remember, I said that I would wait, and I have, six months, eight months.'

'Wasn't Winchester a lovely town? And I'm so glad to have actually seen the Itchen.'

He looked dogged and slightly hurt. 'As a matter of fact, I'm not making conversation — about Winchester.'

'What are you doing?'

'Well, I'm trying to propose.'

They both laughed, and Lanice drew away and considered him. Rather like a bear with his size and rough hair and beard and sagacious triangular eyes. Only his heightened color showed his inner excitement.

'If I were proposing,' she said, 'do you know how I'd do it?'

'Tell me. . . . No, tell me louder. I didn't hear.'

'I said I'd have to *show* you,' she whispered.

She glanced about and listened a minute with upraised hand. 'Sssh,' she said. Gracefully and much to the man's amazement she cast herself on her knees before him, her skirts collapsing in circles about her. Out of the black lace froth, the tight bodice, the sleek head, the arms emerged like stamens from a flower. He saw her face color divinely and grow lovely. Her

[274]

throat and breast swelled. Her mouth, which had not uttered a word, mocked him and the black eyes promised incredible things. He was wild with joy and put out his arms to pick this exotic black flower at his feet, then he realized that she had not once glanced at him during the enactment of her pantomime. Her beautiful, passionate eyes had been fixed steadily on some point behind him, some image or some memory. He drew back from her and her cruelty.

'You do wrong to — torture me,' he said slowly. 'Do not show me — what you can be to — other men, if you cannot be so to me. Get up, Lanice. Some one may come in.'

Shamefacedly she got to her feet and walked over to the table in the window where the Chinese objects of ivory, jade, amethyst, and amber were spread on a heavy piece of gold embroidery. The late afternoon light shone through them and they cast pools of colored shadow.

'I beg your pardon,' she said, and sleeked her hair with a trembling hand.

'My dear,' he said, coming close to her, 'why are you crying?'

'I don't know, but I'll never get what I really want from life, never.'

'Do you know what you want?'

'No.'

'Then how do you know you'll never get it?'

'Oh, I have always known that, really.'

'Lanice, will you let me give you — all I can, and see if that may not be enough?'

She felt his thick, strong arms around her and turned towards him docilely.

'Yes.'

'You know I love you very much . . . too much. I'm afraid when you realize how infatuated I am you will feel contempt for me.'

'Oh, no. I want you to love me — too much. It is such a soft, comfortable thing to sink back into so much love.'

Body and soul he engulfed her. She felt secure and contented.

'I have always liked the smell of horses,' she said, looking up at him.

'Oh, I forgot I had these dirty old things on; but, Lanice, what is it *I* have always liked so much? It smells so clean and yet so subtly wicked!'

'It comes in silk envelopes and I got them in Paris.'

5

On her visits to the Alcotts in Concord, Lanice had often driven or strolled past the four-square yellow house that stood aloof under its elms, bearing upon its door a silver oblong engraved 'Sears Ripley.' She had remembered it as a pleasant place, gardens, paths, long windows with Venetian blinds, wistarias, and within a flutter of ruffled curtains. She had even noticed that there were children, often playing about under the arching elms with a stuffy black pony in a blue halter. This, then, was the place where she would live her life. And when she died the cemetery lay but half a block away. One more weeping willow, one more urn. She would eventually lie between Sears and his Prunella. No, Sears would lie in the middle with a wife on either side. There was no doubt in the world but here she would live, here die, and here her body return to earth. It was fortunate that Louisa and May Alcott lived so near. They would give her some companionship with her own sex, and now that she was definitely contracted to matrimony, she felt a sudden homesickness for all that she was leaving. Friendships never meant the same to married women, so she had noticed. She loved Sears, but she would gladly have put off the marriage for a year.

Early in the month of July in the late afternoon she drove to Concord with what Miss Bigley called 'her intended.' Sears left her sitting in the buggy as he ran across the street to bring back Mrs. Alcott as chaperon. It was with her she would spend the night. 'Marmee' the girls called this stoutish, kindly, intelligent matron. Louisa accompanied her, quite overcome with the romantic aspects of the occasion. She kissed her friend profusely and, awkwardly offering her hand to her old neighbor, began to tell him in the torrential manner of the shy that if ever she could make up a heroine worthy of him she would have her marry him on the last page.

'I can see the scene,' she continued excitedly, 'under a green umbrella — I think I may have him a German, they are so romantic, and then no one would know it was really you! Marmee . . . let's you and I go into the garden and play with Mary and Ridgewood.'

'We'll all go,' said Sears.

It touched him to see how natural was the meeting and how good the *esprit de corps* established between his fiancée and the children of Prunella, yet he realized with half a sigh that this new wife had never had any deep, emotional longing for children; if she had she could not have played with them so naturally. There was in her none of the tight embarrassment that women who love children must so often manifest before they themselves have borne them.

'I love children,' Lanice confided to him; and was surprised when he answered rather wearily,

'Yes — and kittens, too.'

6

They went into the house. It was exquisitely chill after the sun beating down in the garden. The rugs had been rolled up for the summer, and straw matting that smelled sweetly and slightly sickishly had been laid down. There were cool plants, slippery black horsehair, quaint glazed chintzes. The stairway, wide and carved, led off into more cool, quiet rooms where everything was in order. On each washstand the towels hung unused, seemingly unusable. The pattern on the honest yellow soap in the heavy white dishes had never been blurred by water. The curtains were immaculate. The windows shone.

'You must have told your housekeeper I was coming,' she said.

Professor Ripley evidently was so accustomed to this perfection he did not at first understand her remark.

[278]

'Oh, no,' he said in astonishment, 'Mrs. Rice always has it in order.'

Suddenly Lanice felt very homesick. To have seen a necktie on the floor or a picture awry might have made her love the house. She looked at Sears beseechingly.

He laughed and shook his head. 'No, I do not dare to kiss you. If I did I couldn't stop, and I hear "Marmee's" skirts on the stair.'

'But the house is *so* in order; I would always feel like a guest.'

Ripley went to his bureau, pulled out a drawer, and dumped its contents on the floor, stocks, ties, socks, a tobacco pouch, handkerchiefs, and, far back and forgotten, but tactlessly landing on the top of the heap, a faded, broken fan.

'I am, after all, only second choice,' thought Lanice.

Sears Ripley thought of the yellow room at the end of the hall where many a night his inexplicable friend, Anthony Jones, had slept. He suffered dully, and decided not to show this room to Lanice until a later date.

They went downstairs again, and Louisa and Mrs. Alcott tactfully withdrew to the piazza where they busied themselves darning stockings. It grew cool through the garden and Mary and Ridgewood were led off to the kitchen for bread and milk. Lanice and Sears sat in the library on either end of a sofa, facing each other. He wished to make lists. He felt he had to confide in her the exact number of salt cellars that

he possessed and the vintages of his wine. He wished
one of the upstairs rooms done over entirely in
Lanice's own taste.

'Some Chinese lacquer,' he suggested, 'ivory carv-
ings, silks. Captain Poggy has told me that he intends
to give you his collection of carved animals that he
keeps on the living-room table. His daughter cares
nothing for them and I really believe he wants to find
a kind and loving home for them.'

'Oh, I will love them, indeed, and then he will certainly come out to see us. There are some jade fishes
that he never is tired of looking at and touching, but
really I couldn't take them from him.'

'I will always think of them on that gold embroidery with the light shining through them, and you
in black lace standing before them and crying a little
and looking so — alone and powerless.'

'I cried because you were rude to me. Why did you
tell me so peremptorily to "get up, some one may
come in"?'

'I was afraid to let you stir me so deeply, and I felt
that your demonstration — was not for me. The
thought hurt me.'

'No. It was just a demonstration.'

'Not in honor of any one in particular?'

'No, but in honor of life in general. But did you
know that you were going to ask me to marry you
that afternoon?'

'Just as soon as I came into the house and you told
me that the Captain was asleep. The instant I saw
you I knew.'

'You're a funny, spiritual man. You look wise, but not intuitive, and you really are both. If you had asked me only a few months earlier I would not have known what to have said.'

'You would have known if I had asked you out on Bodmin,' he reminded her grimly.

'But how did you know that I was rather . . . expecting something like that, and planning to say "no"? I really thought it all out before I went down to Liskeard. Then you wouldn't and you wouldn't. I was quite provoked.'

He laughed shortly. 'I saw I had to wait. That the time hadn't come — for me. Well, I waited. Then that afternoon I knew immediately, and your demonstration . . . after that I couldn't have stopped even if it had been the wrong time. I'm afraid I am not . . . not a platonic man by nature. I can't manage to kiss lightly and forget it. You had the power, almost from the beginning, to hurt me so much. I could never let my shoulder touch you or caress you in any number of careless ways men caress women.'

Eager as most of her sex to hear that love on his part had been from first sight, she gave him the opportunity to confess it.

'No,' he said slowly, 'not at first, but of course that meeting with Jones was momentous. I can see you now, looking up from your work. Your eyes passed over me, just a glancing blow, and then I saw your face become transfixed as you met *his* gaze, and I knew you were going to love him and going to suffer, and I thought of you a great deal. And later, about

[281]

the time you went daily to his house on West Cedar Street, months later, I knew I loved you, but I felt too old and rather weary. But what good to talk about Jones? You were free, white, and twenty-one. I couldn't intrude. But I suffered, walking every morning past that small house. Oh, yes, I stopped in casually enough, three times. And that last time you were so flushed and lovely, and Jones . . . well, that day I called on you in the afternoon. I wanted to say I loved you. I wanted to forbid you ever to see that man again, wanted to carry you away with me in a hired hack. But I couldn't say and do these manly things. I could only talk about the Mormons and moral codes throughout the world.' He laughed ruefully, and Lanice saw his large hands were gripped into the sofa back until the knuckles whitened.

'Sears,' she said, and leaned towards him, 'it is so inappropriate that you should have suffered because of me. I wasn't worth it. I'm not now. Tell me' — and she looked away — 'does it hurt you now so much — the memory of Anthony Jones?'

'If you had never met him, never loved him, you would be a different person to-day — not you — not the girl I love — some one else. It was seeing you with him that first interested me in you. I couldn't quite understand, and was, perhaps still am, puzzled. Now I can no more wish you different in that respect than I could wish your eyes a different color. It is you.' He leaned towards her rather heavily and gripped her wrists. She realized that if she returned his caress the conversation would be ended. With a pretence of arranging her curls she freed her hand.

'Once I thought, Sears, you believed me to be only a woman whom Anthony had tired of, discarded.'

'No,' he said with a sweet sadness, 'you are only you, and I love you.'

They kissed thoughtfully and sat in silence. The approaching night was gathering through the hollow room. When next they turned back to each other, he saw only a pale oval set with shallow features, and she a dark beard, rough dark hair, and the bulk of his shoulders. Lanice clung to him.

'Sears,' she said, 'I. want to tell you about Anthony,' and pressed her mushroom-smooth cheek to his bearded lips. 'Sears . . . I've never told any one.'

A silence fell and through it the clocks struck, one after the other, each politely waiting until its brother was done. She thought to herself 'How well, sometime, I will know those clocks, lie awake and listen to them, wind them up, perhaps dust them.' Below her resting head she heard the strong heart-beat of her lover.

'If you must,' he said, 'but I'd rather you didn't.'

She rose to her feet, a wan, wistful lady. In the twilight of the room she was a lifeless ghost of some one else.

'I am going now; I am sure the Alcotts want to go to bed.'

'No, wait. Tell me, Lanice . . .'

'Not if you do not wish to know.'

[283]

CHAPTER XIV
HYMEN VINCIT OMNIA
1

IT was Ripley's eccentric friend, Thoreau, who said he had found, south on Cape Cod, farther down than the trains ran, a sandy paradise, permeated by the sea, stranger than much of Europe, and inhabited by men who resembled old sails come to life, women with profiles like sharp *W*'s. 'You stand there on the Cape,' Mr. Thoreau had said, 'and put all America behind you.' The idea of a walking trip upon the Cape with a female companion seemed to the philosophical recluse an idle venture. Much better, he thought, make the trip alone, and then return to Boston and matrimony. Why marry first and drag a woman over the dunes? But it was on this latter course Ripley decided. He had seen his Lanice on Bodmin and knew that its solitary strangeness would delight her.

'I never knew a woman yet,' said Thoreau, 'who would eat a bad breakfast and get sand in her shoes merely for a sight of the grandeurs of nature. And when on the Cape you will have eels and beans and doughnuts and tea three times a day.'

'But we intend to go.'

Thoreau looked pityingly on this intelligent man whom he believed love had demented and shrugged his spare shoulders. But he willingly laid out an itinerary. 'You take a train to Orleans,' he explained, 'and from there on progress by coach. This stage is a narrow one and the three seats really hold but two each. The driver, however, always waits until he has nine passengers without taking the dimensions of any. Then, after several ineffectual slams while you time your inspirations and expirations to help, he gets the door shut.'

Years after, it seemed to the two Ripleys that they had seen the Cape hand in hand. True, the lady's slippers filled with sand, the food was all but poisonous, and the natives smelled much of the fish with which they dealt. Ribs of whales were woven in fences. In places even the baby-carriages were fitted with runners so as to cope with sand. The houses were few and far and the land was desolate. They went beyond the domain of the horse to a far shore where the only commerce was by water. Everywhere was the sea and the sight of its wastes and its richness. The ribs of wrecks antedating the Revolution lay in the sand. The white wings of the fishing fleet flashed like gulls on the horizon. To east and west, and finally to the north, was only the sea. The wind was cold and alive over the wastes of sand.

'Are you as happy, Lanice, as you look?'

'Oh, so much happier! My face is too long and my hair is too dark and straight to show half what I really feel. I wish I had a red face like an apple and little yellow curls, and then perhaps you could tell merely by looking at me how happy I am.'

'Haven't you paddled about in that cold water long enough? Come and sit beside me on this dune.' And he unfurled the big, plum-colored umbrella that had so far theoretically protected the lady's complexion.

2

She wore an odd green dress of glazed chintz speckled over with minute yellow blossoms. Barefooted and bareheaded she climbed the sand and spread her full skirts beside her husband.

'Are you happy, too? Your beard has grown so shaggy it is almost impossible to see what you are really thinking. Isn't this much nicer than a trip to Niagara?'

'We can come here again next summer if you like, or perhaps go over to Paris.'

'Next year, and the next year, and the year after that and the year after that! Can you imagine that *this* is going on forever?'

'This sense of security, completeness, this finality is, I think, marriage. You never felt so at peace with the world before, did you?'

'No,' she answered, and felt a slight, unaccountable dread for the peace she had gained and unreasonable regret for the sometimes unhappy freedom she had lost. 'I will have a great many children,' she thought, 'and move in the best intellectual circles in Concord, Cambridge, and Boston. I will study Italian and aid Sears with his translation of Dante, and hire some one to darn my stockings and go over and help those poor poverty-stricken Alcotts.'

'I feel from now on,' she said aloud, 'that life will be very correct and very certain. And I feel as if you really understand me as no one else ever has. I am like a — glass person, almost. And you know everything, even "what is best," like those unpleasant papas Miss Bigley and I used to put in our stories. You know everything, almost everything I have ever done or thought, and everything I ever will be . . .' Both thought guiltily as she spoke of the sombre young man from Arabia.

'Lanice,' he said, 'once you wanted to tell me something, and I was afraid to hear. But now, no matter what you say, no matter what the truth is, I promise it will make no difference. Because,' he added stubbornly, 'you are you, and nothing else matters.'

'And I love you,' said Lanice rather tigerishly, for marriage had increased a hundred fold her feeling for him, 'and he . . . is nothing now . . . nothing. Would you understand how little he is to me if I told you that for years in Amherst I was really in love with Rochester? "Jane Eyre" was considered a sinful book, but Mamma used to read it. She would try to hide it from me in a dilatory way; I mean, just lay a handkerchief over it, or put it upside down in the bookcase, so of course I read it. Well, at fifteen I loved Rochester. I could not believe he was dead, or rather had never lived. I used to plan how some day I would meet him, and how much more he'd love me than Jane. And later I loved Captain Jones, but now one seems as unreal as the other, and the girl who was so . . . foolishly infatuated is not me — some one else — not Mrs.

Sears Ripley of Concord.' She turned her face in against his shoulder. 'Do you want me to tell you now?'

'Yes, but with your face so out of sight, how can I tell whether or not you are telling me the *exact* truth?' Professor Ripley long ago had discovered that Lanice could, very politely, prevaricate on occasion.

If she told him that Anthony Jones had carelessly possessed and abandoned her, would he ever trust her again? And this belief, she knew, would always hurt him, always ache far down like an incurable open wound deep in his consciousness. He would forgive her and would love her, but she loved him too much to wish to cause him pain. If she told him that Anthony's wild courtship had stopped short of actual possession, he would, she believed, feel too overwhelming a sense of his own right over her. She would never again have any little secret spot, either in her soul or her past, into which she could retreat. Through the most intricate films and fibres of her being he would gaze with clear, comprehending eyes.

'If I had found him at Winchester, then I would have . . . sinned in body as well as soul. But I was too late. Before God, I must be as guilty, however, as if what I really in my wicked heart . . . had hoped . . .' Ripley unaccountably began to laugh.

'Your only wickedness has been in not telling me before,' he exclaimed, 'but of course I always knew. Who but a woman, and a very good one, would consider herself as guilty of a mental crime as of a physical one? Lanice, look at me.'

[288]

He held her delicate chin between his thumb and forefinger and tipped it back so he could gaze into the inscrutable black lacquer of her eyes. Before he stopped to ponder the expression of her face, he fell to kissing it, and when he looked at her again was only conscious of the love and tenderness that suffused it.

3

The March wind staggered about the Concord house, striking at doors, shaking shutters. By its sound you knew that it smelt of melting earth and sticky buds. Inside was a dingy, not unpleasant taint of coke burning in the Franklin grate, and a lingering fragrance of dinner. Bending near the stove for warmth, the gas-lamp at her elbow, sat Mrs. Sears Ripley, crocheting just such baby socks she once had recommended for infants in the pages of 'Hearth and Home.'

Ticking clocks, reptilian hiss of fire, and without, the scampering wind.

She abandoned herself in a yawn, flinging out her long arms, shutting her eyes. Her wool work slipped to the carpet. The clocks ticked. The fire hissed. She leaned forward to pick up the sock, but instead huddled up over the fire, her elbows on her knees, her forehead in her hands.

'I am tired,' she said, 'or sleepy,' and thought of the horsehair sofa out of sight at the back of the room beyond the radiance of the gas-lamp. Sears was above in his study working on Dante. He would finish canto twelve to-night, and she would finish the sock.

[289]

How deathly still is a house in spring when the wind nuzzles the doors, begging to get in. She raised her violet-shadowed eyes reproachfully towards the rattling panes beyond the nimbus of the couch. 'You wouldn't like it, wind,' she said, 'if I should open a window and let you in. Go a long way off, out to sea, or down on the Cape. Concord is not the place for you.' But the wind snuffed like a hound.

The inertia of her body was at the moment too great to allow her to pick up the dropped crocheting or cross the room to the sofa. She yawned again and stretched herself from finger tip to toe-tip, as cats yawn and stretch. Her head sank. She was happy and almost asleep. The wind, the ticking clocks, the hot noises of the fire lulled her. 'Double crochet, seam two and purl two ... women knitting anti-macassars against the Judgment Day. But it is not now what my fingers do, but my body.'

Sometimes it seemed strange to her that there was a live animal growing within her, something insistent that would eventually want to come into life of its own and would not care if it killed her in the process. She did not believe that she would care very much to-night if it did. She was so hypnotized, so sunk in life, she knew no fear of death. She felt no love for the 'little new soul' which the minister had told her God had entrusted to her, but its presence gave her satisfaction, a sense of well-being. Her life should be its life. The things that had hurt and delighted her should in turn hurt and delight the 'little soul.' And in turn this soul would bear or beget more souls who in turn would learn the realities of existence. She thought of Roger and the wind of human experience. She moved with a heavy twist.

Once she would have gotten up to let in the begging wind; now she felt that merely existing and letting this new life spring from her was enough. Footsteps paced the ceiling. One, two, three, four, five, six, seven; then back again, seven, six, five, four, three, two, one; and he was under his student lamp with Dante before him. She dozed.

The ticking of the French clock upon the mantel and the grandfather clock upon the stair ... the ticking of her Swiss watch at her belt, and upstairs the ticking of Sears's big gold Gorham in his waistcoat pocket. One, two, three ... a pause. A door opened and shut. His feet upon the stairs and he was beside her. She really heard his watch at last just above her ear, but was too sleepy to turn her head.

'Yes, dear?'

'I thought I would stop for a breathing spell. It must be past *your* bedtime.'

'Yes, far past.'

He moved restlessly about the room, and Lanice was dully annoyed because he seemed to have something on his mind.

'It is dark in here, Lanice.'

'I know; I like it dark.'

'And your fire is almost out.'

He seated himself upon the arm of her chair, but she moved, so he sat finally in the chair with her in his arms.

'Lanice,' he said, 'you are sure you are happy?'

'Yes.'

'You do not regret what you have given up?'

'I'll never have as nice a figure again.'

'No, no. I don't mean trifles like that. But you are a talented woman.'

She felt by the stiffness of his body that something worried him, and that he was about to speak of it.

'Ah, Lanice. This afternoon I went to your lower desk drawer to find, if I could, a map of Italy, and I found — instead — these.'

She opened her eyes listlessly and saw that he held in his thick hand the four stories that she had written in such delicious frenzy at Porlock Weir.

'Did you read them, Sears?'

'Yes.'

'You didn't like them?'

'No; they are *hideous*. How could you think up such things?'

'You always mistrust fiction.'

'I know, dear. It seems so exaggerated, so unimportant.'

'Well.' She knew that he realized that he held in his hand that part of her nature which he never had possessed, that part which had responded to Anthony. He was afraid of these dark, passionate, and powerful stories about satyrs gambling on the mud flats of Salem, picking up mussels and throwing down the shells, and mortal women who loved devils and bore monsters, and little boys driven into ecstasy by the nymphs in the birch trees by the brook.

'Think how terrible the shock would be if your child should grow up and find these stories, and realize that her *mother* wrote them.'

Lanice moved slightly within his arms. At some future day she might care, but now she did not. Why didn't he tell her to destroy her files of 'Hearth and Home'? Those were the stories that disgraced her.

'But they've never been published; she'll never find them.'

'Oh, my dear. This afternoon, at your desk, I had a premonition of this child, your daughter with all your loveliness, a little girl of fifteen, coming as I did to your desk, finding these stories and reading them.'

'That was why they shocked you so, my dear. You read them, not from your point of view, but from that of a fifteen-year-old child. Truly, Sears, is that a fair basis for literature?'

'I know, but your daughter . . .'

He amazed her sometimes with his absorption in this child which, in due time, she should bear him. It was already a person to him, and from the first he had been sure of its sex. Either his enslavement to his wife made him desire to see her reincarnate in the next generation, or, being a man of habit, he expected first a daughter and then a son because this had been Prunella's conduct.

'What do you want me to do, Sears?'

'Nothing, my love, but I hope that you will wish to . . .'

Her face was pressed against his ear, and her eyes

[293]

were shut. She felt him glance up and towards the fire.

'Burn them?'

'Yes.'

But still she paused a moment; inertia, and the pleasure of inertia came over her.

'I am too sleepy to-night. I'm not quite myself. Let me wait until to-morrow, and then I'll know what I really want to do.'

He said nothing, and she listened to his watch ticking within his pocket, to the shambling wind outside. She moved her head a little and listened to the beating of his heart, deep buried beneath the waistcoat she had embroidered and the fine shirts she had made him, deep within its heavy cage of ribs, through which sometime the worms would crawl . . . She started up a little wildly at the thought and turned towards him her goblin smile. Wantonly she took the manuscript and flung it upon the glowing coals.

'But it will not burn,' said Sears, 'unless it is crumpled up.'

She lay back upon him, closed her eyes, feeling the twists of his body as he managed both to hold her and the poker. The heat sprang up and scorched her slightly. She opened her eyes. The room suddenly was bright. She saw the sofa and the window she had not opened. The gas-lamp looked sickly and green in comparison to the sturdy orange flame. The room sank back into comparative darkness.

'You are almost asleep, my dear.'

'Yes, almost.'

'I'll carry you up to bed.'

But they still waited until the woman slept in her husband's arms, then he reached out and thriftily turned off the gas, picked up his burden in his strong arms, and, looking rather like a fairy bear with a captive sleeping princess, creaked up the stairs on heavy tiptoe.

CHAPTER XV

' TIME STAYS; WE GO!'

THERE had been a girl once, with black silk hair and a high, passionate heart. Where was she now, that the years pass by? The black silk was on the children's heads, and the passion — oh, it was burned in the Franklin stove — four stories had been enough to hold it all.

There had been a girl once . . .

Now a woman rocked a child in her arms, holding it cautiously lest it disturb the next younger growing within her body.

There had been a girl once . . .

But not contented as this woman was contented. A desperate, driven thing that could drink of the cup Anthony Jones offered and wipe her mouth. Break her heart and forget.

'It is through my children I will now see life,' she thought, and felt the unutterable solitude of the human heart that sees only the vast stretch of centuries behind and the burden of time beyond. From her, in all directions, stretched time and space, and she, the least important of all things, stood for a second in the centre of the universe.

'The Romans lived and fought,' she thought, 'so that I might have history to read in school, and the only result of the Napoleonic wars is that once in a long time I think carelessly what a vulgar, little, short fat man Napoleon was. The stars, all the stars, are held up in the heavens so that I may have something to look at just after I've turned out the light and before I get into bed. Christ came and lived beautifully — and died terribly ... Christ on his cross ... to give my soul a few minutes of pity and wonder. And they who lie in the churchyard, what are they but names for me to read on days when I am too lazy to walk far and have no book with me!'

She the centre of it all, and so soon to be but one more name cut in slate for the lazy to ponder over. 'Lanice Ripley.'

What clothes she had had as a girl, and lovers enough — perhaps too many! She shut her eyes and saw herself in brown velvet that looked like a Spanish portrait, and coral earrings to her shoulders. Could see herself wipe her mouth like a greedy child, shake her earrings, and fall asleep, deep in the furs of the Russian sleigh.

'I have loved to live,' she thought, and prayed with sudden passion, 'O God, let my children be happy, too, and their children, and their children's children, forever and ever, Amen!'

THE END